By Debbie Macomber

DEBBIE MACOMBER

Touched by Angels

AVON
An Imprint of HarperCollinsPublishers

This is a work of fiction. Names, characters, places, and incidents are products of the author's imagination or are used fictitiously and are not to be construed as real. Any resemblance to actual events, locales, organizations, or persons, living or dead, is entirely coincidental.

AVON BOOKS
An Imprint of HarperCollins*Publishers*
10 East 53rd Street
New York, New York 10022-5299

Copyright © 1995, 2011 by Debbie Macomber
ISBN 978-0-06-108344-0
www.avonromance.com

First Avon Books mass market printing: November 2011
First HarperTorch special mass market printing: November 1999
First HarperTorch mass market printing: November 1995

Avon Trademark Reg. U.S. Pat. Off. and in Other Countries, Marca Registrada, Hecho en U.S.A.
HarperCollins® is a registered trademark of HarperCollins Publishers.

Printed in the U.S.A.

10 9 8 7 6 5

To Terry and Cheryl Adler.
Happy tenth wedding anniversary little brother.
And I want you to know I've forgiven you
for making copies of my diary
and selling it when I was thirteen.

Dear Friends,

Like many authors, I've received more than one surprise in my writing career. The popularity of my three irrepressible angels is one of them. I wrote *Touched by Angels* over fifteen years ago. Shirley, Goodness, and Mercy were sassy, irreverent, demanding, and totally charming. Good grief, I had teenagers back then who were more than willing to sass back—I didn't need characters doing it. Still, I loved them, and so did my readers, who demanded more and more angel books.

Well, as the saying goes, the rest is history. Over the years there have been a number of angel-themed Christmas stories featuring Shirley, Goodness, and Mercy. And guess what? They aren't finished yet. By this time next year my dynamic trio will be making a fresh appearance in yet another escapade, once again in New York City.

I want to be sure and thank everyone at Avon Books for keeping my angel series alive. Lucia Macro and Esi Sogah have worked tirelessly to give these books another life.

Please take note—because of the advancement of technology, I've gone back and updated where I could without disrupting the story. Can you believe the changes in our world in such a short period of time? I found it jarring not to mention cell phones when nearly everyone has one these days. My hope is that you'll be so caught up in the story you won't even notice.

Christmas blessings, Dear Reader, from Shirley, Goodness, Mercy, and from me.

I so love hearing from my readers, who have been the guiding force in my career. You can reach me at P.O. Box 1458, Port Orchard, WA 98366 or log onto my website and leave me a message on my guest book at *www.debbiemacomber.com*. Die-hard readers can keep up with me on my free phone app. I also have a Facebook page. In fact, I'm so technologically connected, I can hardly believe it myself.

Debbie Macomber

Chapter One

The young man wore a guage in one ear. Brynn Cassidy tried not to stare as he paraded past her and slouched down in the desk in the farthest corner of the classroom. His neck was decorated with a cross tattoo. The fact that his hair was cut in a Mohawk style and dyed red shouldn't faze her. She'd been told what to expect.

Manhattan High School wasn't St. Mary Academy, the parochial girls' high school where she'd taught for the last two years. But teaching here was an opportunity she couldn't let pass her by. She'd accepted this position to test her theories and gain experience in dealing with students from a disadvantaged neighborhood.

Next, a young lady entered the room in a miniskirt, tank top and no bra. Her hair, pitch-black and stringy, covered her far better than her choice of outfits. She glanced around, shrugged, and claimed the seat closest to the door as if it were important to make a fast get-away.

The room filled quickly. The school building itself was said to be dilapidated and run-down, but that didn't trouble Brynn. St. Mary Academy was a turn-of-the-century structure with high ceilings and lovely polished wood floors that smelled of lemon oil.

When Brynn learned Manhattan High in the Washington Heights area had been constructed in the early 1950s, she'd expected it to be an improvement, but she was wrong. Like so many other schools, Manhattan High had been forced to make some difficult budget choices. Thanks to three failed school bond levies, modernizing the classrooms was on the low end of the priority list.

"Will everyone kindly take a seat," Brynn instructed nervously. She stood in front of the class and was ignored, which wasn't surprising since the bell had yet to ring.

Looking for something constructive to do, she walked over to the badly chipped blackboard and wrote out her name.

The bell rang, and several of the kids stopped talking long enough to indicate their irritation at being interrupted. The level of conversation increased once the bell finished.

Brynn returned to the front center of the room

and waited. She'd learned early in her teaching career never to outshout her students. It only made her look foolish, and it didn't work. After five full minutes of being ignored, she went to the wall and flipped the light switch a couple of times. This technique had worked elsewhere but had only a mild effect upon the class. The level of talking decreased momentarily while several glanced her way, then quickly continued their ongoing conversations.

Brynn decided she had no option but to wait them out. It demanded the longest fifteen minutes of her life to stand in front of that classroom until thirty people voluntarily gave her their attention.

It might have taken longer if the boy, Hispanic from the look of him, hadn't raised his right hand and snapped his fingers. Ten or so other Hispanics stopped talking and texting and turned around on their seats. An African American followed suit, and several of the others clustered together went silent.

The class had divided itself along ethnic lines, Brynn noted. The Hispanics sat in the front, the African Americans chose the back.

Once silence reigned, Brynn stepped forward. "Good morning," she said with her brightest smile. "My name's Miss Cassidy."

"Why ain't you married?"

"Because I'm not," she answered simply, preferring not to get trapped in a conversation about herself. "I'm your teacher, and—"

"You're new, ain't you?"

"Yes," Brynn answered politely. "As you already know, we're involved in an experimental program called Interdisciplinary Learning."

"That doesn't sound like something a nice girl like you should be teaching," one of the boys called out.

Despite herself, Brynn smiled. "We'll be spending three hours together each afternoon, exploring senior English, world history, and social science. You'll notice how the classes are grouped along parallel lines."

"Is she speaking English?" one girl whispered loudly, leaning toward another.

Brynn decided it would be best to explain the concept in simpler terms. "The classes we'll be studying are connected by subject. We'll read *The Diary of Anne Frank* for the English portion, the history section will involve the study of World War Two, and in the last part of the session I'd like to discuss the justification for war and other value clarification."

"All three hours will be spent with you?"

"That's right," Brynn said. "You'll know me better than any other teacher, and by the same token, I'll know you. I'd like it if we could work together as a team."

"If we're going to be spending this much time with one teacher, then it only seems right that you tell us something about yourself first," the Hispanic boy who'd quieted the class said. Since she owed him a favor, she agreed.

"What do you want to know?"

"How long you been teaching?"

"This is my third year."

"If she lasts the first week," someone suggested under their breath.

"I'll last," Brynn assured them. "I'm too young to retire and too stubborn to quit."

"Where'd you come from?"

"Rhode Island."

"Why'd you decide to teach here?"

"She's a fool, that's why," someone answered for her.

"That's not true," Brynn countered. "As I explained earlier, we're involved in an experimental program that's being sponsored by the federal government. I was asked to participate."

"Why'd you do it?"

The questions were making her decidedly uncomfortable. "Part of the agreement would be that a portion of my student loan would be forgiven."

"Forgiven?"

"That's the word the government used."

"Where'd you teach before?" a Chinese girl asked, her gaze shyly meeting Brynn's.

"St. Mary Academy. It's a private school for girls near Rochester."

"La de da," one of the boys said in a high-pitched voice. He stood, dropped his wrists, and pranced around his desk.

"Hey, could you set me up with one of those nice Catholic girls?"

Brynn didn't bother to answer.

"Do you color your hair or is it naturally red?"

"It's auburn," Brynn corrected, "and it's as natural as it comes."

"What do you think, dummy, with a name like Cassidy? She's Irish, can't you tell?"

"If he were dumb, he wouldn't be a high school senior. This brings up something I consider vital to this class. Respect. I won't tolerate any name calling, racial slurs, or put-downs."

"You been in girls' school too long, Teach. That's just the way we talk. If Malcolm here wants to call Denzil a nigger, he's got a right 'cause he's a nigger himself."

"Not in this classroom he won't. The only thing I'll ask of you in the way of deportment is mutual respect."

"I don't even know you, how am I supposed to respect you?"

It was a good question and one Brynn couldn't slough off.

"Especially if the only reason you decided to take this job was so you could be forgiven for something you did to the government."

"That's not the only reason I took the job," Brynn pressed, "I want to teach you to dream."

"Excuse me?" A girl with her hair woven into tiny braids all over her head sat upright. "You're making us sound like babies."

"I'm not suggesting naps," Brynn explained. "How many of you know what you're going to do after you graduate from high school?"

One hand went up, from the same Hispanic youth who'd helped her earlier.

"Your name is?"

"Emilio Alcantara."

"Hello, Emilio. Tell me what your dreams are."

"I got plenty of those. I dream about Michelle and Nikki and . . ." His friends made several cat-calls, and Brynn smiled and shook her head.

"I'm talking about the future. After high school, five years down the road. We all need a dream, something to pin our hopes on, something that gives us a reason to wake up in the morning."

"You mean a dream like Martin Luther King?"

"Yes," she said enthusiastically. "An ambition to do something, travel somewhere, or be something."

"Why?" The boy who asked had caught her attention earlier. He seemed indifferent to everything that was going on around him. A couple of the kids had said something to him, but he'd ignored them as if they weren't there or, more appropriately, as if he weren't entirely there himself. Briefly she wondered if he were on drugs.

"Why?" Brynn repeated. "Because dreaming is a necessary part of life, like eating or sleeping. Sometimes we just forget about it, is all. We'll be exploring more about this later, but I guarantee you one thing, by the end of this quarter, there'll be plenty for you to think and dream about."

"You know," said the girl who'd claimed the desk closest to the door, "you might be all right, but it's going to take some doing, getting used to a teacher who doesn't look any older than one of us."

"She isn't married, either. Say, Teach, do you want me to set you up?" Emilio asked. "I got an older brother who could use a chick like you."

"Thanks, but no thanks," Brynn answered, reaching for her attendance book. "Now that you know about me, it's time for me to learn something about each one of you."

"But we don't know you!" two or three protested in turn.

Brynn held the book against her breast and sighed. "What other information do you need?"

Questions were tossed at her in every which direction. She put a stop to them with a wave of her hand. "Listen, I'll give you the basics and then we'll have to get started. My first name is Brynn."

"How many kids in your family?"

"Eight."

"Eight!"

"She's Irish and Catholic, ain't she?"

Brynn ignored the comment. "I'm the fourth oldest and the first girl. My oldest brother is thirty-three and my youngest sister is sixteen." She lowered the grade book and called out, "Yolanda Aguilar."

"Here." The Hispanic girl raised her hand and waved enthusiastically.

Brynn looked at Yolanda and made a notation next to the girl's name. "Emilio Alcantara is here," she said, making a second notation.

"What are you writing down about me?" Emilio

demanded. He sat up on his chair and craned his neck toward her as if that would be enough to read what she'd written.

"I said you sat in the front row and revealed leadership characteristics."

"I do?" He sounded surprised.

"What'd you say about me?" Yolanda asked.

"That you're energetic and personable."

"How'd you know that?"

"Yeah, how'd you figure that about Yolanda?" another boy demanded, then leaned over to the student at the desk next to him. "What's personable mean?"

"Sh-h, I'm next and I want to know what she's gonna say about me."

"Modesto Diaz," Brynn called out, looking at the youth above the grade book.

He curled his upper lip and snarled at her. "Yo."

Brynn added her comment to the book.

"What'd ya say?" Modesto insisted, straightening. He was halfway out of his seat. "I gotta right to know since you told the others."

"I wrote down that you have a flair for the dramatic."

"What's that mean?" Modesto asked Emilio under his breath.

"The hell if I know," Emilio complained. "She's gonna be one weird teacher."

By lunchtime Brynn was convinced Emilio was right. She was completely out of touch with their world. Her vocabulary, which she'd never thought of as especially advanced, served to confuse her students. Half the morning was spent repeating in simpler terms what she'd said previously.

She'd no more than handed out *The Diary of Anne Frank* and briefly described to them Anne's story when the bell rang for their first break. The classroom emptied so fast, one would think the school was on fire.

Brynn sat down at her desk and exhaled sharply, weary to the bone. This was her first day in an inner-city high school, and she was going to need help—lots of help, and she didn't expect it to come in the form of the PTA.

Bowing her head, she murmured a simple prayer, asking for patience and guidance. She yearned to teach her students to dream, to look to the future with enthusiasm. She hungered for them to see beyond the troubles they faced day in and day out and reach for the stars, and she wanted to be the one to show them the way.

Brynn's whispered prayer fluttered past the chipped blackboard, echoed silently through the scarred halls, as it winged its way toward heaven. The request soared, swiftly spanning the distance between man and God. Carried on the brisk winds of faith, guided by devotion, navigated by love, it arrived fresh and bright at the very feet of the Archangel Gabriel.

"Brynn Cassidy," Gabriel repeated slowly as he

flipped through the cumbersome book, marking the entry. He was writing when he glanced up to find Shirley, Goodness, and Mercy standing directly across the desk from him. He'd never seen the three look more—he hated the term—angelic. Their wings were neatly folded in place and they smiled serenely as if the world were at their feet.

"It's that time of year again," Goodness reminded him, grinning broadly.

Gabriel's hand tightened around the quill pen. Heaven help him, he was going to be left to deal with these three lovable troublemakers once more.

"Time of year for what?" he asked. Gabriel was playing dumb in a stalling effort. For the past two years this trio of prayer ambassadors had visited earth, working their own unique brand of miracles. A sort of divine intervention run amuck.

"We'd like to try our hand in the Big Apple," Mercy explained with limited patience. It was apparent she was eager to get her assignment and be on her way. "We've been looking forward to working together again," she reminded him primly. "One would assume that with the success of the past two years we'd have proven ourselves beyond question."

"We don't mean to be impertinent," Goodness inserted, glaring at her fellow prayer ambassador, "but I find myself agreeing with Mercy."

"Brynn Cassidy," Shirley repeated softly, reading over Gabriel's shoulder.

Gabriel deliberately closed the huge book, cutting

off Shirley's view. The last thing he needed was for the former guardian angel to take a hankering for this particular assignment.

The students of Manhattan High would require a far more experienced angel than Shirley. Why, her tender heart would be mush by the end of a week, working with this group of adolescents. Frankly, Gabriel didn't expect Brynn Cassidy to last long herself.

Gabriel knew all about the young teacher. Her mother and grandfather had been praying for her for several years. As far as Gabriel was concerned, Brynn Cassidy was far more suited to teaching the proper young ladies of St. Mary Academy. Manhattan High was a graveyard of lost souls. An unseen storm cloud had settled over the school, feeding on tears yet to be shed and broken promises. Brynn's humble faith was like a newborn lamb placed in the midst of ravenous wolves. She'd quickly be devoured. Naturally Gabriel would do what he could to aid her, but one ill-equipped prayer ambassador would hardly be sufficient.

"Brynn needs me," Shirley said, looking him squarely in the eye.

"She needs an army. I don't mean to discourage you," Gabriel said, feeling mildly guilty, "I'm sure we'll find a more appropriate assignment for you. A less complicated request," he muttered more to himself than to Shirley.

As he recalled, a prayer request had come in that morning from a teenage girl in Boston who needed a date for prom night. Surely Shirley could scrounge up a decent young man. As for Goodness and Mercy, why, there were any number of less demanding requests with which to occupy them.

"Give me a minute," he said, flipping through the unwieldy book, finding a page, and running his index finger down the large number of entries. "I'm sure I'll come up with something appropriate for each of you."

"No arguments?" Goodness asked, her eyes wide with surprise.

"Wow, maybe we have proven ourselves."

"I want to talk to Goodness about Hannah Morganstern," Gabriel said, his brow creased with contemplation.

"Yes," Goodness answered excitedly.

"Her family owns one of the most popular delis in all of New York," the Archangel went on to explain.

Goodness and Mercy looked at each other and squealed with delight. The two joined hands and danced a happy jig around his desk, kicking up their heels.

"What about me?" Mercy asked, breathless with excitement.

"Jenny Lancaster," Gabriel said decisively. "She moved to New York from Custer, Montana, three years ago, hoping to make a name for herself on Broadway."

"Has she?"

"No," Gabriel said with a sigh of regret. "It's time

to go home, only she can't bear to face that. You see, she doesn't want to disappoint her family, and I'm afraid she's stretched the truth and told them things that weren't altogether true. You're going to have to help her make the decision."

"I can do it."

"Without moving the Statue of Liberty?" Gabriel demanded.

"That's kid stuff," Goodness muttered.

"Maybe so, but is Rockefeller Center safe?"

The two found little humor in his question. It was then that Gabriel noticed that Shirley had disappeared.

"Where's Shirley?"

Goodness and Mercy glanced over their shoulders. "I haven't a clue."

"I didn't see her leave."

Gabriel had a sneaking suspicion he already knew where the prayer ambassador had disappeared to. "Wait here," he instructed impatiently. He raised his massive arms and with one wide, sweeping motion parted the clouds of heaven and descended from paradise to the mundane world.

He found Shirley right where he suspected: in an inner-city classroom, keeping a close watch on a young, inexperienced schoolteacher.

Brynn finished her lunch and poured herself a cup of coffee. Standing at the window, she looked out over the concrete jungle that made up the city.

St. Philip's, the cathedral located across the street,

had once been the pride of the diocese. The stained-glass windows, depicting the Stations of the Cross, had aged badly over the years. A flight of concrete steps led to the eight-foot-tall double doors. The church was a magnificent piece of Gothic architecture, but like Manhattan High, it had fallen upon harsh economic times.

When Brynn had first been approached about this assignment, she'd visited New York City and loved it. There was a rhythm to the city, a musical beat that had set her heart to racing.

In her mind's eye came a picture of prosperity and abundance. Not of wealth or riches in the monetary sense, but of purpose. The feeling had stayed with her in the days that followed, and when she'd penned her name to the contract, Brynn had felt instinctively that she was doing the right thing.

Following the break, Brynn headed down the crowded hallway. Several students leaned against their lockers in passionate embraces. This was a foreign element to Brynn, since she'd attended a parochial girls' high school as well as taught in one. It was a bit of a shock to discover how friendly students were allowed to get in the school hallway.

A ruckus broke out at the end of the corridor, and several heated words in Spanish flew at her like fiery darts. Brynn's knowledge of the language was limited, but she was well aware the two boys weren't exchanging pleasantries.

After making her way to the problem, she found Emilio Alcantara and an African American she didn't know staring each other down. A crowd had circled around the two.

"Is there a problem here?" Brynn asked, maneuvering into the tight circle.

"If you know what's good for you, Teach, you'd better leave," Emilio advised.

"I can't do that, and now I suggest you two boys give it up and go about your business. Fighting isn't going to solve anything."

The black boy looked at her with such unadulterated hatred that for a wild second Brynn was caught speechless. She'd never had a student, or anyone else, look at her in quite that way.

A shiver ran up her spine when she noticed both boys had knives. She grabbed Suzie Chang, the shy girl from her class, by the shoulder. "Get help immediately," she ordered, her heart in her throat.

Suzie took off running.

By then the Hispanic youths had lined one side of the hallway and the blacks dominated the second half. The two ethnic groups glared at one another, waiting for an excuse, any excuse, to fight. The atmosphere was explosive, the tension as tightly strung as a fiddle.

Without thinking, Brynn positioned herself between the two boys. Her head was spinning and she felt lightheaded with fear. "Stop," she ordered in her most authoritative voice, but the request sounded hollow even to her own ears.

The sound of footsteps running toward her was so welcome, Brynn nearly collapsed with relief. A male teacher and a janitor exploded onto the scene, and the knives disappeared as if by magic. Emilio and the other youth looked as if they were the best of friends. Emilio wrapped his arm around the black youth.

"What's happening, bro?"

"What's going on here?" Doug Keast, the teacher, demanded, looking to Brynn.

"Emilio and this young man were involved in an exchange of words. Everything's under control now. Thanks for your help."

"Knives?"

Brynn hesitated, not wanting to rat on Emilio but at the same time unwilling to lie. "They both drew out knives, but—"

"I don't need to know anything more than that," Doug barked, escorting both youths to the principal's office. "I'll need you to make a statement."

"What's going to happen?" Brynn asked, scurrying behind Doug and Emilio. A second male teacher appeared to escort the other boy.

"I'm gonna be suspended," Emilio said, glaring at her as if she'd turned traitor on him. "I thought you were different," he spat out. "You ain't no different than any of the other teachers." His dark eyes, leveled at her, were filled with animosity.

"Listen here, Emilio, it wasn't me who got involved in an altercation."

"A what? You know, if you're going to teach English, the least you could do is learn to speak it first."

"A fight," she said, losing her patience. She was

half trotting in order to keep up with Doug's long-legged stride. Her fellow teacher was making haste for Mr. Whalen's office.

"You know the rules about knives on school property," Doug told Emilio.

"What knife?" the youth demanded. "She was seeing things. I didn't have any knife, and neither did Grover, ain't that right, bro?"

"The new teach needs glasses," Grover claimed, sounding as if they'd been strolling through a bed of wildflowers.

"Tell him, Miss Cassidy," Emilio said, staring at her. "There wasn't any sign of knives, now, was there?"

"If you expect me to lie on your behalf, I won't do it," Brynn told him in no uncertain terms. "And if you're both expelled, then—"

"They'll be suspended for three days," Doug interrupted.

"Then you have no one to blame but yourselves," she finished.

"I ain't coming back," Grover announced in chilling tones. "School ain't gonna help me or my homies. I'm outta here, understand?" He jerked his elbow free from the teacher and strolled out the door, letting it slam in his wake.

"Good riddance," the man murmured.

"I'll talk to him," Brynn said, going after Grover.

She hadn't taken two steps when Doug Keast stopped her. "Let him go."

"But—"

"He's right. Grover's nothing but bad news." Doug looked to Emilio as if to suggest the Hispanic boy fell into the same category.

"Emilio's different," Brynn insisted. "Grover's choosing to give up, to fail. Emilio's got a future."

"Yeah," Emilio muttered, pulling himself free of Doug's hold. "Some future. First you tell me what a great leader I am and then you get me kicked out of school." Having made that little speech, he slumped down on the worn vinyl sofa outside Mr. Whalen's office.

"Did you see the knives?" Gabriel asked Shirley gently. "They were real, and the risk to Brynn is equally grave. She could have been seriously hurt."

"The woman's in profound need of heavenly intervention," Shirley said forcefully. "In other words, this teacher needs me."

"Ah . . ." Gabriel hated to be the one to break the news, but Shirley was out of her league. He'd hoped the prayer ambassador would see it for herself, but now he wasn't so sure.

"I know what you're thinking," Shirley said, eager to prove herself. "You think I'm in way over my head."

"My thoughts were running along those lines," Gabriel admitted.

"I believe I could help Brynn," Shirley insisted, and then stiffened her shoulders. "You're the one in charge of handling the prayer assignments, and I have no option but to accept your decision, but I want to help Brynn Cassidy teach her students to dream. I want to stand at her side when their eyes light up with discovery, and I especially long to be there when she tells them about faith in God."

"There are other teachers who need you," Gabriel assured her. "And they aren't trapped in a poor neighborhood school."

"I see," Shirley whispered, hanging her head in defeat.

"Perhaps another year," Gabriel suggested.

"Perhaps." The word was so low, it dragged against the floor.

Gently patting the discouraged angel on her shoulder, Gabriel escorted her back to heaven, where Goodness and Mercy awaited their return.

"I'll find another assignment for Shirley in a moment," he promised, "but first, I want to introduce Goodness to Hannah Morganstern."

Chapter Two

"Hannah who?" Goodness asked, looking puzzled.

"Morganstern," Gabriel supplied. "The prayer request came in from Hannah's mother and grandmother. They want her to make a good marriage." He opened the cumbersome book that listed the incoming prayer requests and smoothly folded back the page. Running his index finger down a list of names, he paused when he located Hannah's.

Gabriel smiled, pleased with himself. This request would be a simple matter and would quickly appease the novice prayer ambassador. The sooner Goodness was back where she belonged, the better for all concerned.

As it happened, Hannah was close to becoming engaged to Carl Rabinsky, the rabbi's son. Carl was a fine, upstanding young man with a bright future.

Hannah's family was delighted that their daughter had chosen such an outstanding marriage candidate. A professional matchmaker couldn't have come up with a better choice. Goodness would soon recognize how advantageous such a marriage would be for Hannah. Naturally the prayer ambassador would accept full credit for the match, which was fine with Gabriel as long as she left well enough alone.

By his best estimate, Gabriel would have Goodness out of harm's way within a day or two. Heaven knew he wouldn't rest until all three were back where they belonged. There was no telling the trouble they could rouse in the Big Apple. Gabriel cringed involuntarily at the thought of Shirley, Goodness, and Mercy loose on the unsuspecting souls of New York City.

They did try. He'd give them that much. The three angels were dear hearts, but frankly they were trouble with a capital T. There was no end to the mischief they managed to muster each Christmas. The season was hectic enough without having to deal with those three.

"When can I see Hannah?" Goodness asked eagerly.

"When are you going to tell me more about Jenny Lancaster?" Mercy asked, crowding her way between him and Goodness. The smallest of the three juggled her elbows until she'd jockeyed herself into position. "I'm looking forward to meeting Jenny."

"It's my turn," Goodness reminded her friend sternly.

"Be patient," Gabriel advised the two. At times he felt like a referee at a hockey match. "Goodness, let me take you down to meet Hannah."

"I want to come," Mercy insisted.

"Me, too." Shirley was determined not to be left behind.

Gabriel hadn't planned on making an expedition out of this. He'd thought it would be a simple matter to point out Hannah to Goodness, then introduce her to Carl. They'd be back before either of Goodness's friends had time to miss her. He was about to reassure Mercy and Shirley of this when he noticed that the three had looped their arms together. They stood before him with a determination that would have shook Moses before that unfortunate incident on Mt. Sinai.

"All right, all right," he grumbled under his breath. These particular prayer ambassadors had a way about them that foiled him at every turn. Only this year, he was simplifying matters. Their assignments were all straightforward requests that would bring them back to heaven in record time. Nothing complicated. Nothing involved. Assignments each one should be able to arrange in record time. This Christmas, Gabriel promised himself, wouldn't be like the past two.

Stepping away from the others, the archangel raised his massive arms and with one sure movement parted the massive clouds of heaven. A thin layer of mist remained, and gradually he was able to make out the earth below. Soon the four of them narrowed in on the big city. Skyscrapers punctured the sky. The top floors of the Empire State Building came clearly into focus. Then he viewed the landmark Brooklyn Bridge, followed by Times Square.

"This is New York City?" Goodness breathed in awe.

"My heavens, what's that?" Mercy asked, pointing to the street below.

Gabriel grinned. His timing couldn't have been better. They'd arrived in time to witness Macy's Thanksgiving Day parade. A giant balloon replica of a popular comic-strip dog floated far above the street, steered by several silly-looking adults dressed in elf costumes.

"It looks like some kind of parade," Shirley answered before he had a chance to explain.

A marching band, the trombone players with their instruments aiming skyward, blared a lively rendition of an easily recognizable Christmas ditty. A fierce pounding of drums added to the excitement of the music.

"This is wonderful," Goodness said, and spread-eagled herself across the top of a blossom-laden float. Six men dressed as toy soldiers stood guard over an open treasure chest filled with a variety of brightly wrapped gifts in gold and silver paper.

"You wanted to meet Hannah," Gabriel reminded her, hiding a smile. Goodness's eyes were as round as a two-year-old child's.

"In a minute," Goodness told him. It was apparent she was more interested in watching the parade than in meeting her young charge.

With a stiff-kneed walk, one of the toy soldiers marched to the end of the float. A fairy princess appeared, with dainty wings strapped to her back, and scooped up handfuls of candy. Smiling, she tossed them into the cheering crowd.

"You call those wings?" Mercy asked on a disdainful note.

"We're here to meet Hannah Morganstern," Gabriel felt obligated to remind the three.

"I'm ready," Goodness announced, reluctantly tearing herself away from the dazzling scene.

"If we must," Mercy added with a decided lack of enthusiasm.

"Do you think Brynn Cassidy's here?" Shirley's gaze scanned the thick crowds that crammed the cement sidewalks. "What about the kids from the school? They'd come, wouldn't they?"

"We're supposed to meet Hannah, remember?" Gabriel reminded Shirley. He should have known it would be a mistake to bring the others. "There's Hannah now," he said in an effort to divert their attention. He motioned toward a group of parade watchers standing along Central Park West.

"Hannah's the petite woman with the blue angel scarf tied around her neck." Gabriel had a soft spot in his heart when it came to the gentle Jewish woman. She reminded him of Rebecca, the young woman God had chosen for Abraham's only son.

"She's lovely."

Gabriel agreed. "Hannah's the only child, born later in life to a devoted couple. Ruth Morganstern prayed faithfully for many years for a daughter."

"Leah Lundberg did the same," Mercy reminded Gabriel. "I don't understand why God makes some couples wait."

"It's not for us to question."

"I know," Mercy agreed. "His timing is always perfect."

"Getting back to Hannah," Gabriel tried again. "The Morgansterns have raised their daughter well. They couldn't be more proud of her, and rightly so. Hannah is well loved by many."

"Do you mind if Shirley and I entertain ourselves for a few moments?" Mercy asked, and her eyes twinkled with mischief. Gabriel noticed the angel was staring at the reader board above Times Square.

"You can go on without us," Shirley insisted.

"No way. Listen, you two. Shirley . . . Mercy," Gabriel stuttered, wanting to stop them before they vanished. Unfortunately he was too late. He clenched his jaw and turned to Goodness.

"You don't have a thing to worry about," Goodness assured him. "They can take care of themselves."

That was what Gabriel was afraid of.

He was about to go after Mercy and Shirley himself when Goodness tugged at his sleeve. "Tell me what you know about Hannah Morganstern.

You said her mother and grandmother are looking for Hannah to make a good marriage."

"Yes," he muttered. He would need his wits to make this assignment sound more difficult than it was.

"Well, if that's the case," Goodness muttered, her shoulders heaving with a deliberate sigh, "I certainly hope she isn't interested in the young man she's with. It's perfectly obvious they aren't the least bit suited."

Gabriel's attention went back to the street corner where he'd last seen Hannah.

"What's wrong with Carl Rabinsky?" he demanded.

"Just look."

"Carl, couldn't we please stay a bit longer?" Hannah asked. She pleaded with him with her eyes, hoping she could find a way to change his mind. Carl had agreed to attend the Thanksgiving Day parade with her, but they'd barely arrived and already he was anxious to leave. She knew he was having trouble with the headmaster at the Hebrew academy where he taught and had been preoccupied most of the day.

"Ten minutes more, then," Carl conceded indulgently. His gloved hand squeezed hers. "I'm sorry, but I told you earlier that this just isn't my thing."

"I know." Hannah was grateful he'd consented to come. She only wished he could enjoy the festivities as much as she did. Hannah found the merrymaking contagious—the children, the excitement, the wonderful silliness that surrounded this time of year.

"Oh, Carl, look," she said, pointing toward the huge float making its way down the wide street. "It's a scene from the *Nutcracker Suite.*"

Carl smiled tolerantly and pointedly glanced at his watch. "Five more minutes," he announced under his breath. "If you want to see more of the parade, you can watch it on television."

Television. Never. Hannah refused to allow his stick-in-the-mud attitude to spoil her fun. Standing on the tips of her toes, she peered down the bustling street, hoping to catch a glimpse of what was coming next. The distinct tones of an approaching band floated toward her.

Unable to see, she edged her way into the crowd until she was wedged against the waist-high barrier to the street. She stayed there until the marching musicians passed, applauding their efforts. The tall, distinguished-looking man standing next to her whistled boisterously. Hannah looked up at him and smiled warmly. Their eyes met, and he returned the friendly gesture.

The man looked vaguely familiar, but then it wasn't uncommon for Hannah to see someone she thought she knew. Working in the family-owned, kosher-style deli, she met literally hundreds of people on a daily basis.

His eyes were a deep, rich shade of coffee brown. They sparkled with delight as he looked down on her. He had a kind face, appealing but not particularly handsome. His hair needed to be trimmed, but that gave him a rumble-tumble look that she found endearing. It was apparent he was some kind of businessman; she could tell that much from the way he dressed and the way he stood. Besides, if he frequented her parents' deli, then chances were he worked in one of the office buildings close by.

"Do I know you?" he asked, frowning slightly.

"I'm Hannah Morganstern," she said. "Most people recognize me from my parents' deli."

"Of course. Your father serves the best pastrami in town." He held out his hand to her. "I'm Joshua Shadduck."

"Hello, Joshua." The noise level made it difficult to carry on a conversation.

They shook hands, and Hannah glanced over her shoulder, looking for Carl. He wasn't there. She scanned the crowd once more, certain he wouldn't have left her intentionally. Carl would never do that, yet he was nowhere in sight. Anxious now, she stood on her tiptoes and looked around.

"Oh, dear," she whispered, and bit into her lower lip.

"Is something wrong?" Joshua lowered his head close to her so she could hear him.

"My friend. I'm afraid we've gotten separated and I forgot my cell phone."

"That happens in crowds like these."

"I know, but . . ." She continued to study the huge throng. The crowd was moving, milling about. "I didn't mean to leave him behind." Carl would be worried and flustered. If she ever hoped to talk him into attending another parade, he'd be sure to remind her of this.

"I'll help you look," Joshua offered.

"You don't need to do that." She was the one to blame. If she hadn't been so impatient to see what was ahead, she wouldn't have lost Carl.

"Tell me what he looks like," Joshua suggested. Since he was head and shoulders taller than she, his chances of finding Carl were far better than her own.

"Let me think," she mumbled. She went with the most obvious: his clothing. "He had on a black wool overcoat."

Joshua leveled his eyes on her, amusement bracketing the sides of his mouth. "Hannah, every man here has on a black wool overcoat."

"Yes . . . I know. He's five ten or so, and . . . he's probably frowning. He only came because I wanted to see the parade, and he's probably annoyed with me for disappearing like this."

"A frowning man, five ten, in a black wool overcoat."

Their eyes met once more, and for no reason Hannah could explain, they both started laughing.

"He's probably given up on me and left," she conceded, and glanced longingly over her shoulder, not wanting to miss the rest of the parade. "I should probably go back myself," she said with regret.

"Why? Your friend can find his own way home, can't he?"

"Yes, but . . ."

"Stay," he urged. His hand cupped her elbow, his touch light and encouraging. His eyes smiled with warmth and pleasure, something she'd found sadly lacking in Carl. Her friend had only tolerated the merriment. Macy's parade was one more thing Carl considered frivolous and impractical. He often mentioned the overwhelming cost of such a production. To Carl's way of thinking, this money would be better spent feeding the hungry or aiding the homeless.

Hannah had no argument to offer. The parade would go on no matter how wasteful Carl found it to be, and she could see no reason not to enjoy it.

"Oh, look," she said, pointing down the street at the oncoming float. She glanced at Joshua and discovered that he viewed the winter festival creation with the same keen enjoyment and wonder that she did.

One lazy snowflake drifted down from the lead gray sky. Another soon followed.

"Snow!" Delighted, Hannah held up her hand to catch a fluffy flake. It melted in the palm of her hand.

"It's a perfect conclusion to the parade, don't you think?" Josh asked. Pressed against him as she was, Hannah couldn't help noticing how warm and close he was.

"Is it over? Already?" She didn't want it to be.

"Do you have to hurry back?" Joshua asked. "We could take a short stroll in Central Park and enjoy the snow."

It went without saying that she shouldn't. Her family would be waiting for her. They assumed she was with Carl, not some strange man she barely recognized. Her father had always been protective of her. She was his jewel. Hannah remembered how pleased her parents had been when she'd first started dating Carl. The fact that he was a rabbi's son added to their endorsement of the young man.

"A stroll in Central Park," she repeated, and then before she could change her mind, she nodded. Her willingness to spend time with him, a man who was little more than a stranger, would be frowned upon by everyone concerned.

"Goodness," Gabriel warned, "don't even think about it."

"About what?" The fact that the archangel was traveling with her had cramped her style considerably.

"I know what you've got up your sleeve."

"What?" Archangels knew so little about romance; what else was she to do? Gabriel thought Carl Rabinsky was the perfect husband for Hannah. Anyone with half a brain could see how ill suited the young couple was. Carl was a determined man, sincere in his faith. Unfortunately he'd fallen into a common trap. He was big on religion and weak on faith.

"I can see what you're thinking and I'm telling you right now, it isn't going to work," Gabriel continued, disapproval beaming from his piercing eyes. "Joshua Shadduck is an important attorney. The two have nothing in common."

"Joshua is Jewish, isn't he?"

"Yes, but that has nothing to do with the issues here. Goodness, listen to me. You're stirring up a hornets' nest if you continue in this vein. I absolutely forbid it, do you understand?"

"Yes, but—"

"There're no buts about it." Gabriel's brow was knit with a thick frown. He opened his mouth and Goodness was convinced he was about to argue further with her when a breathless but elated Shirley arrived.

"I found Brynn Cassidy," the other angel announced gleefully. "She's with Suzie Chang, one of the girls from her class."

"We're discussing something important here," Goodness said. She refused to let Shirley interrupt her now. Not when she was about to make an important point. She glared at the archangel. "Didn't you notice Joshua and Hannah together? It's as plain as the wings on your back that they're right for each other." Anyone with eyes would recognize how lonely Joshua was. Success wasn't all it was cracked up to be. It seemed to her that he'd come to this realization himself recently. As far as Goodness could tell, Hannah Morganstern complemented his life, and she wasn't about to let Gabriel tell her otherwise.

"What I'm saying," Gabriel insisted, "is that you must leave well enough alone. You think I didn't notice the way you manipulated Hannah and Joshua? I'm not blind. You practically steered her right into him."

Goodness released a pent-up sigh. Dealing with Gabriel often required persistence. "I realize you find this difficult to believe, but I'm something of an expert in matters involving the heart. Remember last year?"

"I'm not likely to forget it," the archangel muttered. "I was nearly sent back to singing with the choir because of you three."

Goodness ignored his comment, which she was sure was a gross exaggeration.

"Promise me you'll keep your hands off of Hannah and Joshua," Gabriel warned, "otherwise I'll have you restringing harps for the rest of your days."

The threat was an empty one, and Goodness knew it.

"Did anyone hear me?" Shirley asked excitedly. "I actually located Brynn Cassidy. Don't you realize what a miracle that was in this crowd?"

"I heard you," Gabriel told her with a sour look. "Miracle or not, you won't be working with Brynn Cassidy. The schoolteacher needs far more help than you can offer. You can't work with Brynn and those kids from the high school. I have another assignment waiting for you," Gabriel insisted with a hard edge to his voice.

"But—"

"It's a take-it-or-leave-it situation."

Goodness feared that Shirley was about to blow it. She was relieved when the other angel snapped her mouth closed. At times, Shirley could be downright argumentative. If Shirley made the mistake of debating this Brynn Cassidy issue, the archangel just might pull all three of them out of New York City. Goodness didn't want that to happen just when matters were beginning to look promising.

Without being obvious, she scanned the dispersing crowds, hoping to catch a glimpse of Hannah and Joshua. She found them strolling through Central Park, deep in conversation. The two were oblivious of everything around them. They made a striking couple, she mused, immeasurably pleased with herself. Archangels might be high-and-mighty creatures, but they knew little of dealing with humans and love. When it came to affairs of the heart, Goodness was far more knowledgeable than Gabriel. The problem, and admittedly it was a big one, was convincing him of that.

Joshua wasn't sure what had happened to him. He'd suggested this walk in the park with Hannah for purely selfish reasons. The Thanksgiving Day parade had been enjoyable, but it hadn't been nearly as much fun until Hannah had joined him.

He remembered her with a clarity that surprised him. She was the daughter of the deli owner. When he'd claimed her father made the best pastrami in town, he hadn't been exaggerating. Over the last few years he'd visited the deli a number of times, but generally he had his lunch delivered. Hannah might well have been to his office.

Hannah was a delicate creature, beautiful in ways that struck a man's soul. She wasn't like the crisp, business professionals he knew and worked with on a daily basis. She inspired him with her gentle goodness. Although he'd never met the man she was with—Carl, if he remembered his name correctly—already he found he didn't much like him. If Joshua had become separated from Hannah in a crowd, it would have taken a lot more than a little congestion for him to stop searching for her. Hannah hadn't said a lot, but it was obvious Carl didn't enjoy parades.

Joshua had taken Hannah's hand while strolling through the park. The snow had long since stopped, but the afternoon remained crisp and cold. A perfect winter day.

The moment their hands linked, Joshua experienced a faint stirring of emotion. Faint stirring, nothing, he mused with a bleak smile. It felt as if someone had punched him in the stomach with a pipe iron.

He wondered if this was the woman he'd been searching for all these months. He certainly hadn't expected her to be the daughter of a deli owner. It didn't matter, he decided. Who was he to question fate? They'd met, and being with her, laughing, joking, talking, had felt instinctively right. Never had he been more comfortable with anyone.

It embarrassed him, the way he couldn't stop

staring at her. She had such beautiful eyes, but then everything about Hannah was beautiful. She was guileless and genuine, and when she looked up and blinked, Josh swore he could see all the way to her soul.

"We've been talking all this time and I never asked where you work," Hannah commented.

"I'm an attorney." He would have mentioned the name of the law firm, one of the most prestigious in Manhattan, but he didn't want to sound as though he were bragging. Knowing Hannah, he doubted that it would impress her. More than likely she wouldn't recognize the name of the firm.

"A lawyer." She said this as if the information distressed her.

"You don't like attorneys?"

"No, it's not that. I think there are some wonderful attorneys, only . . ."

"Yes," he prodded.

"My parents were recently involved in a frivolous lawsuit, and my dad's convinced the real culprits in the case were the lawyers. I'm afraid he's developed something of a prejudice, but I don't think that will last long."

"Good. I'd hate to get off on the wrong foot with your family."

At the mention of her parents, Hannah looked at her watch. "Oh, dear," she said anxiously. "I didn't realize how late it was." She took several steps backward. "Thank you for a wonderful time. I'm sorry to rush off like this."

She'd turned and was speed-walking away from him before he'd had time to react. "Hannah," he called.

She spun around.

"I'd like to see you again."

Her eyes were wide, and she seemed to hesitate. Joshua decided it was best not to press her.

"Don't worry," he said. "I'll stop in at the deli and we can talk about it then."

She nodded abruptly, and it was plain she was in a hurry to get away.

"If it'll reassure you, I'll avoid mentioning I'm an attorney."

Her beautiful eyes brightened with a soft smile before she hurried out of the park. Josh buried his hands in his pockets and ambled along the walkway toward Cherry Hill Fountain. He kicked lazily at burnt orange–colored leaves.

Josh found himself smiling broadly. His patience had paid off. For nearly thirty years he'd been waiting to meet a woman like Hannah Morganstern. To think all this time she'd been right under his nose. He threw back his head and laughed. The sound of his delight echoed through the park.

Hannah hurried into the apartment on top of the family deli, stripping the blue scarf from her neck.

"I'm home."

"Thank heaven you're home; I was worried, you're so late," her mother said, planting her hand over her heart as she stepped out of the kitchen. "Your father and I didn't know what to think when Carl phoned and asked if you'd returned safely."

"The parade was wonderful," Hannah said.

"What happened with Carl?" Her father stood with the morning paper clenched in his hands. He studied her over the top of his spectacles.

"I don't know," Hannah told them, walking into the kitchen. The smells of turkey and sage, pumpkin pie and applesauce, that greeted her caused her to pause and inhale deeply. Her stomach growled, reminding her how hungry she was.

"Carl claims you disappeared into the crowd."

"I wanted to get a closer look at the floats," Hannah explained as she lifted the lid off a cast-iron kettle. Broth simmered with a mixture of savory herbs floated on the slowly churning surface.

"There's nothing to worry about now that you're back safe and sound," her father muttered, studying his daughter as though he expected something of her. Hannah knew exactly what her family was hoping. They wanted Carl to ask for her hand in marriage.

"Carl said he'd be by later," Ruth Morganstern said, and shared a secret look with her husband of many years. The exchange confirmed Hannah's suspicions.

"We both think the world of Carl," her father told Hannah unnecessarily. "He's a good man."

"Dependable," her mother added.

"Honorable."

"A righteous man." Her mother nodded for emphasis.

Hannah offered them both a shaky smile and headed toward her bedroom. She didn't want to discuss Carl, not when her head was spinning from her time with another man. "I'm going to change my shoes and then I'll be back to help you with dinner."

Her father looped his arms around Ruth's shoulders. "Take your time," her mother called out after her. "Dinner won't be ready for some time yet."

Inside her bedroom, Hannah slumped on the edge of her mattress. It would be impossible to tell them about meeting Joshua now. He was the man who caused her heart to sing. She couldn't disappoint them. Not with her family extolling Carl's virtues.

Hannah had only briefly discussed marriage with Carl. Their parents had been the ones who frequently spoke of the two entering into an agreement. As far as Carl's family was concerned, the marriage was a foregone conclusion. Her parents seemed to feel the same way.

Hannah lay back and stared up at the bedroom ceiling. Carl was a wonderful man. He was everything her parents had said and much more. Someday she probably would marry Carl.

She closed her eyes and thought about what their lives would be like together. She liked Carl, enjoyed his company. When he kissed her it was something sweet and gentle. But try as she might, Hannah couldn't imagine Carl ever being passionate. A smile cracked her lips, and she chided herself silently.

In her mind's eye she thought about the children she might have with Carl. But instead of conjuring up babies, her mind filled with Joshua Shadduck.

She shook her head in an effort to dispel the image. If only he wasn't an attorney. If only she'd met him last year at this time. If only . . .

"Hannah."

Guiltily she bolted off the bed. "Yes, Mama."

"Carl's on the phone. He wants to know what took you so long. He's been worried. You should have phoned him first thing."

Hurriedly Hannah reached for her shoes. "Tell him I'll be right there."

"Hannah will marry Carl," Gabriel said as if he needed to convince himself.

Goodness was wise enough to say nothing. She'd learned the hard way that it was often more advantageous to hold one's tongue with the archangel.

"You understand this, don't you?" Gabriel asked pointedly.

"I'm sure you're right," the prayer ambassador answered without emotion. It demanded everything she had to hide her true feelings.

Gabriel studied her with a weary look. "You're sure you can handle this case?"

"Positive." She beamed him her brightest, most innocent smile.

"No monkey business."

Goodness's eyes rounded with indignation. "I wouldn't dream of it."

"Just remember that promise."

"Can I please meet Jenny Lancaster now?" Mercy asked.

Goodness wanted to kiss her friend for distracting Gabriel. She didn't know how much longer she would have been able to hide her feelings.

"Ah, yes. Jenny." Gabriel turned his attention away from Goodness and exhaled sharply. "I'd almost forgotten. Now there's a sorry case. Let me take you to her now."

Chapter Three

"Jenny, wake up." Michelle Jordan burst into the bedroom and pulled open the thick drapes. Brilliant sunlight spilled into the room as Jenny Lancaster struggled to an upright position.

"What time is it?" she asked, yawning loudly. It couldn't be morning. Not yet. Not so soon. Her eyes burned and it felt as though she hadn't slept more than an hour or two.

"It's party time." Michelle dramatically threw her arms into the air.

Jenny collapsed against her pillow. "Not for me."

"For both of us, girl." Michelle curled up at the foot of Jenny's bed. "John Peterman's sent out a casting call for a new Lehman musical. He's going to need twenty singers and dancers. I don't know about you, but I intend to be one of those who ends up on stage opening night. Now you can come along and audition with me, or you can sleep the rest of your life away."

Jenny closed her eyes. The choice shouldn't be this difficult. There was a time when she would have leapt out of bed, bright-eyed and bushy-tailed, grabbed her dancing shoes, and headed out the front door. Not so these days. At twenty-three Jenny Lancaster felt like a has-been. Or, more appropriate, a never-was.

"Are you coming or not?"

Another cattle call. Jenny had given up counting the number of times she'd set her heart on getting a bit part on Broadway. Off Broadway, near Broadway. She didn't care. This was her dream. Her goal. Her ambition.

She'd left Custer, Montana, blessedly naive about the cutthroat world of the stage. Three years later she felt washed-out, washed-up, and ready for the wringer.

Three years was a long time to subsist on one's dreams. Jenny would have thrown in the towel a long time before now if it hadn't been for one thing. Her family and friends back home believed in her. She was the bright, shining star the community had pinned its hopes upon. Back home she could outsing, outdance, and outact anyone in town. But in New York she was just another pretty face with talent.

"Twenty singers and dancers," Jenny repeated, still trying to decide if another audition was worth all the pain involved. She wasn't sure her heart could stand another rejection. "Does twenty singers and twenty dancers mean Peterman needs forty people?"

"I don't know," Michelle said with her characteristic boundless energy. "It doesn't matter, does it?"

It did. Jenny sat upright and rubbed a hand down her face. "I don't know if I'm up to this. Rejection hurts. Frankly I'm not sure this is what I really want anymore," she whispered. Admitting this to her best friend was hard, but it needed to be said. She loved New York, but at heart she would always be a country girl.

"You can't think of it like that. Rejections are simply the rungs to the ladder of success," Michelle announced, ever positive, ever confident.

Jenny sighed audibly. "You've been listening to motivational tapes again, haven't you?"

Michelle nodded. "It shows that much?"

"Yes." Almost against her will, Jenny tossed aside the bedding and climbed off the mattress. "All right, I'll go, but I'll need a few minutes to put myself together."

"Good girl." Michelle pulled open her bottom drawer and took out a pair of black leotards. "You don't want to spend the rest of your life waitressing at Arnold's, do you? Sure you get to sing, but it isn't anywhere close to Broadway."

Jenny sincerely hoped her roommate didn't let anyone back in Custer know that. The entire town firmly believed in her talent. Firmly believed in her.

After so much time, she couldn't continue to

make up excuses why her name didn't light up a marquee. So she'd stretched the truth. All right, she'd elasticized it to the point where it was no longer recognizable. Performing in an Off-Broadway musical was a long shot from her job as a singing waitress. Her friends and family believed she was well on the road to becoming a star. Little could be further from the truth. The light of ambition in Jenny's eyes had dimmed considerably in the past three years. Not so long ago she would have jumped at the chance to audition for John Peterman. These days it was difficult to find the energy to drag herself out of bed.

"I don't know if all this trouble is worth the effort," she confessed as she reached for her beige dancing shoes.

"Don't talk like that, Jenny. This is your dream." She hugged her clenched fists to her breast. "Don't let go now. Not when you're so close to making it all come true."

Jenny wished she shared her friend's limitless enthusiasm. Michelle had been spurned as many times as Jenny. Yet her roommate continued to bounce back with renewed optimism, ever hopeful, ever cheerful, ever certain their big break was just around the next corner.

Part of Jenny's reluctance had to do with the season. Christmastime away from her family had always been difficult, but it seemed even more so this year. Not only could she not afford the trip home, but once she was with her family and friends, Jenny realized, she'd never be able to continue with the lie. One look and her parents would guess the truth.

Then there was Trey, their neighbor and long-time family friend. The boy next door, only anyone who met the cattle rancher would be hard-pressed to refer to him as a boy. Whenever Jenny became disheartened, she closed her eyes and remembered Trey.

Trey sitting atop his roan, his Stetson dipped low enough to disguise his eyes. He did that on purpose, she believed, just so she couldn't read his expression. His ranch bordered her father's spread, so Trey had been around for as long as Jenny could remember.

While in school, Jenny had never given much thought to her handsome neighbor. In the years since she'd been away, all that had changed. Whenever Jenny thought about home, it was Trey LaRue who popped into her mind. Trey riding the open range. Trey gentling a startled filly. Trey carrying a sick calf.

Of course he might be married by now, although she doubted it. Surely her mother would have said something if he'd tied the knot. He was at the age—past it, really—when most ranchers married. Three years was a long time to be away from home. Although she remembered him, there was nothing to say he thought about her. A lot of things changed over time.

"Are you ready?" Michelle asked. Her room-mate's eagerness was a burr under Jenny's saddle. By all that was right, she should be in bed. Her feet hadn't stopped hurting, nor had her back ceased to ache. Yet when she'd finished dancing her heart out, singing until her vocal cords were strained, she'd be due back at Arnold's.

"I'm as ready as I'll ever be." Even as she said the words, Jenny felt a sinking sensation in the pit of her stomach. Auditioning seemed a waste of effort. A waste of time. A waste of her heart.

"That's Jenny?" Mercy asked Gabriel, standing in the corner of the tiny apartment.

"That's her."

"Who's been praying for her?" This question came from Goodness.

Mercy glared at her friend as if to say she was the one who would be asking the questions. After all, this was her assignment. Goodness had already met her charge, and as always, her friend was looking to meddle. Mercy knew that look and sincerely hoped Gabriel didn't.

"The prayer originated from her neighbor in Montana," Gabriel answered. He frowned as he said it, as if plowing through his memory to put a name to the request. "Trey LaRue, I believe," he said decisively. "Trey's known Jenny most of his life."

"What has he asked?"

"Trey wants Jenny to come home for the holidays. It seems Jenny's father has been feeling poorly. Dillon Lancaster won't ask his daughter to come home, and neither will Jenny's mother. But both miss her terribly."

"Why don't they visit New York?" The solution seemed obvious to Mercy. She could easily manipulate the couple into heading for the wonders of the big city. Naturally Goodness and Shirley would be willing to lend her a hand. Already she was formulating a plan.

Why, the three of them had gotten so good at this sort of thing that it wouldn't surprise her if the Lancasters never guessed how they'd gotten to New York. A little celestial manipulation never hurt anyone.

"Jenny has discouraged them from coming," Gabriel explained.

"But why . . ." Mercy stopped herself. She already knew the answer. Jenny didn't want her family to know that she'd lied. She wasn't starring in an Off-Broadway production of *Guys and Dolls*. She was a waitress who quite literally sang for her supper. The line of success she'd fed her family was gagging the young woman now. Jenny couldn't allow her parents to see where she worked. Being forced to admit the truth would humiliate her, so she continued to sabotage herself.

Lies were like that, Mercy realized, and wondered why humans so readily fell into that trap. She'd seen for herself how lies tainted human lives. Would they never learn?

What had started out as a slight exaggeration on

Jenny's part had turned into a monster that separated her from those she loved most. All because she hadn't wanted to disappoint her family. Instead she'd disappointed herself.

"This shouldn't be so hard, should it?" Goodness said, looping her arm through Mercy's. "From what we've seen, Jenny's ready to give it up and head back to Montana all on her own. Not just for Christmas, either. After all the disappointment she's suffered, she's more than ready for the green, green pastures of home. I can't say that I blame her. The time has come for her to face up to a few home truths."

Gabriel's brow rose as if Goodness's insight surprised him, and Mercy's friend beamed. "Is that a fact?"

"I wouldn't be so fast to form an opinion about Jenny," Gabriel warned. "She's very talented. I shouldn't need to remind you what God says about the desires of one's heart."

"You mean she isn't ready to relinquish her dream?" Mercy asked. She'd read the situation the same as Goodness. It seemed all Jenny needed was one good excuse to pack her bags and head home to Montana. And to Trey, the young man who cared enough to pray for her return.

"I'm not here to answer those questions," Gabriel said, "but I don't think you should underestimate the power of a dream. Jenny has lived and breathed little else for three long years. It's true she's discouraged, but that doesn't mean she's willing to give up.

You might be surprised to discover just how close she really is to seeing her name in lights. Don't forget," Gabriel warned, "that the darkest hour is just before dawn. She could be on the brink of something big."

"Do you really think so?" Mercy felt the excitement churning inside her. But that enthusiasm slowly ground to a halt as she studied the archangel. "Is there something you know that we don't?" Gabriel occasionally withheld information in a blatant effort to teach them a lesson. Mercy had long suspected it to be so.

"No," the archangel assured them. "Just don't be so quick to assume the obvious."

"My oh my, she is talented," Mercy admitted, watching her young charge's agile leap across the stage.

It was at times like this that Jenny realized how badly she hungered for this dream. Once she stood on stage with the other dancers, her adrenaline started flowing, pumping her deflated hopes until they soared higher and higher.

This was where she belonged, where she longed to be. Her heart hummed with excitement, waiting for the opportunity to prove herself.

"Jenny Lancaster." Her name was called by a man sitting in the theater seating. Since the lights blocked her view, the casting director was no more than a hoarse, detached voice. From her best guess, she figured he was somewhere in the first five or six rows.

Jenny stepped forward and handed the piano man her sheet music.

"What will you be singing?" asked the same uninterested voice.

She moved one step and peered into the dark. " 'Don't Cry for Me, Argentina.' "

"Fine. Give us your best eight bars."

It was always the same. Rarely did it vary. Jenny suspected she could have sung a tune from a *Sesame Street* production and no one would have known the difference, least of all the casting director. He'd made up his mind even before her turn had come, even before she'd been given a chance to prove what she could do.

Argentina might not weep for her, but Jenny felt the tears welling up inside her. Tears of disappointment. Tears of struggle. Tears of a dream that refused to die.

The first chords from the piano filled the silence. Jenny hung her head and closed her eyes, allowing the music to transport her to another world. She drew in a deep breath and slowly lifted her head. No longer was Jenny Lancaster auditioning for a bit part; she was playing the role of her life. Within the magic of a few notes, she was transformed from a disillusioned waitress into the ambitious wife of a South American dictator.

"Wow." Mercy was set back on her wings. "That girl can sing."

"She is talented," Shirley was quick to agree.

"Incredible." Goodness seemed to be at a loss for words, which was completely unlike her.

Mercy knew she could accept no credit for Jenny's skill; nevertheless she experienced a deep sense of pride that she should be assigned to this amazing young woman.

"Her voice, why, it's almost . . ."

"Angelic," Gabriel supplied, grinning broadly. It was a rare treat to find the archangel in such good spirits.

"Yes," Mercy agreed. "Angelic."

"You believe you can handle this request?" he questioned.

Mercy was sure she could. "Yes," she assured him confidently. "Leave everything to me." Somehow, some way, Mercy would come up with the means of helping Jenny fulfill her dreams. With a little help from her friends.

Anyone with this much talent, this much heart, deserved a break. A bit of intercession from the heavenly realm never hurt. Naturally Mercy wasn't about to let Gabriel know her plans, but then what he didn't know couldn't hurt him.

And while she had her hand in Jenny's life, Mercy decided, she might as well do what she could about getting the talented singer home for the holidays.

"No funny stuff," Gabriel warned.

Mercy managed to look offended. "Gabriel, please, you insult me."

"I won't have you hot-wiring cars and sending them where you will."

Mercy's shoulders went back in a display of outrage. "I'd never resort to anything that underhanded."

Gabriel didn't say anything for several moments. Then, scratching his head, he studied the three prayer ambassadors. "Can anyone tell me why I don't believe you?"

Chapter Four

"I'd like everyone to take out a clean piece of paper," Brynn instructed, standing in front of the classroom. It sounded like a simple enough request, one would think. But from the moaning and groaning, it was as if she'd sprung a surprise quiz on them.

"You aren't going to make us write again, are you?" Emilio Alcantara groaned aloud, voicing, Brynn suspected, the thoughts of half the class.

"Yes, I am," she said, unwilling to let her students' lack of enthusiasm dampen her spirits.

Yolanda leaned so far out of her desk toward Denzil Johnson that she nearly toppled onto the floor.

"Yolanda," Brynn said, "is there a problem?"

"I don't have any paper. I wanted to borrow a piece from Denzil."

"Get your own paper, woman," the black youth protested. "What do I look like, a friggin' Wal-Mart?"

"I loaned you paper last week." Yolanda's dark eyes snapped with outrage.

"That's because you were lucky enough to have me sit next to you. I never said nothin' about paying you back."

Yolanda's mouth thinned, and it looked as if she were about to explode when Suzie Chang saved the day.

"I have an extra sheet she can use," the Chinese girl volunteered shyly, tearing off a clean page from her tablet and passing it across the aisle to Yolanda. The Hispanic girl grabbed it and glared at Denzil as if to say it would be a cold day in hell before he got anything from her again.

"Thank you, Suzie," Brynn said, eager to return to the writing assignment.

"What are you going to have us write about this time?" Emilio asked. "Not something stupid, I hope."

Teaching the value clarification portion of the class had proved to be the most difficult for Brynn. She wanted to make this as interesting and as much fun as she could, but she often found herself on a completely different wavelength from her students.

The incident with Emilio in the hallway was a prime example. The teenager had actually expected her to lie on his behalf. Emilio didn't understand why she'd told the truth about the knife. He'd missed three days of school and consequently blamed her. He saw nothing wrong with his own behavior but seemed to feel that she'd been the one to betray his trust.

It had taken the better part of another week for his sullen mood in class to disappear. She wasn't sure even now what she'd done to get back into his good graces. Whatever it was, she was grateful. Emilio was a natural leader, so his attitude was quickly picked up by the others in class.

Ever since the incident with Emilio she'd been subjected to an attitude of mistrust. It was as if she'd fallen from grace in the eyes of her students.

"First off, don't put your name on the top of the page."

"You don't want our names?" This clearly came as a surprise since she'd so often instructed them to remember just that.

"No names," she reiterated. "Now I'd like each of you to write one hundred and fifty words."

"We gotta count them?"

"That's about a page and a half," Brynn explained. "The subject of your paper is this: If I could kiss anyone in this classroom, who would it be, and why."

For a moment the entire class looked at her as if they couldn't believe what she'd said. Someone smothered a giggle and catcalls echoed across the room.

It didn't take anyone long to get involved in

the project. Soon heads were bowed over the paper, and her students wrote feverishly. Brynn liked to involve her students in some type of writing assignment, often on a daily basis. She did this for a number of reasons, but first and foremost was an effort to require them to clarify their thoughts on certain subjects. She attempted to balance a serious topic one day, followed by a lighter one the next.

Although she'd been teaching the class for a number of weeks now, whenever they were asked to write, her students put up a royal stink. Often they bombarded her with silly questions or employed other delay tactics in an effort to forestall the assignment.

Not this time. Looking at them now, writing as fast as their hands would allow, one would think the first student finished would be excused for what remained of the quarter.

"When you're done writing, please bring the papers to my desk." The class was both cooperative and silent. The cooperation part was a welcome relief. Brynn was beginning to feel like a salmon swimming upstream. Every inch was a struggle, every day a challenge.

One by one, her class delivered their papers to her desk. Before long Brynn had accumulated a tidy stack.

Curious whispers followed.

"Aren't you going to read them?" someone asked.

"I will later," she promised, as if this were a normal assignment.

"Wait a minute," Emilio said, slouching down on his seat. "I gotta right to know how many women want me."

Several of the girls booed, suggesting he wasn't the one on their list.

Emilio planted his hand over his heart and looked deeply grieved by their lack of appreciation for his obvious charms.

"Did anyone put me down?" Modesto demanded. "Emilio's got a point, you know."

"One thing's for sure, no one picked Mike," taunted a boy in the back of class.

Mike was a loner and rarely contributed to class discussions. He suffered from a bad case of acne and kept his distance from the others. Brynn had never seen him talk to any of the other students. In many ways her heart went out to Mike, and she struggled to reach him. To have someone taunt him now was cruel and unnecessary. For the first time Brynn wondered about the wisdom of her assignment. It had sounded like such fun when she'd planned it.

"Don't be so sure," Brynn said, and reached for the stack of papers. Her relief was great when she saw that one of the first papers mentioned Mike's name. "Here's a paper for Mike."

"You gotta be kidding." This came from Modesto. The youth sat up and turned around to stare at Mike.

Brynn walked down the aisle and handed Mike the paper.

"How come he gets to read his and I can't have mine?" This came from Emilio.

The corners of Mike's mouth turned up and revealed a brief smile when she laid the sheet down on his desk.

"I'll get to you soon enough," Brynn promised.

"If anyone chose him," Yolanda joked.

"Do bears shit in the woods?"

"Emilio," Brynn admonished. "I won't have that language in my class."

"Sorry, Miss Cassidy."

"Careful," Brynn heard someone say under their breath. "She might get you suspended again."

The next paper listed Emilio's name. She handed it to him and he let out a triumphant cry and punctured the air with his fist. "What did I tell you?" he shouted. "Women are crazy about me." Excited and pleased, he was halfway out of his desk. "I got charisma, you know. Real charisma."

Brynn walked up and down the aisles, delivering the papers. It flustered her a bit when she found her own name toward the top of the page. Emilio's handwriting was immediately recognizable, and she flushed. She'd never intended for anyone to put down her name.

"You aren't going to want these back, are you?" Yolanda pleaded.

"No. Keep them."

"Ms. Cassidy." Denzil's hand waved frantically. "There must be some mistake. I didn't get any papers."

"That's because you're greedy," Yolanda took delight in informing him. "Besides, why would anyone want to kiss you?"

"Hey, you didn't have any problem the other night."

"I'd had too much to drink and you know it."

"That's not what you said earlier."

The bell rang just then, and Brynn was saved from having to break off a spat between the two for the second time that day. Whatever was taking place between Yolanda and Denzil was best settled outside the classroom.

"For your assignment," Brynn said, raising her hand to capture their attention before the room emptied, "read the next chapter of *The Diary of Anne Frank*."

Her words were followed by a loud moan.

"I'll see everyone tomorrow afternoon. Have a good evening."

It never ceased to amaze Brynn how fast her classroom emptied. It was as though her students stampeded toward the door in an effort to escape a nuclear holocaust.

As was her habit at the end of the day, Brynn sat at her desk and graded assignments, but today she didn't have much time because of a dental appointment near her apartment in New Jersey. After a half hour, she tucked what she hadn't finished into her briefcase and headed toward the staff parking lot.

"Yo, Ms. Cassidy!" Emilio raced toward her.

"Hello, Emilio."

His steps soon matched hers. "You probably guessed it was me who wrote down your name, right?"

Brynn could feel her face growing warm.

"Listen, I thought I should explain," he said quickly, looking slightly embarrassed himself. "I gotta be careful paying too much attention to any one chick. You see, there are three or four in the class who've got the hots for me. I was trying to be diplomic about it."

"Diplomatic."

"Yeah, that."

"I understand, Emilio, and applaud your efforts."

"Good, 'cause I don't need chick trouble."

"I figured it was something like that," she assured him.

"Great."

"I'll see you tomorrow," she said, doing her best to disguise her amusement. One thing was certain: she didn't want to be the cause of "chick problems" for Emilio Alcantara.

Emilio turned and hurried across the parking lot toward the basketball hoop where his friends were busy playing two on two.

Brynn climbed inside her car and turned the key. It flickered to life, sputtered, and then quickly died. Surprised, she tried again, with the same results. She hadn't left her lights on that morning, she was sure of that. Her vehicle had recently been serviced. She tried once more, and this time the engine did nothing more than cough and choke.

"No, please, no," Brynn murmured, and pressed her forehead against the steering wheel. Trouble with her car was the last thing she needed.

Hannah shouldn't be this eager to see Joshua again, but she was. Again and again her gaze drifted toward the deli's front door as she waited impatiently for the man she'd met at Macy's Thanksgiving Day parade.

Her heart pounded like a race car piston every time she thought about Joshua. He'd been so gentle and caring. So considerate.

Although they'd only just met, they hadn't lacked for conversation. Joshua was the kind of man she could talk to for hours on end. Generally Hannah found herself tongue-tied and uneasy around men, but not with Joshua. It was as if they'd been friends for a long time.

Friends.

The word comforted her and eased her conscience.

Carl had joined her family for Thanksgiving dinner, and afterward he'd sat in the living room with her father. The two men had talked far into the evening, debating political issues and other matters. Before he'd left, Hannah's parents had discreetly left the room, affording her time alone with her beau. At first Carl and Hannah had seemed awkward with each other, Carl as much as she.

In an effort to ease the discomfort, she apologized for having lost him while at the parade. Carl reminded her that he felt responsible for her safety and suggested that in the years to come they'd watch the parade on television.

Hannah had lowered her head to hide her disappointment. Then, almost as if it were expected of him, Carl had leaned forward and gently pressed his lips to hers.

It was a sweet kiss, undemanding and totally lacking in passion.

Standing in the deli, Hannah closed her eyes and tried to dredge up some emotion, some deep feelings for Carl. But try as she might, she felt nothing. Surely not desire. Definitely no compelling yearning for his company. He was Carl, the rabbi's son. The man her parents felt would make her the perfect husband.

"Hannah," her mother admonished, coming out of the kitchen. Her arms were loaded with a tray of sliced bread. "Are you ill?"

"No, Mama."

"Then why do you stand there with your eyes closed? We have customers."

"I'm sorry." And Hannah was. She didn't know what was wrong with her to dawdle when there was work to be done.

Her mother printed off a list of lunch orders from their website e-mail, smoothed them out on the counter, and went about assembling sandwiches with a skill and dexterity that spoke of many years' experience.

Hannah lent a hand, packing the orders into plain

brown bags and marking each one. The scent of freshly baked bread spilled out of the kitchen and into the front of the deli, mingling with those of sliced pastrami and knishes, her father's specialties.

After a few minutes, Hannah tried again. "Mama, tell me how you met Dad."

Ruth Morganstern slowly lifted her eyes to Hannah. She appeared surprised by the question. "I don't have time for such foolishness now."

Disappointed, Hannah said nothing.

"We have orders and you're asking me about your father and me?" She laughed lightly. "It was so many years ago now. For over forty years I've loved this man. I don't remember when we met."

"You don't remember?" David shouted from the far side of the deli. "Forty-three years and you don't remember? What kind of wife forgets the day she met the man who would be her husband?"

Ruth laughed and dismissed him with a wave. "I remember some things."

"I should hope to God you do."

"He was handsome," Hannah's mother said out of the corner of her mouth.

"I'm still handsome."

"More so then," Ruth added, her eyes crinkling with amusement.

"Your mother was even more beautiful than she is now," Hannah's father called back. "I'd look at her and forget all about slicing meat. The time I courted her I nearly lost two fingers."

Hannah laughed, delighted at the exchange

between her parents. It seemed the lunch crowd, pressed against the glass display case, lost their impatience, and there were shared smiles all around.

Her father handed a thick pastrami sandwich on a paper plate to a young businessman. "You'll have to excuse my daughter," he said under his breath, but loudly enough for Hannah to hear. "She's in love."

In love? This was news to Hannah. But then, if she were to marry Carl, it was implied that they cared deeply for each other. Hannah liked Carl, respected him. He was a good, honorable man and, according to her parents, a fine catch.

Her mother couldn't have been more pleased when Hannah first started dating Carl. A rabbi's son. In Ruth's eyes, Carl was a better catch than a doctor or even an attorney.

An attorney. Automatically Hannah's thoughts drifted back to Joshua, although he'd never been far from her mind since they'd met.

"Here," Ruth said, handing Hannah the bag loaded with Internet orders. "With your head full of romance, can I trust you not to confuse these orders?" she teased affectionately.

"Of course," Hannah answered, and blushed.

"Your head's some place else these days." Her mother leveled her gaze on Hannah. "Your head and your heart." Hannah reached for her hand-knit scarf and wool coat. The deli employed a number of runners, but she was often needed to fill in during the lunch-hour rush.

"I won't be long," she promised before heading out into the cold.

Both her parents stared after her, and Hannah had the distinct impression that they would soon be bragging to their customers about her imminent engagement to Carl.

The wind nipped at her face as she hurried along Front Street in the bustling financial district. Taxis honked with impatience and a bus roared past, leaving her to choke on its exhaust.

Hannah's steps were filled with purpose as she wove her way in and around the foot traffic. She hadn't gone more than a block when she heard someone call her name. After a moment's hesitation, she looked over her shoulder. She didn't see anyone she knew.

"Hannah, wait."

The voice was recognizable now. Joshua.

She scanned the crowd but couldn't see him. Then she found him, standing on the other side of the street. He raised his arm high above his head and waved to attract her attention.

Standing on her tiptoes, Hannah smiled and waved back.

Joshua gestured for her to wait, and as soon as the traffic passed, he jogged across the street.

"Hello again," he said, smiling down on her.

"Hello."

There didn't seem to be anything more to say, but her pulse quickened and she felt as if her heart were trying to escape from inside her chest.

"I was on my way to the deli when I saw you."

"I'm delivering orders," she told him. She didn't have time to talk, not when hungry customers were waiting for their lunches. "I can't visit now." Regret settled over her. All day she'd waited for the opportunity to see Joshua again, and now, when she did happen upon him, she was forced to leave.

"I'll come with you," he suggested.

"But . . ."

"Do you have to get back right away?"

She should. She knew she should. Her parents might need her to make a second run and possibly a third. She hedged, not sure what to do.

"Five minutes," Josh suggested. "Ten. Listen, I'll help you deliver these orders and you won't be away any time at all. Don't say no, Hannah."

Hannah knew she shouldn't, but she found it even more difficult to turn him down, to deny herself the pleasure of this one short encounter. She gave him a barely discernible nod, praying she was doing the right thing.

Even before she had a chance to think the matter through, Joshua reached inside her carrying bag and grabbed three lunch orders. Not giving her time to protest, he rattled off the address to his office and instructed her to meet him there in ten minutes.

Feeling slightly guilty, she hurried to deliver what remained of the orders. Hannah often took a couple of minutes to chat with her customers, many of whom she considered friends, but not this afternoon. She was in and out as fast as she could manage it.

As soon as she could, she made her way to Joshua's office building. Crammed inside an elevator, she headed for the twenty-sixth floor. The elevator doors slid open and she stepped into an office complex lavishly decorated in rich mahogany and earth tones. The names of the law firm partners were elegantly etched in granite across one wall.

Hannah had been inside this complex a number of times and knew it to be one of the most prestigious law firms in Manhattan. She'd had no idea Joshua was a part of this firm.

Law clerks bustled about, and the phone jingled. Clients lingered in the waiting room.

"May I help you?" the receptionist asked. If she recognized Hannah as the girl from the deli, she didn't say anything.

"I'm Hannah Morganstern," she said.

The woman's face relaxed into a smile. "Ah yes, Mr. Shadduck said you'd be here soon. I'll have someone take you right back." She motioned toward one of the law clerks.

Hannah was escorted down a wide hallway. The law clerk gestured toward Joshua's door, which was open. Joshua stood on the far side of the office. He must have sensed her arrival because he turned around and his face brightened with a warm, welcoming smile.

She knew it was impolite to stare, but she couldn't

take her eyes off the framed list of achievements that lined his walls. This was no ordinary man. He was rich and powerful.

"What's wrong?"

She pulled her gaze away from the wall, surprised he had read her so easily. "I've never been inside your office before." She'd delivered his lunch any number of times but had never been past the foyer and the receptionist. She recognized Joshua from the times he'd come into the deli himself.

"Sit down. I'll ring Mary for something hot. Which do you prefer? Coffee or tea?"

"I . . . I really can't stay." To think that she'd allowed this important attorney to deliver lunches on her behalf. Hannah was mortified to the very marrow of her bones.

"You can't stay? Why not? I thought we had this all settled." He walked toward her and reached for her hand. Hannah didn't know if it was from the cold or the shock of seeing Joshua in this environment, but her fingers were icy cold.

"You're freezing." He rubbed her right hand between his own two hands. "You should be wearing gloves."

She felt completely out of her element. Pride prevented her from making up some excuse and rushing away. "I . . . I didn't know," she whispered.

Josh led her to a comfortable brown leather sofa and sat her down. "Didn't know what?"

Hannah held her tongue rather than blurt out the truth. When they'd met at the parade he was a familiar face, someone she recognized. In this office, he was the epitome of the man her father distrusted.

"I've been thinking about you all weekend," he said. "How was your Thanksgiving?"

Now was the perfect opportunity to tell him how close she was to becoming engaged to Carl. She could bring Carl's name up naturally and explain the situation. She could tell him how Carl had joined her family for dinner. How Carl and her father had talked. How Carl had kissed her good night. How they'd met on the Sabbath, after services in the synagogue.

"It was very nice," she said instead, wanting to kick herself. "How about you?"

"I ate with my mother and grandmother."

That started it. Within a matter of minutes he had her laughing over something his grandmother said, and they were immersed in conversation.

Twenty minutes slipped by, and it seemed like only five. "I have to get back," she said, unable to disguise her regret. "Thank you for the tea . . . for everything." She wouldn't indulge herself again. Not with Joshua.

Whatever made her so bold, Hannah would never know. She stood, prepared to walk away, and before she left, she pressed the palm of her hand to Joshua's clean-shaven face.

"Good-bye, Joshua," she said, and not giving him time to answer, she hurried from his office.

Her mother eyed her wearily when Hannah arrived back at the deli. "What took you?" she asked.

"I got sidetracked," Hannah admitted.

"Next time don't visit so long," her father warned her. "We needed you here."

"I'm sorry I'm late. Do you need me to make another run?"

"Don't worry, Louise was able to do it." Her mother rattled off a list of tasks. Hannah was grateful to work in the kitchen the rest of the afternoon.

"Hannah," her father called two hours later. "A package's been delivered for you."

"For me?" Drying her hands on a linen towel, Hannah stepped out to the front of the deli. A freckle-faced delivery boy held out a small, flat box. "Hannah Morganstern?"

"That's me."

"Sign here." He thrust a clipboard at her.

Hannah penned her name and then, with her parents watching, unwrapped the flat, oblong box.

Inside were a pair of expensive leather gloves and a note from Joshua.

"I've never heard you sing better," Michelle said as she and Jenny returned to their shared apartment. "Oh, Jenny, this is the break we've been waiting for. We're going to sing and dance on Broadway. I can feel it in my bones. We're really going to make it."

They often built each other up after an audition. Casting directors weren't known for lavishing potential stars with positive feedback, so they gave it to each other.

"Your voice . . ." Michelle hesitated as though she

had trouble finding the words. "It's different now. There's a depth and maturity that wasn't there six months ago." Michelle set the mail on the kitchen table. "Don't misunderstand me, you've always been good, but this afternoon you were nothing short of brilliant."

Jenny rolled her eyes.

"I'm not blowing smoke out my ears, either." Michelle sounded slightly offended. "I mean it, Jenny. I really think you're going to get a part, maybe even one of the leads."

Jenny knew otherwise. She sang out her heart the way she did for every audition. Nothing was going to change. She refused to build up her hopes again.

"This looks interesting," Michelle said, holding up an envelope and tossing it to her. "It's addressed to you. It might even be a Christmas card. Already? Good grief, it's not even December yet."

Jenny examined the envelope, her gaze scanning the return address. She recognized it immediately, and her breath jammed in her throat.

"Jenny? What is it?"

"It's from Trey," she whispered.

"Trey who?"

She stood and walked around the table while motioning with her hands, unable to formulate the words. "Trey LaRue . . . my neighbor, or rather my parents' neighbor."

"You've never mentioned him before," Michelle said.

"I haven't?" That seemed impossible. He was an integral part of what she considered home and family.

"Well, open it and find out what he has to say," Michelle encouraged.

That seemed the most logical thing to do. Jenny's hand trembled as she peeled back the flap and withdrew a card. A colorful turkey decorated the front, its plumage fanned out across the top. She opened the card and found Trey had written only one short sentence: "I'm eager to see you this Christmas." His name was listed below in smooth, even strokes of the fountain pen.

Jenny's heart sank to the pit of her stomach. She handed the card to Michelle.

"You're going home for the holidays?"

Jenny shook her head. "You know I can't. Not with money so tight." Not after she'd let everyone believe she had a starring role in an Off-Broadway production.

"I like his signature," Michelle said, studying the card. "You can tell a lot about a man by the way he signs his name." Her look was thoughtful. "But," she continued, grinning at Jenny, "I'd rather have you tell me all about him yourself."

"What can I say?" Jenny murmured, surprised to discover she didn't want to discuss Trey with her best friend.

She'd never missed home more than she did right at that moment. She longed to gaze into a night sky where the stars weren't obliterated by city lights.

She wanted to close her eyes and smell the scent of fresh hay. Home was cattle and mud and frustration. Home was love. Home was Trey.

"He hasn't written you before, has he?" Michelle pressed.

"No."

"Why now?"

Jenny shrugged. "I don't know. He owns the spread next to ours," she volunteered, hoping her friend would help her reason it out. A smile touched the edges of her mouth. "He's a cowboy from head to foot. Full of grit and mettle. Stubborn and determined, with skin as tan as leather and a constitution of iron."

"Did you date him?"

"No . . . he's older than me by several years." Eight years had made a world of difference when she was in high school, but it didn't seem all that important now. "He's probably one of the most decent, hardworking men I've ever known."

"It's obvious he's wants you to come home."

Jenny set aside the card and exhaled a long, slow breath. "Well, I can't, so there's no use sitting around here stewing about it."

"It seems a shame, after him writing and all."

"I can't go home," Jenny said forcefully. "You can't, either, because the both of us are going to have plum roles in the new Lehman musical, and we'll be in the thick of rehearsals."

"You're right," Michelle said as if this were something she hadn't considered.

"We'll be stars."

"Stars," Michelle repeated. "Our names will light up the marquee."

"Bright lights, and bright futures." But even as she said the words, they rang false in her ears.

"Goodness." Gabriel was furious. Shirley, Goodness, and Mercy had ignored him at every turn, and he wasn't putting up with it this year. His schedule was busy enough without those three meddling in matters that were none of their concern.

"You called?" The three shot up to heaven, looking as innocent as newborn lambs. Their feathery wings were tucked firmly in place, and their expressions were filled with guileless innocence.

"Shirley," he roared. "Did I or did I not tell you to stay away from Brynn Cassidy?" He didn't give her a chance to reply. "Might I ask what you were doing in her classroom this afternoon? This is your assignment," he said, handing her a slip of paper. "Now I expect you to help Craig Houle. If I see you anywhere close to Manhattan High School again, it will be cause for disciplinary action."

The three gasped.

Gabriel refused to allow these prayer ambassadors to manipulate him any further.

"Goodness, what did I tell you about Hannah? You don't think I know that you had a hand in Joshua Shadduck running into her this afternoon? Well, I'm on to your games. You will keep your fingers out of her life, is that understood?"

Goodness nodded.

"As for you, Mercy . . ." He looked down over his notes and, flustered, ran a hand over his face. He glanced up at the third angel. "Oh my, you're going to need all the help you can get."

Chapter Five

"Gabriel handed you an assignment on a piece of paper." Goodness was offended on Shirley's behalf, and rightly so. Never in their two-year history of working the Christmas holiday prayer rush had they been treated so shabbily. It was downright degrading.

"It might not be so bad," Mercy suggested, gathering close to her friend's side. The third angel was the peacemaker of the group. "The least we can do is give Gabriel the benefit of the doubt."

Shirley peeled open the folded sheet. Goodness and Mercy crowded close in an effort to read over her shoulder.

"The prayer request is from Craig Houle," the angel told them. "He's ten and has asked God for a chess set for Christmas."

"You've got to be kidding." Mercy

flapped her wings in a display of disgust. "A chess set for a ten-year-old boy. Why, that's an insult to our good names."

"We have a tradition to uphold."

Goodness couldn't stay in one spot, not when she was this angry. "It's a matter of pride. If anyone could help Brynn Cassidy with those high schoolers, it's Shirley. This other stuff is child's play."

"Exactly!" Shirley declared. "We have something to prove, so let's do it."

Indignant, the three returned to earth, their feathers in a dither, swirling down on the unsuspecting city like the Horsemen due from the Apocalypse.

"Exactly where does this Craig Houle live?" Goodness demanded as the three hovered over the Queensboro Bridge. Gabriel should count his blessings. There was a time, not so long past, when Goodness would have taken delight in dallying with streetlights and rerouting New York City traffic.

"According to this, Craig lives on Roosevelt Island," Shirley answered, reading over the request form. "At this time of day, he's most likely in school."

"Yes, but it's his parents we need to influence, right?" Mercy asked, thinking on her feet—er, wings.

"Right," the other two agreed.

"Then all we need do is convince his mother or father to do a little pre-Christmas shopping."

Goodness made a tsk-tsk sound. "I think it's time we taught Gabriel a lesson on just how good we are."

"I don't believe I've ever been more offended," Shirley said as the three briskly headed toward Roosevelt Island.

Peggy Houle walked down the quiet hospital corridor and sat at the nurses' station. Her rubber soles barely made a sound on the polished tile floor.

She started to make a notation in one of her patient's charts when she noticed a newspaper spread open across the top of the counter.

"That's odd," she mumbled to herself, and scooted the paper aside.

She looked around, wondering who'd left it. One thing was certain: none of the nurses were accorded the luxury of sitting down and reading. Not while on duty, at any rate. The hospital was short staffed as it was, and breaks, even the ones allotted them in the terms of their contract, were often few and far between.

"My dogs are barking." Ellen Freeman, another nurse, joined Peggy. She slipped off her shoe and rubbed her sore toes. "This is what I get for not breaking in these new shoes first." She reached for the newspaper. "Who left this?"

"I don't know. It wasn't here five minutes ago."

"Look," Ellen said, pointing to the printed page. "There's a gigantic toy sale going on for the next couple of days. I haven't even started my Christmas shopping."

"I was finished last week," Peggy said, feeling almost smug. She'd hit the stores her first day off following Thanksgiving and finished it all in one fell swoop—wrapping paper, new decorations, tinsel, the whole nine yards.

There wasn't a reason on this earth good enough for her to voluntarily step inside a store again in the whole month of December. Not when it seemed the entire city had gone crazy. At the end of her shift all Peggy wanted to do was head home.

"I've been thinking I'd buy the kids educational gifts this year," Ellen murmured. "Something that will stir their minds instead of those brainless television games. I can't tell you how sick I am of them sitting like zombies holding on to their joysticks."

"A chess set?" Peggy said, and snapped her head back, startled.

"A chess set," Ellen repeated, oblivious of her friend's chagrin. "Now that I think about it, you're right. A chess set is an excellent idea."

"What did I just say?"

"A chess set." Ellen looked up, surprised. "Is something wrong?"

"No . . . the funniest thing just happened." Peggy slapped the side of her head, hoping that would help.

"What?" Ellen was curious now.

"The words *a chess set* echoed in my ear. Three times, and each time I swear I was hearing a different voice."

"I still think it's an excellent idea," Ellen said, and replaced her shoe. "Are you sure you won't come to the toy store with me?"

"Ah . . ." Peggy hesitated, then found herself agreeing. "Sure," she mumbled, "why not?" For the life of her, she couldn't imagine why she was doing such a thing. "Who knows, maybe Craig would be interested in learning how to play chess himself," she said to justify her actions. After all, it was a good idea. Her son would enjoy learning the game.

Peggy leaned back on her chair. Abruptly she shook her head, then repeatedly slapped her hand against her ear. "It happened again," she said incredulously.

"You heard the words *a chess set?*"

"No," Peggy said, and shook her head like a dog fresh out of the water. "It was the same three voices, only this time they said . . ."

"Yes," Ellen prodded.

"You aren't going to believe this." Peggy wasn't entirely sure she believed it herself. "*Piece of cake,*" she mumbled, and shrugged, completely baffled.

"Oh, my," Shirley said, pointing into the distance. "Brynn Cassidy's in trouble." It was just what she'd expected would happen.

"Trouble?" Mercy repeated. "What's wrong?"

Cocky with their success, Goodness brushed the grit from her hands. "Trouble's our middle name. Brynn doesn't have a thing to worry about."

"Brynn might not, but we do," Mercy said, looking skeptical. "Gabriel isn't going to like this one bit. Not after the warning he gave us to stay away from her."

"Brynn's car won't start," Shirley informed her friends, her voice growing more concerned. "And I don't like the looks of those men, either." Clad in black leather jackets, two men stood on the other side of the chain-link fence, watching her.

Brynn climbed out of her car and opened the hood. She cast a wary eye toward the men.

"If ever I've seen anyone with evil intentions, it's those two," Shirley informed her friends.

"They've got knives," Mercy said, tugging on Goodness's sleeve.

"We've got to do something," Shirley cried, hoping to hide her panic.

"You don't dare," Goodness insisted, gripping Shirley by the arm and stopping her. "Mercy's right. If Gabriel finds out, it'd be just the excuse he's looking for to stick us with guard duty."

"Then I'll take matters into my own hands," Shirley insisted.

"Talk to Gabriel," Mercy suggested. "Goodness and I can keep those two thugs occupied while you reason this out with him."

"Did I hear someone mention my name?" Gabriel appeared just then, startling the three angels.

"Gabriel," Shirley said boldly, "we need to talk."

"Indeed we do. What's this I hear about Peggy Houle experiencing hearing problems?"

Shirley, Goodness, and Mercy clammed up *so* fast their teeth made clicking sounds when their jaws closed.

"I strongly suspect a bit of . . . intercession."

"I have a question of my own." Shirley stepped forward and bravely confronted the archangel. "Exactly whom have you assigned to work with Brynn Cassidy?"

Gabriel hesitated. "As a matter of course, I hadn't gotten around to choosing anyone just yet."

This was all Shirley needed to hear. "It's exactly as I suspected," she turned to inform her two friends with an indignant huff. "In the meantime Brynn Cassidy flounders, while heaven looks on unconcerned."

When she dared, Shirley chanced a look in his direction. "I want in," she informed Gabriel, her hand braced against her hip.

"What makes you think you can handle this case?" Gabriel's intense eyes burned holes straight into her.

"I can't," Shirley admitted. "At least not alone, but I have two friends who can help. In addition to . . ."

"Yes," Gabriel prodded.

"In addition to my friends, there's you."

"Me?"

"And a host of heavenly assistance that's always on call."

Gabriel sighed. "You just might need it."

Shirley opened her mouth to further her argument, then realized what the archangel had said. "You mean to say you're willing to give me the assignment?" The winds of indignity that had ruffled her sails fell slack. "Really?"

From the tight set of his mouth, the archangel looked as if he already regretted this. "One condition. You must agree to call for help when you need it."

"I promise," Shirley said solemnly, and smiled at her two friends.

"Just remember we can accomplish all things with the power of God."

"All things," Shirley, Goodness, and Mercy repeated.

"We'll start right now," Gabriel suggested. "I'll let you take care of the problem of those two malcontents."

"Sure thing," Shirley said, eager to get started on the assignment now that it was officially hers. She eyed the two men watching Brynn, and almost felt sorry for them. It seemed to her they were prime candidates for a bit of intervention. Perhaps they should meet up with an old friend, one they weren't eager to see. Like their parole officer. Angel Shirley in disguise.

"I sincerely hope you know a good mechanic." Gabriel cast his gaze over to the disabled vehicle; then without a sound, without a clue, he disappeared.

"We do know a good mechanic, don't we?" Shirley asked, looking to her friends.

Goodness and Mercy stared back blankly.

"No," said Mercy to Shirley. "We thought you did."

* * *

It was barely after four and already the sky was growing dark. Within a half hour night would settle over the city like a black velvet quilt.

Brynn Cassidy had long since given up the idea of seeing her dentist. Missing the appointment to have her teeth cleaned was a minor inconvenience compared to the hassles of dealing with car troubles.

She couldn't leave her Ford Escort here overnight, that much she knew. In this high-crime area, she'd be fortunate to find the shell of her vehicle left by morning. Nor did she know of a good garage, especially one close by. She cast a look across the street, surprised and grateful that the two men lingering there moments earlier had disappeared.

"Are you having trouble, Miss Cassidy?" Emilio walked up to her, a basketball tucked under one arm.

Brynn was so grateful that someone had asked that it was all she could do to keep from blurting out her troubles. "It won't start, and I haven't got a clue what could be wrong."

Emilio walked around her vehicle as though inspecting it. "I know a little bit about engines."

"Do you think you might look at it?"

"Sure thing." Emilio slid halfway inside the driver's seat. One foot remained on the asphalt parking lot while he turned the ignition key. He pumped the gas pedal a couple of times while her car made a sick grinding sound.

"Do you know what's wrong?" Brynn asked expectantly.

"You sure it isn't your battery?" Emilio asked.

"Good grief, I wouldn't know."

The teenager seemed to find her answer amusing. "You know all them fancy words, Teach, but you aren't so smart when it comes to cars, are you?"

Brynn was more than willing to admit it. "Is it serious?" she asked.

Emilio shrugged. "I haven't got a clue."

"I thought you said you knew something about cars."

"I do, but I ain't no Mr. Goodwrench."

"Thanks anyway, Emilio. I appreciate your help." He'd done a lot more than her fellow teachers. Most had walked right past her.

Brynn closed the hood and locked up the car. She didn't want to leave it, but she didn't have any choice. Its hood shut with a bang that echoed through the darkening afternoon. She swung the strap of her purse over her shoulder, and with her back stiff, not knowing where to turn, she started out of the parking lot.

"Where you going?" Emilio asked, bouncing the basketball and weaving it in and out of his legs as he walked alongside her.

"I'd better get a tow truck."

"My brother can do that."

Brynn paused. "Your brother?"

"Roberto. He's owns a mechanic shop. If you want, I'll take you there. He'll know what to do."

Frankly, Brynn wished Emilio had said something about his brother sooner. "That would be great."

"Yeah, well, remember how much I helped you the next time you're tempted to have me suspended."

The three-block walk took only a matter of minutes. Brynn spied Roberto's shop when they turned the corner. It looked as if the garage had once been a neighborhood gas station. The corners of the cement building were chipped and the entire structure was badly in need of a fresh coat of paint.

Emilio opened the glass front door and walked inside. "Roberto!" he shouted.

His brother's reply was muffled.

"He's in the garage," Emilio said, gesturing to the narrow doorway that led to a large open area that served as the repair shop. Brynn followed her student inside.

"I drummed up some business for you," Emilio announced proudly, and motioned toward Brynn.

Roberto Alcantara slowly unfolded from a quarter panel of the blue Civic and reached for the pink rag tucked inside his coveralls pocket.

"Hello, Mr. Alcantara."

"Call him Roberto," Emilio insisted. "This is Miss Cassidy," he continued, looking well pleased with himself. "She's the teacher I was telling you about."

"Hello."

Roberto nodded and wiped his hands. His face remained emotionless.

"Ms. Cassidy's having car troubles."

"My car won't start," she elaborated. "I doubt that it's the battery. It ran perfectly fine this morning . . . at least I thought it had."

"She doesn't know anything about cars," Emilio inserted. "Her specialty is dangling particles."

"Participles," Brynn corrected.

Emilio chuckled. "See what I mean?"

"I'm pleased to meet you, Miss Cassidy," Roberto said coolly, and tossed the rag onto his tool bench.

"I left my car in the school parking lot." She twisted her arm around and pointed in the direction of the school, which was completely unnecessary. Roberto Alcantara knew very well where the high school was.

Roberto said something to Emilio in Spanish. Emilio nodded quickly, then turned abruptly and hurried out of the garage. Within a matter of a minute she heard the youth talking on the phone, again in Spanish. Before he left, he collected her car keys.

"I've had Emilio call for a tow truck," Roberto informed her. "He'll meet the driver over at the school."

"Thank you. I can't tell you how much I appreciate your help."

Roberto said nothing.

Without being obvious, Brynn studied Emilio's brother. Roberto was tall and lean. His skin was the color of warm honey, his eyes and hair as dark a shade of brown as she'd ever seen. She guessed him to be around her own age, perhaps a year or two older. He wasn't openly hostile, but he did nothing to put her at ease. Every attempt at conversation was dead-ended.

As the minutes passed, the silence became more and more strained. Brynn wondered what she could have done to earn his disapproval, then realized it must be the incident with Emilio in the hall the first day she was at the school.

"I imagine you're upset with me because I was the one responsible for Emilio's suspension," she tried again. She wouldn't apologize, but she was prepared to state her side of the case. If he was willing to listen, that was.

"I'm not the least bit upset," he surprised her by answering. "Emilio knows the rules. He deserved what he got." He returned to working on the Civic and ignored her.

The next time he straightened, Brynn asked, "You don't like me, do you?" Normally she wouldn't be so confrontational, but it had been one of those days. If she'd done something to offend him, she wanted to know about it.

"That's right," he concurred.

"Do you mind telling me why?"

Apparently this was just the doorway he'd been waiting to walk through. Roberto met her look brazenly and continued. "Because you're filling my brother's head with nonsense."

"How do you mean?" Brynn struggled not to sound defensive and doubted that she'd succeeded.

He flung his arm in the air. "All your talk about the importance of an education. A high school diploma isn't going to help Emilio any more than it did me. Tell me, Miss Cassidy, exactly how is the history of World War Two going to feed a family? Will reading about Anne Frank get him a decent job?"

"Yes . . . well, not directly," she faltered. "Education is the answer for Emilio." She couldn't believe Roberto would say such a thing.

"Emilio would be better off if he dropped out of school now and learned a trade." He turned his back on her and appeared to be looking for something on his tool bench. He carelessly tossed aside a wrench and reached for another.

"I soundly disagree," Brynn said.

"That's your right."

In all her years, Brynn had never heard anyone discourage someone from an education. "Don't tell me you actually want your brother to quit school. Surely your parents object to that."

"I'm the only family Emilio's got," Roberto announced.

"I'm sorry to hear that, especially if you think he shouldn't complete his education."

"I nearly had him convinced to come work with me here in the garage, but then you arrived and all of a sudden he's talking about goals and dreams and other such nonsense."

"It isn't nonsense," she argued.

Roberto threw down a rag and shook his head. "No matter what happens, my brother and I will live and die in this neighborhood. All your talk isn't going to change one damn thing."

*   *   *

Hannah knew it was coming. The minute Carl arrived with his parents, following synagogue, she knew. He'd come to ask her to be his wife. Come to stake his claim. She didn't know why he'd chosen now; then again, perhaps she did. Hannah knew that Carl had experienced pressure from his own family. They had dated several months now, and it was time to make a decision. He taught at the local Hebrew academy, and his position there was secure, despite his differences with the headmaster.

Together with her mother and father, Hannah led Carl's family into the compact living room. An expectant silence settled over the group as the two sets of parents exchanged happy glances.

Carl looked to Hannah, and she read the apology in his eyes. He hadn't wanted it to be like this, either. He would have preferred for them to speak privately first, but like her, he was caught in the trap of obligation and family tradition.

"Carl." The rabbi looked to his son.

Carl cleared his throat. "Hannah and I have been seeing each other exclusively now for several months," he began. His hands were clasped in his lap, and he seemed to be as uncomfortable with this as Hannah was. "It should come as no surprise that I have deep feelings for your daughter."

David and Ruth smiled and nodded.

Hannah read the delight in their eyes. This was their dream for her, what they'd been anxiously waiting to happen for weeks. If anything, they seemed surprised it had taken this long.

"Our Hannah has deep feelings for Carl as well," her father assured the rabbi and his wife. He looked to his daughter for confirmation.

Hannah had no option but to agree, and really, it wasn't a stretch of the truth. She did care for Carl. He had been both generous and considerate.

"I have a good job and make a respectable income," Carl said.

Her father nodded.

"I can afford to care for Hannah."

Again her father confirmed his approval with a quick nod.

The room went silent as everyone waited with breathless anticipation for what was to come next.

"With your permission, David and Ruth," Carl continued, his voice low and firm, "I would like to ask Hannah to be my wife."

Hannah watched as her sensible mother dissolved into tears of happiness and, perhaps, relief. Her father's face beamed with love and pride.

David cleared his throat as if to say his words were those of importance. "We couldn't ask for a better man for our only child. You have our permission and our heartfelt approval. May God deeply bless you both."

"Hannah?" Carl turned his attention to her.

Five people looked to her. She held their dreams in the palm of her hand. With everything in her she wanted to ask Carl to give her time before she decided. But to do so now would embarrass him and deeply disappoint their families.

"Hannah?" her mother asked softly.

Hannah glanced toward her parents. All her life she'd done as they wanted. She'd been a good daughter, an obedient child.

"Oh, Carl," she whispered.

Her mother dabbed at her eyes. Carl's mother sniffled.

"I couldn't be more honored than to be your wife."

The tension in the room evaporated as Carl's and her parents leapt to their feet and hugged each other. The only two not embracing were Carl and Hannah.

Carl moved to her side and knelt on the floor next to her chair. His eyes held hers captive. "I'll make you a good husband, Hannah."

She lowered her gaze. "And I'll be a good wife."

Joshua glanced at his watch and was surprised at the time. He'd been held up in court earlier that morning and been playing catch-up the rest of the day. Earlier he'd decided to stop off at the deli and be sure Hannah had received his gift. Frankly he'd been surprised not to hear from her before now.

It came as something of a surprise the way Hannah had filled his mind and his heart. For too many years he'd been whizzing down the fast lane of life, building his career and making a name for himself.

Then one morning, out of the blue, he'd woken with a hollow feeling in the pit of his stomach. This feeling, this emptiness, was something his grandmother's cooking wasn't going to satisfy.

It was then Joshua realized that what he was missing was a wife and family. He knew his mother had been wanting him to marry for a good long while. Only he had a certain type of woman in mind, and he didn't know if such a woman existed in this modern age.

First and foremost he sought a woman who shared his faith. One who would stand devotedly at his side through the years. A woman who would make his dreams hers and allow him to be part of hers. One who was kind and gentle. Loving and tender. Sensible.

He'd searched for months for this paragon of virtue, until he was convinced a woman such as this no longer existed.

Then he'd met Hannah.

After their first afternoon together, he'd realized she was exactly the type of woman he'd been longing to meet. To think all this time she'd been right under his nose. The local deli owner's daughter.

Joshua reached for his coat, and after telling his secretary where he'd be, he headed toward what many in New York considered to be the best deli in town.

When he was less than a block away from the deli, Joshua spied Hannah. She was walking with an older woman, whom he assumed must be her mother.

It was hard not to raise his arm and attract her attention the way he had at their previous meeting. But since she was advancing toward him, there didn't seem to be much point.

Joshua frowned when he noticed Hannah wasn't wearing the gloves he'd had delivered. Then he noticed her eyes. How easy she was to read. Whatever she was doing didn't please her. Even from this distance he felt her resistance.

Just then she looked up, and he caught her gaze. Briefly her eyes widened with alarm and she gnawed on her lower lip as though she weren't sure what to do.

Without her saying a word, Joshua received her message. She didn't want him to greet her. Silently she pleaded with him to walk on past. It offended him, but he didn't question her request.

Without a word they strolled past each other like total strangers. Three steps on the other side of Hannah, Joshua turned, hoping for some telltale sign that would clue him to what was wrong.

She glanced over her shoulder, and in that briefest of seconds, Joshua read her eyes. She was grateful. Later, when she could, she promised silently, she would explain everything.

It probably had something to do with what she'd told him the day of the parade. Her parents had been involved in a frivolous lawsuit. The fact that her family didn't take kindly to attorneys wouldn't dissuade him. He was very much interested in knowing Hannah better. Once her family had an opportunity to know him, they'd be willing to overlook the fact that he was an attorney. Joshua smiled to himself.

He would be patient, because Hannah Morganstern was well worth the effort. After all, he'd been looking for her most of his adult life.

"This must be old home week," Michelle said as she walked into the apartment and tossed the mail on the kitchen table. "There's another letter with a postmark from Custer, Montana."

"There is?" Dressed in her slip and standing in front of the ironing board, Jenny set aside the iron and walked over to the table. She reached for the envelope and read the return address. "It's from my mother."

"At least you hear from your mother," Michelle complained as she shucked off her coat and scarf. "It's been three months since my mother last wrote me."

"But she calls once a week."

"True."

But Jenny understood what her friend was saying. It was a relief to get something in the mail other than bills.

She opened the envelope and withdrew the letter. It was exactly what she expected. Her mother had broken her silence and joined Trey to ask her to come home for the holidays.

It hurt more than words could voice having to explain that she couldn't leave New York. Jenny had long since run out of money, out of excuses, and, worse yet, out of ideas.

"What'd she say?" Michelle asked. Her roommate stood in front of the open refrigerator and stared at its meager contents. Rather than explain, Jenny handed the single sheet of stationery to her friend. Michelle scanned the page, then raised her eyes to Jenny.

"Your mother wants you to come home for Christmas."

Jenny sank onto the sofa and tucked her feet beneath her. "Christmas has always been so special with our family. I don't think I've met anyone who could put on a spread the way Mom does. She makes this incredible sage dressing for the turkey, and the scent of it fills the house." She closed her eyes, and the memory was so powerful, she could almost smell the pungent herbs right then.

"Maybe there's a way you could manage to make it home," Michelle said sympathetically.

"There isn't," Jenny said, unwilling even to listen to suggestions. No one needed to tell her that she'd done this to herself.

Christmas with her mom and dad and little brother. A lump formed in her throat.

Christmas on the range. Snow glistening in the moonlight, sleigh rides every December. Decorating the tree together had long been a family tradition. Her father would set a pot of wassail to warm over the fireplace, and they'd sing carols while they strung the lights and added the tinsel. The ranch hands and neighbors would stop over for a cup of her father's special brew. Trey came every year.

"Jenny?"

Her eyes popped open. "Sorry. I guess I got carried away there for a moment."

"Why hasn't your family come to see you?"

"Mom and Dad?" Jenny supposed she should have considered that a long time ago, but try as she might she couldn't picture her parents in New York. To the best of her knowledge they'd never been more than three hundred miles away from the ranch. Their lives revolved around the care and feeding of a thousand head of cattle. It would be unheard of for her father to leave the ranch unattended.

There'd been a time when Jenny hated the mere mention of the word *beef*. How eager she'd been to escape to the big city and find her way in the world. How eager she'd been to disassociate herself from the Flying L Ranch.

"Did you hear anything from Peterman?" she asked Michelle, needing to change the subject before she became downright maudlin.

"Not a word. Rumor has it he's looking for a particular kind of girl."

"Oh?" Jenny feigned interest. It went without saying that whatever character type the famous director sought wasn't likely to be Jenny. She had lost count of the number of times she'd auditioned for John Peterman. He hadn't chosen her yet, and she doubted he would this time.

She didn't know when she'd started all this

stinking thinking. About the time she'd told the first lie to her parents. Negative thoughts had crowded her mind ever since.

"I can't shake the feeling you're going to be offered one of the major roles," Michelle said. "Mark my words, Jenny Lancaster. We're both headed for Broadway."

"This is the saddest thing I've ever seen," Mercy told her two friends. "Jenny wants nothing more than to go home for the holidays, and can't."

"Surely there's a way we can help her."

"I'm convinced there is." Goodness spoke with utter confidence. "All we may need to do is pull a few strings. That shouldn't be so difficult."

Mercy smiled. "We've been doing that for years, haven't we?"

"Maybe we should make it impossible for Jenny to refuse her mother."

Mercy looked to the former guardian angel. "What do you mean?"

Shirley pointed to the Thanksgiving card tucked in Jenny's bedroom mirror. "Perhaps all we really need to do is give her a good enough excuse to head home."

Chapter Six

Jenny didn't want to do it. Her heart ached every time she thought about refusing her mother's plea. The list of fabricated excuses was as long as her arm.

She waited until she had the apartment to herself and then sat down at the computer. She bolstered herself with a cup of hot chocolate and a plate of butter cookies, and began to type.

Dearest Mom and Dad,

You don't know how it pains me to tell you I won't make it home for the holidays. I love you both more than words can say. I think of you every day. Know that my heart will be with you, but this is the price of success. . . .

Jenny stopped and unceremoniously hit the Backspace key. She tried again, and after six or seven lines the second attempt followed the path of the first.

A half hour later, Jenny was no closer to crafting a response to her parents. It hadn't been this difficult to answer Trey's card. Her brief note to her former neighbor had been cheerful and witty when she'd sent along her regrets.

Anyone who knew her well might have been able to read between the lines of her lighthearted message. But not Trey, she decided. Her witty note would amuse him.

In the end, Jenny wrote three short lines to her parents and left it at that. She couldn't come. She was sorry, and she'd miss them terribly.

Not once did she mention the Off-Broadway production she'd told them she was in. Jenny refused to perpetrate the lie any further than she had already.

By the time Michelle returned from her errands, Jenny was in a real funk. Depressed and miserable, she battled off a case of the blues, determined not to get caught in the trap of feeling sorry for herself.

"You know what we need?" her friend said.

"What?"

"A little fun. It's the season of joy, and yet here we are, moping around waiting for the phone to ring." Their agent hadn't called, and Jenny didn't care what people said. No news was not good news. No news was no news. And this time the waiting had never seemed more interminable.

"What if we had a party?" Michelle asked.

"A Christmas party," Jenny added, warming to the idea. "That's perfect." Then reality set in. "But how would we possibly feed all our friends?" It was difficult enough to scrounge up meals for the two of them.

"We'll make it a pot luck," Michelle suggested. "All we need supply are the drinks, plus plates and silverware. Between us we could manage that, couldn't we?"

"Sure we could." Jenny's nod was eager. Her spirits lifted just thinking about the celebration. She needed this, needed something to take her mind off how much she would miss Montana. "We can make the invitations ourselves."

"Let's hand them out. That way we could save on postage," Michelle said, offering another money-saving idea.

"Who should we invite?"

"Bill and Susan," Michelle suggested.

The couple had met in drama school and had married that summer. Jenny and Michelle had been bridesmaids. Jenny had joked about how the two of them always seemed to end up as bridesmaids.

"What about Cliff?" Jenny asked.

"Abby, too."

The list continued until they were afraid they'd forget, so they decided to write them all down.

Michelle sat at the table and reached for a pen. "What have you been doing all day?"

The tightness gripped Jenny's throat. "I finally

wrote my parents and told them I wouldn't be home." Just saying the words aloud increased the ache.

"Next year you'll be with your family," Michelle said with confidence.

"You're right," Jenny said, forcing herself to think positive thoughts. Surely living in the same city in which Norman Vincent Peale had preached his philosophy of positive thinking should teach her something. Yet here she was doing it again: stinking thinking.

"Bill and Susan," Michelle mumbled as she repeated the names of their mutual friends. "Abby. Cliff. John."

The phone pealed and they froze.

Michelle looked to Jenny.

Jenny to Michelle.

"You answer it," her roommate instructed.

"You," Jenny insisted, shaking her head. It had been like this all week. The instant the phone jingled they hoped, prayed, it was Irene, their agent. If it wasn't Irene, then perhaps it was the casting director and maybe even the great and mighty John Peterman himself. It wasn't likely, but they could dream.

"It's probably some schmuck wanting to sell us aluminum siding," Michelle joked.

"Or someone doing a survey on cat food."

But Jenny noticed that neither one of them took their eyes away from the kitchen telephone.

Michelle edged herself from the chair on the third ring and reached the phone. "Hello, this is Jenny and Michelle's place," she said cheerfully in a perfect rendition of the efficient secretary.

Jenny studied her friend. Afraid to hope. Afraid to care.

"It's for you," Michelle stated, and handed her the receiver. Then she mouthed, "It's a man."

Jenny pointed her finger at her heart, wondering if she'd misunderstood. "For me?"

Michelle nodded.

She took the phone and said in a friendly but professional-sounding voice, "This is Jenny Lancaster."

"Hello, Jenny."

Trey.

Jenny couldn't have been more shocked if it'd been Andrew Lloyd Webber himself, wanting her to star in his next musical.

"Trey!" she said, barely managing to hide her shock.

"I got your note," he announced.

"It was a surprise to get your Thanksgiving card," she said, holding the receiver with both hands. She felt lightheaded and wasn't sure if it was the shock of Trey's call or the fact that she hadn't eaten all day.

"You aren't coming home for the holidays."

Trey, her family. Everyone seemed to be pressuring her. It felt as if the walls were closing in around her. "I can't come," she told him, unable to disguise her own bitter disappointment. "I want to be there. More than anything, but I can't."

"That's what your note said. So the bright lights of the city have blinded you?"

"No." She longed to tell him how she hungered for the peace and solitude of Montana. New York City held its own excitement, its own energy. So often she'd walked down the crowded avenues and felt a rhythm, a cadence, that all but sang up from the asphalt. For three years she'd marched to that beat and hummed its special brand of music.

Yet the lone cry in the barren hills of home played longingly to her soul, its melody haunting her.

"Your family misses you," Trey said, tightening the screws of her regrets.

Jenny bit into her lower lip.

"I miss you," Trey added.

Jenny's eyes flew open. Trey, the man who'd invaded her dreams for weeks, admitted to missing her. He'd as much as said he wanted her home.

Regrets clamored against her chest, their fists sharp and pain filled. "I can't come," she whispered miserably.

Her words were met with silence.

"Can't or won't?" he asked starkly.

Brynn Cassidy crossed the street in front of Manhattan High and St. Philip's Cathedral. She found Father Grady, the gray-haired priest who'd become her friend, in the vestibule.

"Hello, Father," she said.

"Brynn, it's good to see you, my girl." His green Irish eyes lit up with warm delight.

"I got your message. You wanted to see me?"

"Yes. Come over to the rectory and I'll have Mrs. Houghton brew us a pot of tea."

Brynn glanced at her watch. She enjoyed visiting with Father Grady, but the older priest liked to talk and she didn't have time that afternoon.

Father Grady's eyes followed hers. "Do you have an appointment?"

"I have to stop off at Roberto Alcantara's this afternoon and pick up my car."

"I know Roberto well," Father Grady said, and motioned for her to precede him out of the church. "He's a fine young man." He paused to glance her way, and it seemed to Brynn that the priest was looking for her to elaborate. She didn't.

"Emilio's in my class."

"Ah, yes, Emilio. Roberto's done his best to keep his brother out of trouble. There haven't been problems with Emilio, have there?"

"No, no," Brynn was quick to tell him.

Father Grady's face relaxed.

Brynn lowered her gaze. It wasn't Emilio she'd clashed with, but Roberto. "I'm afraid Roberto doesn't think much of me."

Father Grady opened the door to the rectory. "I'm sure you're mistaken."

Brynn followed him inside. She preferred not

to tell him about their brief confrontation. It rankled still. Roberto Alcantara had been both rude and unreasonable. But more than that, he'd been wrong.

"I'm not sure I have time for tea," she reiterated when she realized that Father Grady fully intended for her to stay and chat anyway.

"Nonsense." He escorted Brynn into the parlor and left her while he went in search of Mrs. Houghton, the elderly housekeeper who cared for Father Grady and the bishop when he was in residence.

Father Grady returned shortly with a tray and two cups. "I was hoping you'd be able to stop over this afternoon," he said as he set the tray on the coffee table. He handed Brynn a delicate china cup and took one himself before sitting across from her on the velvet settee. "The church is sponsoring a dance this Friday evening for the youth group."

Brynn had seen the posters. "I've heard several of the kids mention it."

"We generally have a good turnout."

Brynn was sure that was true.

"I was wondering," Father Grady said, studying her above the china cup, "if you'd agree to be one of the chaperones."

The request took Brynn by surprise, although in retrospect she supposed it shouldn't.

"The children are quite fond of you," he added as if he felt flattering her would be necessary. "Modesto Diaz mentioned your name the other day. He said . . ." Father Grady paused, and his eyes sparkled with humor.

"Yes?" Brynn prodded.

"Well, Modesto did say you were a little weird, but that he liked you anyway."

Brynn was sure her students didn't quite know what to make of her teaching methods.

"I realize it's an imposition asking you at this late date," Father Grady continued. "I'd consider it a personal favor if you could come."

"I'll be happy to chaperone the dance," Brynn murmured.

"Now," Father Grady said, and set down his teacup. "Tell me what happened between you and Roberto Alcantara."

"It's nothing," she said, preferring to make light of their differences. "Actually Roberto's been most helpful. My car broke down and he's fixing it for me."

Father Grady said nothing.

"I was on my way to pick it up now."

"Roberto's been through some difficult times," the priest told her. "I'm not at liberty to tell you all the circumstances, but . . ."

"Oh, please, no. I wouldn't want you to break a confidence. It's nothing, really."

"If Roberto offended you . . ."

"He didn't. We had a difference of opinion."

Father Grady seemed relieved. "I'm glad to hear that. If you do find him disagreeable, all I ask is that you give him a bit of slack. He's a good man. I'd vouch for him any day."

"I'm sure what you say is true." Brynn stood and set the teacup back on the tray. "Now I really must be going."

Father Grady escorted her to the front door. "I'll see you Friday evening, then, around seven?"

Brynn nodded. "I'll be here."

The priest's eyes brightened with a smile. "Thank you, Brynn, I promise you won't regret this."

Brynn briskly walked the few blocks to Roberto Alcantara's garage. Earlier that afternoon, Emilio had personally delivered the message that her car was ready for her. The youth made sure the entire class heard him, as though the two of them had a personal business arrangement. Brynn had been forced to conceal her irritation.

As the afternoon progressed, she discovered she wasn't looking forward to another encounter with Emilio's older brother. The man was way off base. It was impossible to reason with anyone who regarded education as a waste of time. The fact that he'd actually urged his younger brother to drop out of school was nothing short of criminal.

"Yo, Miss Cassidy." Emilio, Modesto, and a few more of the boys from her class drove past her slowly and waved.

Brynn returned the gesture automatically. It wasn't until they'd turned the corner that she realized the boys were joyriding in her car.

Brynn bristled and hurried the last block to Roberto's. When she reached the garage, she stormed in the door. "Emilio's driving around in my car."

Roberto, who was working on another car, straightened. "Yes, I know."

She blinked. "You know."

"Yes, I gave him the keys myself."

The man had a way of flustering her unlike anyone she'd ever encountered. "Well, I want it back."

"You'll get it." He returned to the truck he was working on, disappearing behind the hood.

"Do you generally allow Emilio to ride around in your customer's cars?"

"No." His answer was clipped and didn't invite further inquiries.

His attitude—in fact, everything about Roberto—irritated Brynn. "I want my car returned," she insisted, her voice raised and tight. No matter what Father Grady claimed, it was plain to her that this man didn't have one shred of responsibility.

"And you'll have it."

Brynn crossed her arms and started to pace. Twice she made a show of looking at her watch.

"Emilio will be back any moment," Roberto said, continuing to work on another vehicle.

Bent over the engine as he was, Brynn couldn't see his face, but she had the distinct impression the mechanic was smiling. Her irritation amused him. That infuriated Brynn all the more.

"I want you to know that I don't appreciate being kept waiting."

Roberto straightened and reached for an oil

rag; his dark, intense eyes meshed with hers. "I'm not one of your students, Miss Cassidy, so there's no need to yell."

"I was not yelling." She realized she was and lowered her voice immediately.

Roberto grinned broadly. "I suppose you'd like to send me to the principal."

"Ah-ha!" Her arm flew out and she pointed at him with her index finger, wagging it while she gathered her thoughts. "I thought as much. You blame me because your brother was suspended."

"On the contrary. Emilio knows not to fight on school grounds. What is it the law enforcement people are so fond of quoting? Do the crime, pay the time. My brother deserved what he got."

"But you blame me?"

"No, I just wish you'd quit filling my brother's head with garbage."

Brynn clenched her jaw in an effort not to argue. This was the same mine-riddled ground they'd covered earlier. Brynn had no desire to do battle with Roberto a second time.

From the corner of her eye, she saw her car pull into an empty parking slot in front of the garage.

"Yo, Miss Cassidy," Emilio called out. "Your car's running like a dream."

Despite her misgivings, Brynn managed a smile. "If I could please have my bill," she said with stiff politeness.

Roberto gestured toward his brother. "Emilio will take care of that."

Brynn hesitated before leaving the garage for the small outer office where Emilio stood. Although Roberto had been deliberately rude, she felt obligated to him. "I want you to know I appreciate your help."

Involved once again with another vehicle, Roberto didn't bother to answer. It was almost as if he were ignoring her. His lack of a response to her peace offering offended her pride. Swallowing the small hurt, Brynn brushed the hair from her face.

"Your car runs like new," Emilio told her as he stepped behind the cash register. "Roberto asked me to test-drive it around the block. I hope you don't mind that I let a couple of my posse join me."

"Four is more than a couple," she informed him primly.

"I know," the youth said with a flash of pearly white teeth. "But it isn't every day that we can say we rode in a teacher's car."

Brynn decided it was best to not comment.

Emilio located the work order for her vehicle and scanned its contents. Brynn had been waiting for this moment, praying that the expense wouldn't wipe out the meager remainder of her budget for the month. The Escort had well over two hundred thousand miles on it and thus far had been relatively problem free. With the dread building up inside her, she opened her purse and took out her checkbook.

Something didn't appear to be right, because Emilio looked up from the bill. "I need to ask Roberto something," he said, and walked around from behind the counter. In the other room, the two brothers talked in hushed tones.

Emilio returned, wearing a wide grin. "It's on the house," he announced.

Brynn wasn't sure she understood. "What do you mean?"

Pride gleamed in the youth's dark eyes. "You don't owe us anything."

"But I can't let you do that. . . ."

"Roberto insists."

Still Brynn argued. "That wouldn't be right."

"It's a gift, Ms. Cassidy," Emilio said with a deep sigh of frustration. "Didn't you ever learn you're not supposed to question someone when they give you a gift? Some lady with manners wrote it up in a book. You read all the time . . . you must have read that."

Brynn was uncertain. "Let me at least pay for any parts."

"No way." The teenager held up both hands as though she were holding him up.

"But carburetors can be expensive." She didn't want Roberto absorbing the cost of this.

"Roberto says he found another carburetor at the junkyard and got it for next to nothing. Besides, he let me do most of the work myself." His dark eyes pleaded with her to accept this small gift.

"Emilio, I don't know how to thank you."

His face erupted in a wide smile. "I'll think of something."

Roberto shouted from the other room, and Emilio's smart smile disappeared. "Think nothing of it, Miss Cassidy."

"Thank you both again." Brynn felt like a fool for having made such an issue of Emilio driving her vehicle. She glanced toward the garage, but Roberto was bent over the side of the truck, busy at work. "Tell your brother that I'm grateful."

"I will." Emilio followed her outside and held open her car door for her.

When she couldn't find her car keys, she eyed the youth. A desperate look came over him, and he slapped his hands over his shirt and pants pockets, then laughed and withdrew them from his hip pocket. "I had you worried there, didn't I?"

Brynn rolled her eyes, then started the engine. As Emilio had said earlier, it purred like new. Her car sounded better than it had in years. She backed out of the driveway. It was as she started down the street that she noticed Roberto Alcantara watching her from inside the building.

He owed her an apology, Roberto reasoned. He'd been angry and frustrated the day they'd met, and he'd taken his irritation out on her. True, he believed the things he'd said, but generally he kept his opinions to himself. It had helped relieve his irritation to sound off at Emilio's teacher; but it hadn't been fair.

An hour before he'd met Brynn, Roberto had learned his offer to lease a building in another neighborhood had been rejected. It hadn't been the first time a landlord had refused to rent to him. Naturally he'd been given some flimsy excuse, but Roberto had learned long ago the real reason. No one wanted a Hispanic taking up residence nearby.

Brynn Cassidy was everything Emilio had said. Bright. Intelligent. Pretty. Roberto feared his younger brother was half in love with her himself. But this spunky teacher was off-limits to the both of them, and Roberto knew it. It would be best if he never saw her again.

Funny how a woman could be so dangerous; but Roberto had recognized it from the first moment they'd met. Brynn Cassidy just might teach him to dream, too.

Friday evening Brynn arrived at the gymnasium behind St. Philip's. She walked in the gaily decorated room and stopped to admire the decorations. Red and green streamers were looped across the ceiling from one end of the room to the other. A refreshment table was set up alongside the folded bleachers.

"Hello, Miss Cassidy." The first one to greet her was Suzie Chang, who looked exceptionally pretty in a dark blue silk pants suit.

"Oh, Suzie, you look so nice."

The Chinese girl lowered her head and blushed. "So do you."

Brynn hadn't been exactly sure what to wear and

had opted for a blouse and skirt and patent-leather flats. Although she'd attended a number of school dances at St. Mary's, she'd never actually served as a chaperone. Generally the girls' school relied on parents and members of the PTA.

"Miss Cassidy," Emilio called. He helped himself to a handful of cookies. "What are you doing here?"

"I'm a chaperone."

"Hey, that's cool. So's my brother."

Brynn hadn't recognized Roberto without his coveralls. She hadn't given Roberto much notice before, but now . . . caught by his piercing dark eyes, Brynn found it difficult to look away.

"Hello, Roberto."

"Miss Cassidy." He nodded politely in her direction.

The music started. It came from a sound system with large speakers that blared from the front of the stage. No one seemed to want to be the first one on the dance floor.

"Hey, you two," Emilio said. "Shouldn't you start the dancing or something?"

Hannah needed to talk to Joshua. It was important that she return the gloves as soon as possible. It was wrong of her to have kept them this long. Then to walk past him on the street and pretend that she didn't know him was a terrible insult. She'd witnessed for herself the surprise and confusion in his gaze. Yet she was forever grateful that he'd read her silent message and hadn't greeted her. Hannah didn't know how she would explain knowing him to her mother.

For herself, Hannah was both bewildered and guilty, and she felt like a coward. It was unfair to Joshua to lead him to believe that she was free to care for him. Unfair to Carl, who'd courted her faithfully these many months. She'd juggled with her conscience until she couldn't think straight any longer.

"I do wish we weren't doing this," Hannah said to her mother.

"Doing what?" Ruth questioned. "Buying my daughter a trousseau? Don't be ridiculous."

"We haven't set the wedding date yet."

"You will soon enough." In the eyes of her parents she was all but married to Carl Rabinsky.

"Your father and I have patiently waited all these years for a man who was worthy of you."

A lifetime of accepting what her parents felt was right was what helped Hannah hold her tongue.

"Such a wedding you'll have," Ruth promised, her eyes alight with excitement.

Hannah found she couldn't look at her mother.

"Your father's already talking about the food for the reception. I promise you it will be one that people will talk about for years to come. You are our only child. God's gift to us. Our joy."

"Mama, what if I don't love Carl?"

Her mother hesitated, but for only a moment. "Nonsense. I know you, Hannah, you wouldn't have agreed to be his wife if you didn't love him. Carl will make you a good husband. Every girl has doubts when it comes time to pledge her heart to one man."

"What if I'd met another man?"

"Who?" her mother demanded as if this were impossible.

"Someone I liked very much and would like to know better."

Her mother frowned and shook her head. "You won't. But if you do, then talk to Carl. Tell him your thoughts."

"I will," Hannah promised, but she had the feeling that it would be even more difficult to discuss this matter with Carl than with her mother.

"Now come along, we have lots to buy."

Hannah shuffled along beside her mother. Never had she dreamed that she would dread a shopping expedition the way she did this one.

It was in Saks Fifth Avenue that her mother stopped. "Shall we look at wedding dresses?" Ruth asked, her eyes warm and gentle.

"Don't you think that would be premature?" Already Hannah's arms were burdened with packages. "I'm tired, Mama, can we go home?"

Ruth released a low sigh. "Yes, perhaps that would be for the best."

Outside once more, Hannah felt invigorated as the cold hit against her cheeks. She matched her steps with those of her mother, who walked along, humming softly to herself. It took Hannah a moment to realize where the melody was coming from.

"You're singing," Hannah commented.

Ruth laughed and nodded. "So I am. I do when I'm especially happy." As they stopped for traffic, Ruth placed her hands against Hannah's pink cheeks. "You're going to be the most beautiful bride in all of New York. Mark my words, Hannah Morganstern. I get excited every time I think about planning your wedding."

Once they were back at the deli, Hannah escaped to her room. As soon as she could, she made an excuse to go out. Almost always she told her parents where she was going, but not this time.

When she arrived at Joshua's office the receptionist recognized her.

"Is Mr. Shadduck available?" she asked.

The woman looked down at the schedule. "He left no more than a minute ago."

"Oh." She wasn't able to hide her frustration.

"You might be able to catch him."

"Thank you." Hannah rushed out of the office and hurried into the first available elevator. Her heart felt as though it would explode as she made her way to the front of the office building. On the sidewalk, she looked both ways and sighed with relief when she spied Joshua walking away from her, carrying a briefcase.

"Joshua," she called.

He turned at the sound of her voice, and his face lit up with pleasure. "Hannah." He started toward her.

"I'm so sorry," she said in a breathless rush. She

planted her hand over her heart in an effort to regain her breath.

Joshua wrapped his arm around her shoulders and steered her out of the heavy foot traffic. "Don't worry about it," he said gently.

"But . . ." She'd been unforgivably rude.

"Let's sit down a minute and talk this out," he suggested.

Hannah knew his idea was much better than her handing him back his gift in the middle of a New York sidewalk. At the same time, she feared that spending time with Joshua, even a short amount, would make it all the more difficult to do what she knew she must.

They strolled until Joshua pointed across the street to a five-star hotel famous for its afternoon teas.

Hannah wanted to protest that a cafe would serve just as well, but she wasn't given the opportunity. Before she could suggest someplace else, Joshua had taken her by the arm. Together they raced across the street.

The hotel lobby was filled with polished crystal. Enormous chandeliers gleamed from above, their glittering lights transforming the entire area.

Huge floral wreaths decorated in gold lamé bows hung from marble columns. The registration desk was checkered with poinsettias. Light music swirled about them like a cool autumn mist. Before Hannah had a chance to comment, she was led into a private dining room.

Before Joshua could give the man instructions, the waiter handed them a gold-tasseled menu. Joshua ordered the tea, and the other man quietly slipped away.

Joshua smiled at her. "You said there was something you wanted to tell me?"

Chapter Seven

This meeting with Joshua was so much more difficult than Hannah thought it would be. But there was no help for it. She had to tell him she was engaged to Carl. To delay any longer would be a grave disservice to them both. As they sat in the elegant hotel restaurant waiting for the tea to be served, Hannah struggled to find the words.

"Joshua," she said, dragging a deep breath through her lungs, her heart heavy.

"You received the gloves?"

"Yes, thank you, but I can't accept—"

"Joshua Shadduck?"

Hannah was cut off midsentence by a well-dressed middle-aged woman who stopped at their table. Her gaze drifted from Joshua to Hannah, and her eyes were marked with warm approval.

"Gloria." Joshua stood and enthusiastically hugged the white-haired woman. He turned to Hannah. "Hannah Morganstern, meet Judge Fowler."

Impressed to meet a judge, Hannah smiled and said, "I'm honored."

"I've been meaning to get in touch with you all week," Gloria said. Her gaze connected briefly with Hannah's once again. "But I can see that now isn't a good time. I promise I'll call you soon."

"I'll look forward to hearing from you," Joshua returned. Before he could reseat himself, the judge whispered something in his ear, then turned away.

Joshua grinned broadly, then explained to Hannah. "She approves."

"Approves?"

"Of you. She told me it was high time I . . . well, never mind."

"Joshua." A stout figure of a man approached their table next. "By George, it's good to see you," he said, sounding genuinely pleased.

"Hello, Tom." Although Hannah didn't know Joshua well, she could hear the frustration in his voice.

The other man studied Hannah with barely disguised admiration. His blue eyes twinkled. Before Joshua could introduce him properly, he stretched his hand across the table. "Tom Colfax," he said.

"Hannah Morganstern," she replied, and they exchanged brief handshakes.

Tom's admiration was straightforward. "I know this sounds like a worn-out line, but have we met?"

"I don't think so," Hannah replied.

Tom rubbed the side of his jaw, then shook his head as if to say he was certain he'd seen her someplace before.

The two men exchanged information, then Tom drifted away. He continued to wear a puzzled look and glanced over his shoulder once.

Joshua exhaled sharply. "This isn't going to work," he muttered.

That was what Hannah had been struggling to tell him since they'd met, but she hadn't been able to put it into words.

Joshua set the linen napkin on the table. "Come on, let's get out of here."

Hannah's first instinct was to argue, but she wasn't given the chance as she followed Joshua through the elegantly decorated lobby to the street outside. "Where are we going?" she asked, a little breathless.

He turned as though he hadn't given the matter a second thought. "I don't know. My apartment is a short walk from here."

"I can't," she said, her heart in her throat. "I have to be back shortly."

Joshua's gaze narrowed as if to suggest he didn't believe her. "Already?"

"Yes." She should have told him earlier and been done with it, but each time she shared his company it became more difficult. Now she found herself frantic to say what she must.

"Joshua, please listen to me." She hardly sounded

like herself. Her voice was tight with emotion as she brushed the hair from her cheek. She opened her purse and handed him the soft deerskin gloves. "I can't keep these. They're a lovely, thoughtful gift, but I can't accept them."

He took the gloves, but his eyes revealed his disappointment. "Why not?"

People wove their way around them, and her throat tightened with regret. "I'm so sorry, Joshua, so very sorry, but I'm . . . There's someone else." That sounded much better than announcing she was engaged.

Joshua's face revealed nothing. "The man you were with at the parade?"

"Yes."

"The one who abandoned you?" His feelings for Carl were more than clear.

"Carl didn't abandon me, we simply lost each other." Carl hadn't deserted her, not on purpose, and she found it important that Joshua know that. Carl might have his faults, but nearly everyone was flawed in one way or another. He'd gotten separated from her on Thanksgiving Day, and with so many people crowding the sidewalks, watching the parade, it had been impossible for him to find her again.

For a long time Joshua said nothing. Then, "Are you going to marry him?"

A definitive answer was her only recourse. Joshua deserved the truth. To hedge now might give him reason to believe there was a chance for them.

"We're engaged."

"That wasn't my question. I asked if you were going to marry him."

"Yes . . . of course." But she sounded unsure even to her own ears.

He hesitated, but only for a moment. "I see."

Now was the time to turn away. To end any kind of relationship before it began. One thing was certain: she shouldn't have paused. But she did. "I like you, Joshua." More than she should. More than she wanted to. "I misled you, and I regret that."

"Carl isn't right for you." His words were stark and cool, his gaze intense.

"You don't know that," she argued. "You've never even met Carl."

"I know you."

She lowered her eyes because meeting his gaze had become impossible. Her throat felt as if it were about to close up on her. "I have to go."

"Not yet," he said, stopping her. He backed her into the shadows until her shoulders butted against the side of the brick structure. Instinctively she clenched the lapels of his overcoat. Even when she realized he intended to kiss her, she couldn't find the words to object. Being inherently honest, Hannah realized this was exactly what she'd wanted for a long time.

Slowly, as though he expected her to protest, Joshua lowered his mouth to hers. She assumed his kiss would be hard and demanding, a penance required for having misled him. A penalty to be paid.

But she was wrong.

He pressed his lips gently over hers in the lightest, the tenderest, of contacts. So sweet. So smooth. The pressure increased, so gradual at first that she didn't notice. His lips worked over hers, sliding, then deepening, encouraging her to open to him.

With him as her tutor, Hannah eased open her mouth and moaned. This was nothing like the quick pecks and almost apologetic exchanges she'd experienced with Carl. Nothing like anything she'd experienced with anyone. Her nails dug into his coat, and she responded with a lifetime of pent-up longings.

It seemed to require a great deal of effort for Joshua to break off the kiss. Even then he seemed to ease himself away from her with a series of short but equally potent kisses.

He held her against him, and she stayed, the ragged edge of his breathing echoing in her ear. Her own breathing was just as unstable. Wrapped in the warm cocoon of his arms, Hannah never wanted to leave.

"Please . . . my family is waiting. They don't know where I am." It was pointless to continue. Pointless to torture themselves.

His arms tightened before he released her. "Meet me," he whispered against her cheek. "Monday evening at eight at the skating rink at Rockefeller Center."

"I can't. You know I can't."

"Be there, Hannah," he pleaded. "I need time to think. We both do. You don't love Carl."

"Joshua . . ."

"You don't love him," he returned with conviction, "otherwise you'd never have allowed me to kiss you like that." With that he turned away.

Hannah wanted to run after him and explain that she wouldn't show. She had no intention of continuing this charade. That was why she'd told him about Carl. It was too late for them. Much too late.

"Joshua," she called.

He ignored her, and because she was forced into it, she raced after him. She was out of breath by the time she reached him.

"I won't be there," she cried. "I won't."

He turned, and for the first time since she'd told him about her commitment to Carl, he smiled, saying without words that he believed otherwise.

"You'll be wasting your time," she argued heatedly.

Joshua said nothing, then wrapped his arm around her waist and dragged her to him. His kiss was short but thorough. When he finished, he exhaled slowly. "You'll be there," he said with supreme confidence. "You won't be able to stay away."

"Will Hannah meet Joshua?" Shirley asked Goodness. The two had parked themselves atop a light fixture in the Morgansterns' deli. Hannah's father was locking the doors while her mother was upstairs preparing the evening meal.

"What do you think?" Goodness was downright gleeful.

"What do I think?" Shirley repeated. "I think you're headed for serious trouble with Gabriel, that's what I think."

Goodness couldn't have disagreed more. "Gabriel knew exactly what was going to happen," she insisted. "He might think Carl Rabinsky is the cat's meow, but you and I both know he isn't the right man for Hannah."

Shirley's look was skeptical. "Why isn't he?"

"It's clear to me that Carl's as confused about all this as Hannah. The poor boy's parents had more to do with the engagement than he did. They pushed him into it."

"How do you know that?"

"I don't," Goodness confessed reluctantly, "but I'd wager a good deal that was the case."

"What you're wagering," Shirley seemed to feel obliged to tell her, "is our futures. You've done this before, you know. My heaven," she continued, wringing her hands. "I can't get involved in your prayer request, not when I've got troubles of my own."

"Oh?"

"It's Brynn and Roberto. This is simply not the time for her to walk around with her head in the clouds. She needs her wits about her. I'm afraid something serious is about to happen, and I can't be constantly fretting about what you're getting into."

"Me?" If she didn't know better, Goodness would be insulted.

"Yes, you. I beg of you, Goodness, kindly leave matters be with Carl and Hannah."

Goodness considered it seriously, but not for long. She didn't mean to be a rabble-rouser, but there were some matters that one couldn't ignore. Unfortunately this was one of those times.

"I can't."

Shirley groaned, and her head slumped forward. "Why did I know you were going to say that?"

"I'm sorry, really I am. But I asked myself exactly why Gabriel would assign this particular prayer request to me."

"What do you mean?"

"Think about it," Goodness said, crossing her arms. "Ruth Morganstern prayed that Hannah would make a good marriage."

"Yes," Shirley agreed impatiently.

"It was as clear as the feathers in our wings that Carl was about to ask for Hannah's hand in marriage. Both Hannah's parents are nuts about Carl, and his family about her."

"So?"

Goodness had a hard time believing that her fellow prayer ambassador could be so thickheaded. "Don't you see?"

"Obviously not."

"Well," Goodness said with a sorry lack of patience, "Gabriel assumed the assignment would be a snap. An engagement to Carl was in the cards already. Really all that was required was for me to stand back and let it happen. Once Hannah was formally engaged to Carl I was supposed to pretend it was all my doing and promptly return to heaven, the assignment complete."

"Hannah is formally engaged to Carl," Shirley reminded her.

Shirley was missing her point entirely. "That's true, but Gabriel doesn't know that."

"In other words," Shirley said, walking circles around Goodness as she mulled over the situation, "you think this job is another one of Gabriel's little token assignments."

Goodness folded her arms and nodded with a good deal of ceremony. "I do indeed, and frankly I'm insulted."

"You mean like the chess set for Craig?"

Goodness nodded. "Exactly."

This information seemed to fluster her friend. "My oh my, I don't know what to think."

"Well, I do," Goodness returned with a hint of self-righteousness. "It was clear to me from the first that Carl Rabinsky isn't the right husband for Hannah. In good conscience I can't idly stand by and let her marry the wrong man."

"What are you going to do?" Shirley asked, and then crunched up her face as if she were afraid of the answer.

Goodness relaxed and smiled. "I'm not sure yet, but I do know one thing."

"What's that?"

"She's not going to marry Carl."

* * *

Sunday morning Brynn quietly slipped inside the pew at St. Philip's, crossed herself, and knelt on the padded kneeler. She closed her eyes and bowed her head, fully intending to pray. But it wasn't thoughts of God that filled her mind. Instead she found herself mulling over the night before with the church youth group and Roberto Alcantara.

Every time Brynn remembered the dance in which they'd shared the duty as chaperones, a warm, expectant feeling stole over her. It had all started innocently enough when they'd first danced together. No one seemed to want to be the first couple on the floor, so Roberto, stiffly, had asked her. She knew from the way his lips tightened that he wasn't keen on being her partner. Taking it personally, she'd glared back at him, letting it be known that she didn't relish his company, either.

Yet from that shaky beginning, something fragile and exciting had blossomed. As the music started, Roberto had held her awkwardly in his arms, his body rigid, as if to avoid touching her.

Then gradually, as they'd warmed to the rhythm of the music, he'd relaxed. Because he had, she had too. Slowly, almost without being aware of what was happening, she'd found herself tucked securely in Roberto's arms. It amazed her how well they performed together, how easy his steps were to follow. Anyone looking at them would have assumed they were longtime partners. Halfway through the dance Roberto had smiled, and she'd shyly returned the gesture. Then he'd tucked his head close to hers, and they'd continued to sway gracefully across the polished gym floor.

From that point forward in the evening, Brynn had looked for an excuse to dance with Roberto a second time. Unfortunately their duties had prevented them from spending any more time together. The teenage dance had gone on until almost midnight, and the high schoolers couldn't have kept them apart more had they plotted to do so.

From the silent messages Roberto had sent her way, from the quick exchanges of eye contact, she'd realized that he was as eager to be with her as she was with him.

After the dance, Roberto had walked her to her car. At first they'd been shy with each other, not knowing what to say. But gradually that had changed, and they'd chatted freely. Brynn was certain Roberto had meant to ask her for a date, but before he'd had a chance, a fight had broken out between two boys. In his frustration, Roberto had closed his eyes and forcefully released his breath. Brynn had felt the regret in him as he'd turned away and hurried toward the scuffle.

Long after she was home, Brynn had found it impossible to sleep. Again and again her mind had reviewed the one dance she'd shared with Roberto. The memory had left her hungering to learn what would have happened had they been free to enjoy one another's company.

The more she thought about Roberto, the more she admired his accomplishments. He worked hard and seemed determined to make his business a successful enterprise. He genuinely cared about his brother's welfare and took an active role in the community. Father Grady, whom Brynn considered to be an excellent judge of character, couldn't say enough good about Roberto.

True, they'd started off on the wrong foot, but Brynn was eager to make up for that and start again. If she did have God's attention, then what she sought was for Roberto to be at church this morning.

Giving up the pretense of praying, Brynn opened her eyes and sat on the hard wooden pew. She didn't see Roberto and couldn't swivel around to look without being obvious.

Triumphant organ music announced the beginning of mass, which Father Grady celebrated. Not until Brynn stood to follow the others to the altar for communion did she spy Roberto. Instantly her heart gladdened.

He saw her too, because she watched as a brief smile touched his eyes.

After mass Roberto was waiting on the top of the church steps for her. Following the throng of the faithful out of the large double-wide doors, Brynn saw Roberto almost immediately and waved.

"So we meet again," she said. She hated the breathless quality to her voice, but she couldn't hide how pleased she was to see him.

He acknowledged her with a short nod.

"Did the boys give you any trouble last night?" she asked, wanting to learn the outcome of the fight.

He shrugged as though to say it wasn't anything serious. "I separated them and had Emilio take Modesto with him."

"I'm glad."

Once again Brynn noted what a fine figure of a man Roberto made. She didn't know what had blinded her earlier.

"So it was Modesto," she murmured. That didn't surprise her.

"Mike and Modesto were going at it until—"

"Mike?" Brynn interrupted. "Not Mike Glasser?"

"That's the name."

Brynn hadn't seen the morose young man all evening. But then it would be characteristic of Mike to conceal himself in the shadows. If he had come to the dance, then perhaps some girl had caught his eye. Brynn hoped that was the case. She genuinely liked Mike and wished she knew how to reach him.

"It surprises me that Mike would fight anyone, especially Modesto." Although she said the words aloud, she didn't expect Roberto to comment. Mike wasn't a fighter. Modesto was much more savvy when it came to such matters. The Hispanic youth would have dropped Mike in record time.

"Whatever plagued him was a hot issue," Roberto commented. "From what the others told me, Mike went after Modesto without provocation. The funny thing is, I don't think Modesto really wanted to fight him."

"But you were able to break it up before anyone was hurt?" she asked, unable to hide her concern.

Roberto nodded, and a hint of a smile turned up the edges of his mouth. "No problem."

Brynn relaxed.

Roberto was about to say something when Emilio strolled past casually and stopped as though surprised to find his older brother spending time with his teacher. "Mornin', Miss Cassidy."

"Morning, Emilio."

The teenager turned to his brother. "Have you asked her yet?"

Roberto answered in Spanish, his voice low and threatening.

Emilio ignored him. "He's going to invite you over to the apartment for breakfast. I'm supposed to make myself scarce." He grinned boyishly and added in a low voice, "I'd be careful if I were you, 'cause it looks to me like my big brother intends to put the make on you."

Brynn couldn't keep from laughing, but Roberto wasn't amused. He spoke again, and his tone was clear. He wanted his brother to shut up and leave them alone.

If Emilio felt the least bit threatened by his brother, he didn't let it show. If anything, the younger Alcantara couldn't have looked more pleased.

"You should have seen Roberto this morning," he continued undaunted. His smile was full and cocky.

"He was up at the crack of dawn, shaving and splashing on that fancy cologne he likes so well."

"Emilio." Again Roberto threatened him.

"He likes you, Teach, big time."

Brynn knew smiling was probably the worst thing she could do, but she couldn't make herself stop. Emilio was telling her everything she wanted to hear.

Disgruntled, Roberto pulled his wallet from his hip pocket and jerked out a twenty-dollar bill. "Get lost for a couple of hours," he instructed.

A wide grin split Emilio's face. "I'm outta here." He looked to Brynn and winked. "Have fun, you two." With that he was gone.

"I apologize for my brother," Roberto said flatly.

Brynn arched one brow. "Was what Emilio said true? Do you intend to put the make on me?"

His intensely dark eyes didn't waver from hers. "That depends."

"On what?"

"Several matters," he said, and cleared his throat. "Mostly on if you feel the same way about me as I do you." He reached for her hand and laced his fingers with hers. "I'd be honored if you'd join me for breakfast."

"Does that mean you're volunteering to cook?"

He didn't hesitate. "Yes."

"Then I accept."

Hand in hand they strolled down the sidewalk.

"We have nothing in common." It was as though he felt obligated to remind her of that.

"I certainly don't agree with your views on education," she added. If he was looking for reasons they shouldn't see each other, she had a list of her own.

Roberto's chest deflated as he released a pent-up breath. "You're Irish, I'm Hispanic. I have no business bringing you home with me."

"But you are, aren't you?"

"Yes," he said, as though admitting to a fault.

"Why?" Perhaps she should leave matters as they are and not ask.

"Because I had to know." His voice was gruff with impatience, but Brynn understood. She was equally curious. Equally fascinated with him.

"I needed to know, too," she admitted softly.

Roberto's hand squeezed hers, and when she looked up, he smiled.

He brought her to the apartment he shared with his brother. The compact unit was decorated with large overstuffed pieces of furniture. The royal blue material had several crocheted doilies flattened across the back.

"My mother made those," Roberto explained when Brynn ran her finger over the delicately crafted cotton threads.

"They're lovely."

"So are you."

Before Brynn could comment, Roberto turned her in his arms. She came willingly, without a qualm, eager for his kiss. He didn't disappoint her. Soon his mouth settled firmly over hers. His kiss was both hot and compelling. Brynn's breath caught in her throat as he wrapped her securely in his arms. She buried her face in the hollow of his neck and breathed in the warm, spicy rum scent of him. The bay cologne reminded her of what Emilio had said, and she smiled softly and pressed her lips against his smoothly shaven skin.

"I meant to wait to kiss you," he confessed, his lips in her hair. "At least until after breakfast."

"I didn't want to wait."

He continued to caress her back. "We shouldn't be doing this."

"You're right," she agreed, and stepped up onto the tips of her toes to kiss him again. The world dissolved, melting away any resistance that might have remained. "We're both crazy."

"The world is crazy," Roberto agreed, "but I haven't the strength to resist you."

Brynn closed her eyes and pressed her head against the solid strength of his shoulder. She was content to stay as they were, but she wasn't blind to their differences. What Roberto said was true. They had little in common other than the fact that they were crazy about each other.

Jenny was convinced she was coming down with a cold. Her throat ached, and she alternated between hot flashes and the chills. And she swore every bone in her body ached. A cold complicated by the flu.

She managed to sing her way through the two production numbers she was involved in from *South*

Pacific. She smiled as if she hadn't a care in the world, delivered the dinners to her customers, and counted the minutes until she'd finished her shift.

When she returned to the apartment the first thing she did was take a long, hot shower. Even with the comfort of warm water raining down on her, she developed a hacking cough.

"You don't sound so good," Michelle called from the other side of the bathroom.

"I'm miserable."

"Do you want me to get you some aspirin?" her roommate offered.

"No thanks," Jenny said as she opened the door. "I took some when I got home." Dressed in a thick terry-cloth robe, she ambled into the living room and buried herself under the wool afghan her mother had mailed her last Christmas.

"I bet a nice hot bowl of chicken soup would help you to feel better."

"I'm fine, Nurse Michelle," Jenny teased.

"You need something," her roommate insisted.

What she needed, Jenny realized, wasn't to be easily found. More than at any other time since her arrival in New York, Jenny needed her family.

Jenny could feel a sneeze coming on, and she reached for a tissue and nearly blew a hole through it with the force of her misery.

"My goodness." Michelle laughed.

"What about the Christmas party?" Jenny asked, wanting to take her mind off her woes. She needed to divert Michelle before she whipped out a thermometer and dispensed massive doses of TLC. Struggling as she was against bouts of self-pity, Jenny preferred to suffer alone.

"Oh, my goodness, the party! I nearly forgot." Michelle walked over to her purse and took out a list. "I talked to Paul. You remember Paul Fredricks, don't you?"

Jenny nodded, although she hadn't a clue who Paul was. She'd figure it out in a moment.

"Anyway, Paul says the fifth would work out great."

"The fifth is fine with me." For the life of her, Jenny couldn't figure out why they would need to clear the date with Paul Fredricks, but again that was something she would leave to reason out later.

"Do you agree?"

"Sure." One day was as good as any other as far as she was concerned. "I'll make sure I have the fifth off."

"Good. I added Paul's name to the list while I was at it. You don't object, do you?"

"Of course he can come. The more the merrier." Paul Fredricks, of course. He was the actor who'd captured Michelle's attention and her heart after one short meeting. Her roommate seemed to think no one had noticed. Perhaps no one else had, but Jenny wasn't as easily fooled.

"Look," Michelle said, standing inside the kitchen. "The message machine is blinking."

"I forgot to check," Jenny admitted. The first

order of business when she'd returned home was aspirin and a hot shower. "Who called?"

"I don't know." Michelle pushed down the button and reached for a pad and pen.

"It's Irene," Michelle cried.

It would be just like their agent to leave the most important news of their careers on the answering machine.

"I don't know where you girls are," Irene's elevated voice said, "but I sincerely hope you'll be home soon. Now listen up! I talked to John Peterman this afternoon, and he wants you both back for a second audition first thing in the morning. I repeat, he wants to see you both again."

Michelle looked to Jenny.

Jenny looked to Michelle.

Michelle threw open her arms and screamed.

Her cold forgotten, Jenny tossed aside the quilt and raced over to her friend's open arms. Together they danced around the living room, screaming at the top of their lungs.

Then Jenny started to cough again.

Chapter Eight

"Suzie, can I see you after class?" Brynn asked the Chinese girl. Of all her students, Brynn found real encouragement in watching this particular teenager's progress. Suzie's written essays revealed a quick, analytical mind and a thirst for knowledge. Brynn hadn't said anything to Suzie, but she'd taken it upon herself to inquire about the possibility of a full-ride scholarship for the girl.

Suzie glanced up from her desk and blinked. "Did I do something wrong?"

"No, not at all," Brynn quickly assured her. She patted Suzie's shoulder, and the girl returned to her writing assignment.

"Do you want to see me, too?" Malcolm called from the back of the classroom, disrupting the calm. That was Malcolm's specialty.

"Not today," she said.

Malcolm folded his muscular arms and leaned back on his desk chair until his shoulders were braced against the wall. His eyes were round with irritation. "I heard you stopped by my place yesterday and asked to speak to my mother. If you got something to say to her, you can say it to me first." He lifted his chin an inch in open defiance.

It was clear Malcolm didn't trust her. Brynn doubted that many of her students did, although she'd worked hard to gain their confidence. Again and again she butted her head against the thick walls of doubt and suspicion. To the best of her knowledge she hadn't gone against her word once, yet her students acted as if they were waiting for her to knife them in the back. Certainly the incident with Emilio that first day hadn't helped matters any.

"My stepdad said you stopped by my place, too." This was from Yolanda.

"Are you looking to make trouble for us?" It was Malcolm again.

"What'd you want with my mom?"

"Yeah. You ain't got no right to talk about me behind my back."

Brynn could see that she'd best explain the purpose of those afterschool visits. She'd hoped meeting her students' families would be a positive experience; instead she'd incurred the mistrust and ire of her class.

Emilio sat up and looked over his shoulder. "Miss Cassidy comes to my apartment most every afternoon, and I ain't making no fuss about it."

His remark was followed by several boos and hisses. Emilio just smiled. He reveled in the fact that Brynn had been seeing a good deal of Roberto. What he said, however, wasn't true.

"All right, all right," Brynn said, holding up her hands. "It looks like I owe you an explanation."

"You're damn right you do."

Brynn looked into a sea of angry faces. "Malcolm, you're right. I did stop off at your place yesterday afternoon. I wanted to tell your mother it was a pleasure to have you in my class and report to her that your progress in the last few weeks has been nothing short of amazing."

Malcolm's mouth snapped closed. He looked confused, then relieved. "You wanted to tell her good things about me?"

"Is that why you came to my house?" Yolanda asked.

"Yes. I'd hoped to visit everyone's family by the end of the quarter. Yolanda, I couldn't be more pleased with how well you're doing. You've maintained a B average, and I wanted your family to know how hard you've been working."

"You won't be able to say that about me."

Denzil was right about that. His grades had been dismal, and he gave little if any thought or effort to his assignments. His contributions to the class were limited to disruptions and arguments.

"Well," she said, thinking on her feet. "I thought I'd tell your parents how I've noticed your ability to argue an issue from any point. That's the quality of a good attorney. If you were the least bit interested, you could make a career learning the law."

"An attorney?" Denzil sat up straighter on his chair. "Me, an attorney?" He laughed under his breath. "I've had lots of experience with the law, and I've met some of those fast-talkin' lawyers, too. Only they were looking to toss my butt in jail."

"There are other kinds of attorneys," Brynn told him.

"I could wear one of those fancy silk suits, couldn't I?"

"Of course. Listen, Denzil," she said, her convictions causing her voice to grow strong and sure, "this is exactly what I've been telling you all quarter. You can be anything you want. The power is right here inside you." She held her clenched fist against her breast. "All you've got to do is want it bad enough."

"I ain't never had anyone tell my mother good things about me," Yolanda said. "The only time a teacher ever came to my house was because she thought I took something out of her stinking purse." Looking away, she sighed loudly. "I did it, too, because that teacher was a real jerk. She wasn't even fair."

"You got any good things to tell Roberto about me?" Emilio asked, and draped his elbows over the back of his seat. He was sitting proud.

"I have plenty to tell Roberto about you," Brynn teased as she rubbed the chalk dust from the palms of her hands.

The class laughed, just as Brynn intended they should.

"Now that I've answered your questions, please return to your writing assignment." Generally, when she directed her students' attention back to a written task, a grumble of discontent would spread across the room. Not this time.

After the bell rang, dismissing the class, Suzie Chang made her way to Brynn's desk. The shy girl clenched her books tightly. "You wanted to talk to me, Miss Cassidy?"

"Yes," Brynn said, scooting the chair back. "Suzie, you're an excellent student. This last paper you wrote about Anne Frank is as good as anything I've read on the subject. You revealed both insight and sensitivity to the Jewish girl's plight."

Uncomfortable with the praise, the teenager lowered her gaze. "Thank you."

"I'd like to know if you plan on attending college next year."

"College." The girl's eyes lit up briefly, then she sobered and slowly shook her head. "I can't."

"But Suzie, you're exactly the kind of student who should continue their education. I can feel the hunger in you, the desire to learn. There's a way, I promise you. I can help you if you want."

The girl shifted her weight from one foot to the

other. She kept her head lowered and refused to meet Brynn's eyes. "I can't, Miss Cassidy."

"Suzie, didn't you hear what I said to Denzil earlier? Where there's a will, there's a way. Now if you're worried about the money, there are scholarships. I'll help you fill out the applications. and . . ."

Suzie's head snapped up, and Brynn noticed that the teenager's face was streaked with tears. "A scholarship isn't going to help me, Miss Cassidy. Nothing will." Having said that, Suzie turned and raced out of the classroom.

Stunned, Brynn sat at her desk for several moments, pondering Suzie's words. Nothing would help her? That made no sense.

Feeling as though she'd somehow failed her brightest student, Brynn left the building, determined to try again to meet Denzil's and Malcolm's parents. Perhaps she'd have more success now that the word was out that she wanted to compliment the teens instead of complain.

A block away from the school the streets were dirty, filled with litter and broken glass. A discarded davenport was turned upside down and garbage dumped in the ripped undercarriage. The smells of rotting food were potent enough to cause Brynn to turn her head away.

Dusk settled over the city. The streetlights that weren't broken blinked on, casting a clouded yellow glow to the filth on the sidewalk.

From the distance, Brynn watched as a man

approached her. She stiffened, then reminded herself she had nothing to fear. This was a violent neighborhood, but like Father Grady, Brynn had faith in the goodwill of those who occupied the tenements.

As the figure of the man grew near, Brynn recognized Roberto. When he realized it was she, his steps became quick and filled with purpose. The tension drained from her, and Brynn relaxed. They'd met twice in the last week, swift snatches of time they'd stolen in an effort to be together. Five minutes. Ten. Just long enough to convey that they wished it could be longer.

"Roberto." She didn't bother to disguise her happiness.

Roberto was frowning. "It's true, then," he said, sounding none too pleased.

"What is?" she asked, surprised by his attitude.

"Emilio stopped off at the garage to tell me you were parading around these streets after school visiting families."

"I wanted—"

"Don't you realize it's dark now by four-thirty?" he barked. He jerked off his baseball cap and slapped it against his knee in a display of disgust.

"Roberto, what's wrong?"

"Are you crazy, woman?" He said something in Spanish, and from his tone, it was just as well she didn't understand. "You're inviting trouble. I thought you had more sense than this."

"Roberto, if you'd only listen."

"To what? Don't you realize this is New York

City? You're targeting yourself to be the next crime victim. You're inviting trouble. I can't follow you around and protect you."

She didn't appreciate his attitude, but she didn't want to argue, not when they'd come so far. She stiffened her shoulders and glared right back at him. The cold wind whipped about her face as she struggled with her composure. "I know what I'm doing."

"You haven't got a clue," Roberto snapped. "What could possibly be so important for you to risk your life?"

She tried to tell herself that he was so angry because he cared, but his attitude stung. The people in this neighborhood knew her. She couldn't go more than a few houses before she met someone she recognized from either the school or the church.

"Don't you understand?" Roberto said, gripping her by the shoulders. "You can't change the world on your own."

"But I can help these kids."

"Brynn, oh, my darling fool." Briefly he closed his eyes, struggling to hold on to his temper. "You can do nothing. You can change nothing. Denzil, Malcolm, and all the rest will live and die in this neighborhood the same way Emilio and I will."

"That's not true," she argued. She could make a difference. She believed that with all her heart. That was the reason she was here.

"Grow up," he said, his fingers biting deep into her coat. "You've got to step out of this dream world you're living in. Look around you. Can't you see?"

Brynn refused to believe what he said. "We have a difference of opinion, Roberto, but that's no reason to treat me like a child."

He seemed to be struggling within himself. After a moment, he dropped his hands and his features hardened. "Go home, Brynn. For the love of God, go home where you belong. You don't fit in here. Just go!" he shouted, and gave her a light push.

She blanched. "You don't mean that."

"I've never been more serious in my life. Pack your bags and head back to Rhode Island or wherever it was you came from before you get yourself killed. Please, Brynn." This last part came on a rush of emotion.

The pain his words produced sucked the breath from her lungs. At first she could barely think, and when she spoke her voice betrayed her pain. "You want me to leave?"

He held himself stiffly away from her and didn't answer for several moments. Then something broke within him, and he expelled his breath forcefully. Before her heart beat again, before she could take another breath, Roberto brought her into his arms. "No, I don't want you to go."

Her arms circled his waist, and he relaxed. Nothing had ever felt more right than to be in Roberto's arms.

"Promise me, if you're so anxious to go out nights, you'll let either me or Emilio accompany you."

She remembered his words about not having the

time to be her bodyguard and knew he'd said those hurtful things only because he was worried for her.

"Promise?" he demanded.

She nodded, and he kissed the top of her head.

Beneath the warm, golden glow of the street-light, the man who'd shouted at her only moments earlier now bent his head to kiss her. "What am I going to do with you?" he said.

Brynn smiled to herself, content in his arms. In time he'd realize she could make a difference. If it was only to be in one life, then so be it, but she wouldn't walk away from her students, nor would she leave this neighborhood, no matter what Roberto thought.

Jenny stood on stage, dressed in her tights and dancing shoes. Five others stood with her, including Michelle. All triple threats. Each one accomplished in singing, dancing, and acting. Each one eager to be John Peterman's latest Broadway discovery. Each one pleading silently to be chosen for this role. Any role. A chance.

Bright lights blinded her, but Jenny was accustomed to not being able to view her audience. Her throat was raw and her head throbbed, but she ignored the cold and flu symptoms as best she could.

"Miss Lancaster."

The man with the booming voice called her name. Jenny stepped forward and shaded her eyes with her hand. "Yes."

"You sang 'Don't Cry for Me, Argentina' in the first audition, is that correct?"

"Yes." Her voice quivered with the strain of answering his questions.

"Did you bring your sheet music with you?"

"Yes." She looked to the man sitting at the piano.

"What will you be singing this time?"

With her cold and her throat feeling the way it did, Jenny knew her voice wouldn't carry any musical number with more than a two-octave range. Normally her voice was able to scale four octaves, something that had amazed and thrilled her music teachers in Custer, Montana. But such versatility wasn't uncommon here in New York.

"I'll be singing 'Rainy Days and Mondays,'" Jenny told the faceless voice. The first piano notes broke into the silence. She was forced to clear her throat, which had tightened up on her to where she could barely speak, let alone sing.

The piano player looked at her when she didn't come in on cue and played the introduction a second time. She opened her mouth and nothing came out. She tried again, and what sound did escape wasn't anywhere close to being considered musical.

Miserable, Jenny raised her hand and stopped the piano player. There was no use continuing. Not now. She couldn't do it.

"I'm sorry," she mumbled, wavered, and reached out blindly, afraid she was about to collapse.

Michelle gripped her hand. "Jenny's sick . . . she shouldn't even be here."

Her roommate placed her arm around Jenny's shoulders, and she slumped against Michelle, needing her friend's support to remain upright.

"She has a fever of a hundred and two," Michelle informed the casting director.

"And you are?" the loud voice boomed.

Michelle stiffened. "Her roommate. I realize this is none of my business, but I'm afraid Jenny's sick. If you want to hear her sing, our agent can supply you with any number of tapes. Come on, Jenny," Michelle said, steering her off the stage. "I'm taking you home."

"No," Jenny protested. It was bad enough that her best chance of ever appearing on Broadway was being taken away, but she wouldn't allow her own misfortune to ruin Michelle's chances, too. "You stay here."

"But—"

"I insist. Don't argue with me. This is your chance."

"But, Jenny—"

"Michelle Jordan!" the voice shouted.

Michelle wavered and looked over her shoulder.

"Are you staying or going?" the voice asked.

"Staying," Jenny answered for her. She'd meant to shout. She'd put all her effort into making herself heard, but what remained of her voice was shockingly weak.

"Oh, Jenny, are you sure you'll be all right?"

"Of course. All I need is a little rest." She managed to put on a bright smile, which depleted what little energy remained. "I'll get a taxi," she promised a second time. A real luxury, considering her finances.

"You promise?"

"Yes. Now break a leg, kid," she said in her best Humphrey Bogart imitation. "You'll have to make it for both of us." She felt like weeping but managed to keep the tears at bay until she was outside the theater.

It was snowing. Wouldn't you know it? Every man, woman, and child in New York would be looking for a cab. Jenny stepped halfway out into the street and raised her arm in an effort to hail a taxi. The cold snow was a welcome coolant as it drifted onto her upturned face.

"You're going to help her, aren't you?" Goodness asked Mercy. "That poor girl's sick and miserable."

"Of course I'm going to help her." Mercy was indignant that her friend would believe otherwise. "It's just that this is the worst time imaginable for her to find an empty taxi."

"Well, do something."

"What would you suggest?" Mercy snapped, impatient herself.

"Stop traffic."

Mercy grinned. Why hadn't she thought of that herself? It wouldn't be so difficult to create a distraction. Not with Goodness there to help her. Naturally it would work; she just hoped Gabriel didn't find out about this.

"Come on," she said, sharing a gleeful smile with her friend.

"Where are we going?"

"Times Square," Mercy answered.

"Yes, but . . ."

Even Goodness looked surprised, and Mercy grinned sheepishly. "Don't worry, Gabriel will never hear of it." Well, at least she hoped that was the case.

"Look." Someone near Jenny stretched out their arm and pointed toward the huge electronic billboard above Times Square. "What in heaven's name is going on?"

Jenny looked up and did a double take. The sign that had flashed a huge Santa drinking a bottle of Coca-Cola only minutes earlier had disappeared. In its stead stood a picture of her own face, with the words flashing "Jenny needs a cab. Help Jenny."

She blinked, certain she was seeing things. Her fever must be higher than she realized for her to hallucinate this way. Obviously she'd stepped over the edge of reality.

Cars slowed to a crawl. Any number of people paused and pointed to the sign.

"Are you Jenny?" a bag lady who was nearly bent in half asked her. She wore a ragged wool coat. A worn shopping bag was draped over her forearm.

"Yes," Jenny whispered.

"I'm here to help you," the old woman proclaimed. "I'll get you that cab, now don't you worry none."

"I'm sick," Jenny whispered.

"Yes, I know, dear, now don't you fret. You'll be home soon enough." Holding Jenny by the arm, the old woman marched her out into the middle of midtown traffic and stood in front of the first yellow cab she spied.

The cabdriver stuck his head out the window and shouted angrily. Apparently he hadn't been in the country long, because his accent was so thick that it was nearly impossible to understand him.

"This is Jenny." The bag lady opened the cab door and stuck her head inside. "She's sick and needs to get home."

"I don't care if she's the president," the man inside the cab muttered, clenching his briefcase as if he expected the woman to snatch it from him. "I'm not giving up this cab. Driver," he instructed, "do something."

The driver twisted around and placed his hands over his ears. "Only been in America one day."

The passenger said something under his breath.

Undeterred, the bag lady tried a second time. "That sign up there says this woman needs help. Now get out."

The dignified-looking businessman bristled. "What sign?"

"Look at the billboard!" she shouted. "Now do as I say."

Jenny remained in a daze, barely able to decipher what was happening around her. Horns blared.

People stopped and stared. Traffic snarled even worse than it normally did. No one moved.

"You're Jenny?" the businessman leaned half-way out of the cab to ask her.

"Yes," she whispered.

"Oh, all right," he muttered, and with that he hopped out of the cab.

Jenny turned to thank the bag lady who'd helped her, but she'd disappeared into the crowd. Safe and warm, Jenny climbed inside the cab, laid back her head, and closed her eyes. The next thing she knew the driver pulled up in front of her apartment complex. She couldn't remember giving him her address.

"How'd you know where I lived?" she asked as she pulled out her limited cash reserve to pay him.

"The old lady told me."

"But . . ." Jenny shook her head, hoping to clear her thoughts. She'd never seen that woman before in her life. How could the bag lady have known where she lived?

"Good job," Goodness said, standing under the blinking lights of Times Square.

Mercy was downright proud of herself. She'd pulled off the role of the bag lady with the finesse that had done all angels proud. "Jenny never even guessed she was dealing with an angel," she bragged to her friend.

"I see you had a bit of a problem with that

businessman, though. He didn't seem willing to give up his seat."

"A nonbeliever," Mercy explained. "He prefers to take care of matters himself. Poor fellow. He doesn't know what he's missing."

"It looks to me like he's missing his cab." Goodness chuckled and pointed to the street below. The man stood with his shoulders hunched against the cold, his arm raised in a desperate effort to hail a taxi.

Joshua was about to give up hope that Hannah would show. He'd waited a half hour and was tempted to admit he'd been wrong. His face stung with cold and his fingers were numb. He might have left if it hadn't been for the skaters gliding over the ice and all the bright lights on the fifty-foot-tall Christmas tree. Both held his attention and kept him from dwelling on his disappointment.

This was the first day of Hanukkah, the Jewish holiday that observed the freedom of religion. These few days in December celebrated the hope for peace. This night Jewish families around the world lit the first candle of the menorah, commemorating the Jewish recapture of the Temple in Jerusalem from the Hellenic Syrians in 164 B.C. It was the holiday honoring "the miracle of the oil."

If Joshua remembered his history correctly, only one small jar of undefiled oil could be found for the Temple's menorah. It should have been enough for only one day, but the jar lasted eight days, until a fresh supply could be delivered.

Joshua had never considered himself a particularly religious man. He preferred to think of himself as a man of faith. In the darkness of winter, his people celebrated the return of light.

That was the way Joshua thought of Hannah. She was a ray of sunshine in a world that had been filled with dark ambition. A ray of hope. He hated placing Hannah in the awkward position of having to choose between him and Carl, but he was confident she didn't love the other man. He would have staked his career on that.

This evening would be telling. What he'd said to Hannah earlier about her not being able to stay away was true. If she truly cared for him the way he suspected, she'd find a means of meeting him.

Rockefeller Center was big, but somehow, some way, they'd connect. Joshua checked his watch one last time: 8:40.

His disappointment was keen. He'd wanted her to come. Willed her there. But it was apparent now that he'd been wrong. He had no option but to release her; she'd made her choice. He'd found her too late.

He'd turned away from the ice-skating rink when out of the blue he saw her. In that moment, it was as though the weight of the world lifted from his shoulders and his heart sang.

Hannah saw him, too, but her beautiful blue

eyes were devoid of emotion. She hurried toward him, and he held out his hands to greet her.

By the time she'd gripped his fingers with her own, she was breathless and barely able to talk. Her eyes were bright with questions. With doubts and confusion. Without speaking, she told him everything he needed to know. She hadn't wanted to come. Had decided to stay away . . . and found she couldn't.

"You were right," she said with a sadness that was nearly his undoing. "I had to come. A hundred times I told myself the best thing for both of us was if I stayed away. What have you done to me, Joshua? What have you done?"

It was difficult not to pull her into his arms and comfort her. It was what he wanted. His heart was full, spilling over. The fact that his love brought her unhappiness wasn't lost on him. In time he'd make up for the unpleasantness he'd caused her. If only she would be patient, he'd prove to her she'd made the right decision.

"I think we should talk this out," she suggested. She seemed to harbor the hope that they could sit across from each other and reason away their mutual attraction. It wasn't as simple as that, but she'd need to reach that realization herself.

"All right." He sought nothing more than to be with her. It wouldn't have mattered what they did. In many ways, he felt he was already fully acquainted with Hannah. He knew he loved her. He knew he wanted her to be his wife and the mother of his children.

How or when he'd come to realize all this, he couldn't answer. He was a man who dealt with facts, who argued cases. A man who generally was uncomfortable defining feelings. But when it came to Hannah Morganstern, Joshua found he was an expert on identifying his emotions.

"Come on," he said, tucking her hand in the crook of his arm. "I'll buy us a cup of hot chocolate."

A fragile, tentative smile touched her mouth. Her beautiful, kissable mouth.

"I'm beginning to think we're both a little nuts," she said.

"I couldn't agree with you more, but it's a good kind of crazy. Being with you makes me happy, Hannah. You're beautiful and generous and loving."

She lowered her head, uneasy with compliments.

Joshua found a table, and after she was seated, he walked over to the refreshment booth and bought two steaming cups of hot chocolate.

When he returned, she glanced up at him shyly. "The most amazing thing happened this evening."

"Oh?" He sipped from the edge of the paper cup, the steam wafting upward.

"When I told you I couldn't meet you, it wasn't because I didn't want to. Carl had asked me to attend the candle-lighting ceremony with him. It's the first day of Hanukkah," she told him unnecessarily.

"I know."

"I knew there wasn't any way I could possibly break our date. Then at the last minute Carl phoned. He came down with the flu."

That explained why Hannah was late. She'd been at the synagogue with her family and then rushed from there to Rockefeller Center.

"When I left in such a hurry, I'm sure my parents thought I was going to see Carl . . . instead I'm meeting another man." Sadness coated her words. It was clear she hated deceiving those she loved.

"I'm sure that given time, your family will learn to like me as much as they do Carl," he assured her gently. He regretted bringing the other man into the conversation. It seemed they spent half their precious time together discussing the rabbi's son.

Hannah's gaze drifted to the ice skaters and then back to him. "I hardly know you myself."

"Ask me anything you like," he invited her.

"You've never married?"

"No. I've been waiting for you, Hannah Morganstern." By the way the color drained from her face, Joshua realized he'd said the wrong thing. He didn't mean to rush Hannah. Because he was confident didn't mean he had to get cocky.

"I'm engaged to Carl," she whispered. "Doesn't that matter to you?"

"It matters a great deal." He wasn't going to lie. When she'd told him, he'd been both frustrated and angry. Later he'd realized just how fortunate it was that they'd met before the wedding. "I figure I found you just in time."

He didn't ask her if she felt the same way. Didn't bombard her with questions. That wasn't necessary. He already knew. She felt everything he did, only for her, it wasn't so simple. Tied up with her feelings for him was a lifetime of adhering to her parents' wishes.

"I'll go to your family," Joshua offered, "and explain."

"Explain what?" she asked miserably. "There's nothing to tell them, Joshua. I haven't changed my mind about anything."

Chapter Nine

Hannah had no intention of staying with Joshua. Her only purpose in meeting him was to explain once and for all that a relationship between them was impossible. It was too late for them. She was engaged to Carl now, and they'd soon be planning their wedding.

That had been the reason she'd decided to meet Joshua: so he'd know. Yet the moment she'd found him, her heart had been filled with a yearning, a wonder, that she couldn't reason away.

She couldn't look at him, she feared, and not reveal what was in her heart, so she focused her attention on the ice skaters. As a child she'd loved it when her mother had taken her to this very rink. Although she'd struggled to remain upright, Hannah had enjoyed the simple pleasure of gliding freely over the ice.

When she'd tired, she'd sat and watched others, admiring the skillful athletes as they'd leapt and spun their way across the rink. In her child's mind, she'd dreamed about someday being as graceful and talented.

"Come," Joshua said, and reached for her hand. He'd been silent since she'd announced that she fully intended to marry Carl. Hannah hoped he would accept her decision graciously and let matters drop between them. It was as difficult for him as it was for her, but she couldn't tell him that. She willed him to leave because she hadn't the strength to do it herself.

"Where are we going?"

His eyes revealed nothing, then he smiled in that gentle way of his. "Ice skating."

"But, Joshua, it's been years. I'm not sure I even remember how."

"It's been years for me, too."

"I can't," she insisted. "Really. I should get back before Mama asks questions. I can't lie."

Joshua stiffened. Surely he understood that she'd intended never to see him again. Surely he realized that she'd come this evening only because Carl had canceled at the last moment. Even now that surprised her.

"I'm not asking you to lie," Joshua explained, his hand clasping hers firmly. "All I want is for you to skate with me."

Hannah gazed longingly toward the ice. She was tempted. Oh, heaven, she was tempted. It wasn't so much to ask, she decided, not when she wanted this so badly herself.

"All right," she agreed. "But for only a short time."

"Agreed."

Joshua left her briefly, after checking her shoe size, and returned a few moments later with two pairs of ice skates. After lacing up his own, he knelt in front of her to be sure her skates were tied properly.

"You may well regret this," she said, linking her arm through his. Her legs wobbled when they stepped onto the ice, but Joshua's grip about her waist was firm.

Her first few steps were tentative and awkward. If not for Joshua, she was sure she would have fallen. "I can't believe I let you talk me into doing this," she said, concentrating on staying on her feet.

"You're doing just fine."

He was being kind, and she said so. Their first whirl around the rink was marked with her clumsy attempts to remain upright. Even with Joshua holding on to her, Hannah's arms flailed out in front of her a number of times in an effort to maintain her balance.

Before long she found a certain rhythm and glided over the smooth surface. Gaining confidence, she relaxed her grip on Joshua's arm, and he gradually released her. Skating backward in front of her, he smiled and praised her skill.

"Do you think anyone from the Ice Capades is watching?" she joked.

Joshua chuckled.

Thinking herself clever, Hannah decided to speed past Joshua. Unfortunately, in her effort to impress him, she lost her footing. Her feet slipped out from under her so quickly that she didn't have time to react. Arms flailing, she landed butt first on the hard, cold ice.

Joshua nearly fell on top of her, trying to keep her from losing her balance. By some minor miracle he managed to remain on his feet. Smiling broadly, he skated wide circles around her.

"You think this is funny, do you?" she asked, her dignity sadly bruised.

"Hilarious."

Hannah's rear end was getting wet and cold from the ice. She stretched out her arm, silently seeking his assistance. Joshua ignored her hand. Bracing his fists against his hips, his skates perpendicular to each other, he circled her.

"Joshua," she pleaded.

Chuckling, he helped her to her feet.

They skated for more than an hour, and then afterward, because she was unbelievably hungry, they ate huge hot dogs. Mustard dripped onto Hannah's forearm, and Joshua dabbed it away with a paper napkin, teasing her about being so messy.

Time seemed to drift away from them. Never could Hannah remember enjoying anyone's company more. It had been like this from the first moment they'd met.

"I have to go," she said sadly when she noticed

the time. It seemed she was always saying that to him.

He hailed a taxi and sat next to her on the seat. When they arrived outside her parents' deli, Joshua paid the driver and climbed out of the cab with her.

On the abandoned sidewalk, Hannah stood with her head bowed, her heart thudding hard and heavy with dread against her chest.

"I can't see you again." The best way was to say it flat out and leave no room for speculation. It was difficult, but necessary.

"Hannah . . ."

"I'm engaged to another man," she said as firmly as she could manage, afraid her voice would catch with emotion. "I can't string you along. It isn't fair to you. Please, Joshua, try to understand."

"Can't do this to me?" he repeated, and it seemed to her that he found encouragement in her words.

She didn't want to argue with him. She glanced longingly toward the door, wanting this last farewell to be over as quickly as possible. Not wanting to dwell on the unpleasantness of hurting him.

"Good-bye, Joshua."

He caught her by the shoulders and brought her into his arms. She didn't resist him. Hadn't the strength. His kiss was more potent than Irish whiskey. More heady than fine wine.

"Don't you think you should be more worried about hurting Carl than me?" he asked, his lips against her hair. "You said you couldn't do this to *me*."

"I can't do this to Carl, either," she said in a rush, her words dwindling to a mere whisper. She squeezed her eyes closed, realizing her mistake. Her first thought had been of Joshua, not Carl.

"You don't love him," Joshua insisted.

Hannah backed away from him. "Please accept this, Joshua. I can't . . . I won't see you again."

He opened his mouth, then snapped it closed as if biting off an argument. "It isn't in me to make you miserable, Hannah. Nor can I force you into a relationship against your will. I'm here night or day, whenever you need me." He pulled a business card from his wallet, then wrote something on the back of it. "Here's my address and phone number. You can reach me twenty-four hours a day. Call me when you're ready."

"I won't call."

"Take the card anyway."

He opened her hand and planted it in her palm, then folded her fingers over it.

Having done that, he kissed her again until her knees felt as though they would give out on her. She could barely manage to breathe when he lifted his head from hers. He reached up and tenderly slid his index finger down the side of her face.

"Call me," he whispered, his voice low and seductive.

Pride demanded that she tell him she wouldn't be making that phone call, but his kiss had stolen her breath away. By the time her lungs had recovered, he'd turned and walked away.

Realizing she was still clutching the business card, she buried it in her coat pocket and as silently as possible unlocked the door to the deli.

Soundlessly she made her way up the backstairs to the family apartment. All the lights were out, and Hannah sighed with relief. Her parents had gone to bed.

Guided by what little moonlight was available, she crept toward her bedroom. Just when she thought she was home free, her father spoke from behind her.

"Hannah?"

She swallowed tightly.

"For the love of heaven, where have you been? Don't you have a clue what time it is? Your mother and I have been half sick worrying about you."

All through the afternoon, Brynn noticed that Suzie Chang's eyes avoided hers. Although the teenager didn't contribute freely to class discussions, if Brynn called upon her, Suzie would willingly share her thoughts.

Often Brynn had been grateful for Suzie's contributions. Her other students tended to get sidetracked easily. Brynn had come to rely on Suzie to subtly steer the topic back on course. Reading the teenager generally wasn't difficult, and Brynn knew from the way Suzie's eyes brightened when she had something she wanted to say.

It wasn't that way this afternoon, however. Suzie

seemed to be trapped in a world all her own. Knowing the girl was miserable nearly broke Brynn's heart.

Brynn blamed herself. It had been wrong for her to look into scholarship possibilities without first discussing the idea with Suzie. Her intentions had been good, but in the process she'd somehow managed to hurt the girl.

The bell rang, and Brynn stopped Suzie on her way out the door.

"Could I speak to you for a few moments?" Brynn asked, hoping her voice didn't betray her worries.

"I can't this afternoon, Miss Cassidy," the teenager mumbled, her head bowed.

"It'll only take a moment, Suzie."

The room emptied, and Suzie stood just inside the classroom, her gaze fastened to the floor. She trembled like a frightened rabbit.

"It's about our discussion from the other day," Brynn began. "Remember I asked you if you had any plans for higher education."

"I can't go to college, Miss Cassidy."

"Suzie, if I said something to offend you, then I'm truly sorry."

The teenager bit into her lower lip, then slowly lifted her head. She offered Brynn a weak smile. "You didn't offend me. I was honored that you felt I . . ." She paused, and her dark eyes filled with tears.

"Suzie?"

The girl turned away and would have rushed from the room, Brynn suspected, if she hadn't stopped her.

"Can you tell me what's wrong?" Brynn asked gently.

Suzie trembled as she ran the back of her hand under each eye. "I don't want to trouble you with my problems."

"It's no trouble," Brynn assured her gently. "I'll do anything I can to help you."

"You can't help me, Miss Cassidy. No one can."

"I can try." With her arm around Suzie's shoulder, Brynn steered the girl to her desk and handed her a tissue.

Suzie's thin shoulders shook with repressed sobs. "Oh, Miss Cassidy, I don't know what I'm going to do."

"The first thing is to dry your eyes. There isn't anything so terrible that you can't tell me."

Suzie looked up and studied Brynn as though to gauge her sincerity. Brynn met her look without flinching. She hadn't a clue why Suzie was so unhappy. Naturally she had her suspicions, but she hoped it wasn't as traumatic as the girl seemed to feel.

"I can't go to college," Suzie announced on a wobbly, emotion-laden breath. "I don't even know if I'll be able to graduate from high school."

Brynn waited, giving the teenager the freedom to continue without the interruption of questions.

Suzie stiffened and looked away, as if meeting her eyes were more than she could manage. "I haven't told anyone." The words were low and filled with trepidation.

Brynn gripped the younger girl's hand, and Suzie squeezed her fingers hard enough to cause her pain.

"I'm pregnant," she whispered.

The news shouldn't have surprised Brynn, but it did. Suzie didn't have a boyfriend at school—in fact, to the best of Brynn's knowledge, the only social activity Suzie had ever participated in had been the dance at the church.

"How far along are you?"

"Almost six months."

"Six months!" Brynn couldn't disguise her surprise.

"I realize I barely show. . . . I've lost weight because I didn't want anyone to know. I was afraid if my father found out, he'd make me have an abortion," she said in a rush, her voice barely audible. "I don't want to kill my baby."

"Of course you don't."

"I want this baby, Miss Cassidy. I love him so much already. When I first realized I was pregnant, I thought I would die; then later, after I felt him move . . . it was such an incredible feeling."

"The father?" Brynn didn't want to pry, but surely the baby's father should be helping Suzie with some of these difficult decisions. Surely he could stand with her when she told her parents.

"I . . . haven't told him either." This was admitted with the same downcast look Suzie had worn earlier.

"But, Suzie . . ."

"He's got his own troubles, and I don't want to burden him with my news."

"Burden him?" Brynn couldn't keep the irritation out of her voice. "Suzie, this child is his responsibility, too. You shouldn't have to deal with this alone. There are decisions to be made. For one thing, you won't be able to hide your condition much longer."

"I know, but I don't want him to worry about me. He can't help, and . . . and if I told him about the baby, it would only make him feel worse. He loves me. I know he does." She buried her face in her hands, and her shoulders shook with silent tears.

Brynn patted Suzie's back gently.

"I don't know what I'm going to do, Miss Cassidy. I don't know what will happen when my family learns about the baby."

"You're going to have to tell your parents."

Suzie wiped the tears from her face. "I'm afraid my father will make me leave home, and I won't have anywhere to live. I want to finish high school, and what you said about me getting a scholarship for college, well, I never thought I could do anything like that."

"But of course you can. Your grades are excellent, but more than that, you have a clear desire to learn. Did you take the SAT test?"

Suzie shook her head.

"But before you consider college, you're going to need to make a decision about your future, yours and the baby's. I can't help you with that, but I do know that the school counselor can help guide you. Will you talk with her?"

Suzie hesitated, then nodded. "I like Mrs. Christian."

Brynn walked down to the office with her and waited while Suzie made an appointment with the school counselor for the next day.

"If there's anything more I can do, let me know, okay?" Brynn asked when Suzie had finished.

The teenage girl started to cry once more, and Brynn hugged her close and whispered reassurances. "Everything will work out, Suzie, don't worry."

The teenager sniffled and left the school. Silently Brynn returned to her classroom and sagged onto her seat, her heart heavy with Suzie's news.

Suzie was pregnant. The girl was little more than a child herself. So tiny and delicate, it was a wonder she'd been able to disguise her pregnancy this long. The fact that she'd gone without prenatal care hadn't escaped Brynn's notice, either.

The desire to wrap her arms around the teenage girl and protect her from the harsh reality of being a single mother nearly overwhelmed Brynn. More than one of her students was a mother. Brynn had been surprised to learn Yolanda had a two-year-old son. The boy stayed with Yolanda's mother while Yolanda attended classes to complete her education. Denzil had bragged to her about fathering three children. He'd done so in an effort to shock her. The fact that he was sexually active didn't astound her, but his attitude toward the number of children he'd fathered with different girls did.

By the time Brynn left the school, she felt as

though she carried the weight of the world on her shoulders. It seemed only natural to seek out Father Grady, but the parish priest was gone for the afternoon.

Mrs. Houghton, his housekeeper, seemed to sense Brynn had come for more than their usual friendly chat. "Do you want me to try to reach Father Grady?" the kindly older woman asked.

Brynn stood outside on the rectory steps. She shook her head. "No, that won't be necessary. I'll talk to him later."

"Are you all right, dearie?"

"I'm fine," Brynn assured her, but she wasn't.

Blindly she made her way toward the subway station, but as she neared the entrance, she hesitated. The thought of returning to an empty apartment held no appeal. With no clear destination in mind, she turned back, her shoulders slumped and her steps slow.

Roberto. She needed him. Although she trusted Roberto, she couldn't tell him about Suzie's condition. That would be breaking the teenager's confidence.

By the time she arrived at his garage, her eyes burned with unshed tears. The tight knot in her throat made it difficult to speak.

Roberto was bent over the hood of a car, and when she walked into the shop, he glanced up. He knew immediately that something wasn't right.

"Brynn, what's wrong?"

"Nothing," she lied. "Would you mind holding me for a little bit?" she asked, and her voice cracked.

He didn't hesitate, didn't question her, but simply did as she requested. Gently he laid aside his tools and brought her into the wide circle of his arms. "I'm greasy," he advised with regret, his touch light and tender.

Brynn burrowed deeper, needing his comfort. "I don't care."

His arms came fully around her then as he brought her against his solid strength. The hurt and fear, the disappointment and doubt, produced a hard, bitter tightness in her chest, and she clung to him.

"Brynn," Roberto whispered against her hair, stroking it away from her face, "can you tell me what's upset you so?"

She shook her head. The dream she'd had for her students seemed to have crumbled at her feet. Suzie had shown such promise, and Brynn had wanted so much for her. An unplanned pregnancy wasn't the end of the world, but Brynn didn't want Suzie caught in the trap like so many others. The teenager loved and wanted this child, enough to hide her pregnancy past the time she could have had an abortion. Enough to stand up against the wrath of her family.

As best she could, Brynn swallowed the emotion. "It was just one of those days," she said, drawing in a quick, stabilizing breath.

"It was more than that." He led her to a stool next to his work bench, and when she was seated, he paced the floor in front of her. "It's this neighborhood, isn't it?" His voice was gruff with anger. "You don't belong here. I told you that before and you refused to listen." He continued muttering in Spanish, knowing full well she couldn't understand him.

"Roberto." She reached out to him, but he ignored her. "Stop talking like that. Nothing you say is going to convince me to leave."

He rubbed his hands clean on a pink flannel rag and then burrowed his splayed fingers through his thick hair, leaving deep indentations.

"If I'd known this would upset you, I wouldn't have come." Brynn felt bad about that now. "I'm fine, really. There's nothing you can do except . . ."

"Yes?" he prodded.

She hesitated and held her arms open to him. "Could you please kiss me?" The world felt right when Roberto held her and loved her.

The beginnings of a smile edged up the fringes of his mouth. He walked over to where she sat and captured her upturned face between his callused hands. Her own hands found the curves of his shoulders. He felt stable and strong, and she needed that security. Someone to hold on to while trapped in one of life's storms.

"Roberto." His name came as soft as mist across a Scottish moor.

He closed his eyes as if struggling against her. She felt his breath against her face and touched his lip with the pad of her index finger. His mouth was moist and warm.

The simple action was all he seemed to need. Roberto bent forward and claimed her mouth in a long, leisurely kiss. Since the night of the dance, he'd kissed her any number of times. Each episode taught her something more about this man. He'd enthralled her from the first. He felt strongly about his younger brother, accepting responsibility for Emilio's welfare. At the same time, Roberto cared deeply about the neighborhood, confronting injustice, prejudice, and hatred. Every time she met Father Grady, the priest sang Roberto's praises. Already she was half in love with him herself.

She knew a part of Roberto wanted her to quit teaching at Manhattan High. He didn't want her to deal with the squalor and misery he confronted day in and day out. He'd rather she returned to teaching at the prim and proper girls' school. Yet at the same time, he was learning, just as she was, that they had a good deal in common. The barriers that had kept them apart seemed to shrink a bit more each time they were together.

"I hope you'll listen to reason this time." His lips were less than an inch from her own.

Brynn linked her arms around his neck and bounced her mouth against his. "Just being with you makes everything seem better. Thank you."

His face tightened. "Brynn, for the love of—"

She stopped him cold with a long, lingering kiss. When she regained her voice, she whispered, "I'm falling in love with you, Roberto Alcantara."

He reacted as if she'd pulled out a gun and fired at him. He groaned and rubbed his hand down his face. "That's the last thing I wanted to happen." He edged away from her until his backside collided with the side panel of the car on which he'd been working moments earlier.

"Roberto . . ."

"Don't you know not to tell a man that?" he asked gruffly. Then he whirled around and walked out of the shop as if she'd deeply insulted him.

The fever felt as if it were about to take the top of her head off as Jenny struggled out of her clothes and into her pajamas. The fever or the bitter pill of disappointment, she didn't know which.

Someone knocked against the apartment door.

"Michelle, can you get that?" Jenny called out before she remembered that her roommate was still at the audition with John Peterman and company.

Struggling out of bed, Jenny reached for her robe. She'd never looked or felt worse in her life and was in no mood to deal with a door-to-door salesman.

The knock came a second time, sharp and impatient.

Grumbling under her breath, she tied the sash

loosely around her waist and then unlatched the door lock without checking the peephole first. "Whatever you're selling, I'm not interested."

The words left her mouth and collided with a solid male chest. Jenny frowned and slowly looked up.

If she hadn't been feeling lightheaded earlier, she felt that way now.

"Trey," she whispered, so shocked there was no sound in her voice. He stood bold as life directly in front of her, all six feet four of him. With his Stetson adding another couple of inches to his height, he made for an intimidating figure.

"Jenny?"

Another woman might have fainted then and there, but by this point Jenny had endured so much that another shock barely fazed her.

"I've been sick."

"It certainly looks that way. Can I come inside?"

She nodded, too numb and too confused to find an excuse to refuse him. Not that she wanted to. He was a hundred times more compelling than she remembered. A hundred times more devastating. He didn't seem to realize that in New York a man this good-looking generally appeared in fashion magazines.

"You should be in bed," he commented as he walked inside the tiny apartment. He glanced around, and his gaze narrowed as if to say he found it impossible to understand why anyone would choose to live in a place this small. A man who rode the wide-open range would have to feel claustrophobic in New York City, Jenny reflected.

Despite her shock at seeing him, she maintained her wits. It would serve him right if she told him that she *had* been in bed and had been forced out of it in order to answer the door.

"What are you doing in town?" she asked. She gestured toward the sofa.

Gingerly he sat on the edge of the thin cushion and held on to his cowboy hat with both hands between his parted knees. "What am I doing in New York?" he said. "What else would someone like me come to this crazy town for? I came to see you, Jenny Lancaster."

"See me?" Now that the excitement had started to fade, Jenny felt the dread take over.

"You wrote and said you wouldn't be home for Christmas, remember? I thought about that, then decided if you wouldn't come to me, there was no option but for me to visit you."

She lowered her head, and her hair, stringy and damp from the snow, fell forward. "I can't go home, Trey, I just can't." The dread was replaced with a heavy sadness.

He didn't say anything for several tense minutes. "Your parents were terribly disappointed."

The pain tightened her chest. "I know."

"I was disappointed, too."

Slowly she lifted her gaze until their eyes met and held. A woman could get lost and wish never to be found in eyes that dark. Funny she'd never noticed that when she was growing up.

He continued to hold her look for several breathless moments. "I've missed you, Jenny."

She bit into her lower lip.

Trey had never been a man for a lot of words. And the years apart hadn't improved the situation, Jenny noticed. He rotated the brim of his hat in his hands.

"When you first left Custer I thought you'd come to New York and get this singing and dancing craze out of your head. Then when you became so successful, it seemed this was your destiny. But I always counted on seeing you again."

She couldn't bear to listen to him repeat the lies she'd fed her family and friends. She bent forward and buried her face in her hands.

"Jenny?" he asked gently, his tender concern ripping at her heart. "Do you need a doctor?"

She shook her head. What she really needed was a priest. Someone who could absolve her from the guilt. Someone who could help her repair the damage she'd done to herself and her family. Someone to show her what to do now.

He moved from the sofa and knelt on the thin carpet in front of her. As though he weren't sure what to do next, he placed his hand on her back. "Jenny, are you crying?"

She didn't answer him, although there wasn't any use trying to hide it.

He hesitated, stood, and then reached down and

gathered her in his arms. Then, as if she weighed next to nothing, he lifted her from the chair. One moment she was doubled over, struggling to hold back the giant sobs, and the next thing she knew she was being carried.

"Trey, what are you doing?" she demanded.

"Taking care of you." He sat back down on the sofa, holding her in his lap, his arms around her. "I never was much good at dealing with a woman's tears. Holding you just seemed the right thing to do."

She wrapped her arms around his neck and buried her face in his shoulder. For the longest time he did nothing but hold her, and she did nothing but let him.

"Tell me about Charlie," she begged, wanting to hear everything he could say about her family. Her brother wrote the least of anyone.

Trey chuckled and rubbed his hand down the side of his lean jaw. "I suspect you've heard he's sweet on Mary Lou."

Jenny's head came off Trey's chest. "Mary Lou Perkins?" That seemed impossible. First off, Mary Lou had been engaged to Brad Harper when Jenny had left Custer. Then she'd learned that the wedding had been called off at the last minute—word was Brad had gotten cold feet. But Jenny had assumed that the two would eventually marry.

Trey grinned. "Charlie's right sweet on her, and after three years Brad may just have lost his girl."

"It serves Brad Harper right. He had his chance," she said, siding with her brother.

She felt Trey's smile against her hair. "Last I heard, Charlie and Mary Lou had decided to announce their engagement to the community on Christmas Day."

"Oh." She wouldn't be there. One more nail in the coffin of her guilt.

"If you won't be there for Christmas, Jenny, will you come home for your brother's wedding?"

Chapter Ten

"Aren't you going to help Jenny?" Goodness asked. The three crowded in the corner of the tiny living room, hovering over Trey and Jenny.

Mercy knew that her friend had a soft heart. In fact, it was Goodness's tender nature plus her weakness for electronic devices that had been the main source of their difficulties over the last couple of years. To be fair, Goodness had matured. Either that or she'd become accustomed to such things as fifty-two-inch television screens. Not once in the past two Christmases had Goodness appeared on pay-per-view. Mercy was downright proud of her friend's progress.

"Mercy," Goodness snapped. "I asked you something important."

The warm thoughts Mercy had entertained about her fellow prayer ambassador vanished. "I brought Trey LaRue to New York, didn't I?"

"You did that?" Shirley joined them and sounded downright impressed. Mercy's evaluation of the third angel rose by several degrees.

Mercy was proud of her efforts and grateful someone had noticed. She tucked her thumbs in her waistband and rocked back on her heels. "You're darn tootin' I brought Trey LaRue to town."

"She's been hanging around cowpokes again," Goodness whispered out of the side of her mouth. "She's starting to talk just like one of 'em. The next thing we know she'll be wearing a buckle as big as a chastity belt and bragging about her rat-chasing dog."

"Not me," Mercy contradicted. "I've been too busy arranging Trey's trip east. I found he isn't as susceptible to suggestion as some humans are, especially schoolteachers and young Jewish women—if you catch my drift. I had my work cut out just getting him to New York. Must've taken three or four people suggesting he visit Jenny for him to take the hint."

Goodness frowned and apparently didn't take Mercy's words kindly.

"But look what happened to Jenny while you were away," Shirley commented glumly. "She's sick. My goodness, the poor girl looks wretched."

"That couldn't be helped." There was only so much one angel could do, and no one seemed to appreciate

Mercy's efforts on this assignment. Least of all her two best friends.

"Has Jenny told him the truth yet?" Goodness asked, making herself comfortable. She usually preferred to dangle from light fixtures, but not in these tight quarters. "She isn't going to be able to keep it from him, is she?"

"Not now," Mercy agreed. It wouldn't do any good to remind her companions that she could lead a horse to water, but she couldn't make him saddle himself. She paused. Was that how the saying went? She'd heard some smart-talkin' fellow in Montana say something along those lines, and at the time it had made perfect sense.

"What's this I heard about Jenny's brother?" Shirley asked impatiently. "Is he really getting engaged?"

"That's another thing." Mercy flung herself across the back of a living room chair and supported her head with the palm of her hand. "Does anyone here understand what I had to go through to arrange this last-minute romance between Charles Lancaster and Mary Lou Perkins?"

"You did that?" Shirley asked, amazed.

"Well, not entirely," Mercy admitted with some reluctance, although she'd be willing to accept a certain amount of credit. "All Charlie really needed was a little encouragement."

"And you supplied that?"

Mercy shrugged. "Some."

Goodness beamed her approval. "Good thinking."

"What about poor Jenny?" Shirley asked, studying the down-and-out actress.

"I don't know," Mercy admitted. "What she does and doesn't tell Trey is up to her."

"How long will Trey be in town?"

Mercy didn't have the answer to that, either. "Your guess is as good as mine."

"He'll be here for the party, won't he?" Goodness wanted to know.

It took Mercy a moment to remember the Christmas potluck Jenny and Michelle were holding. She hadn't a clue where the two young actresses intended on putting everyone, but they seemed to think they could manage.

"I don't know what Trey's plans are," she muttered. It seemed her friends insisted upon asking her questions she couldn't answer. "All I know is that however long he stays, it'll be long enough."

Her words were followed by a short silence. "Are you saying you know something we don't?" Shirley inquired.

Mercy's smug smile was all the answer she intended to give them.

Brynn stood in front of her class, and her gaze rested on Suzie Chang's empty desk in the middle of the room. It seemed as if the space were magnified until it appeared to crowd everyone against the walls.

The lessons that day involved the history of the Second World War, and although Brynn was prepared to discuss the Battle of the Bulge, her mind was elsewhere.

All she could think about was Suzie.

"This afternoon," Brynn said, forcing her attention back to the history lesson, "we are going to be talking about . . . sex." The word raced out of her mouth before she could stop herself.

Modesto cheered and sat up straighter on his desk chair. "Hey, Miss Cassidy, I bet I could teach you more than you could teach me." He laughed, thinking himself downright comical.

"Not if my brother hears about it," Emilio warned, his eyes narrowing. "Miss Cassidy is his woman."

"I'm no one's woman," Brynn corrected evenly.

"No one owns another person," Pearl Washington insisted righteously. To the best of Brynn's knowledge, this was the first time the young black girl had freely contributed to any class discussion. "A woman's body is her own, just the way a boy's body is his own."

"You're right, sister."

"I didn't plan this talk," Brynn admitted, wondering if she was treading over a mine field. "But this is a subject that's been on my mind lately, and I'd like us to have an open discussion. I'll share my thoughts with you, and you can share your feelings with me."

"Ask me anything you want," Emilio said proudly.

"In other words, you've got all the answers?"

"Sure." Emilio glanced over his shoulder to be

sure he had his friends' support. "Most of us in class do. Come on, Miss Cassidy, we been around, you know?"

"Yeah, I do know. But making love isn't like sampling chocolates. It's much more involved than that. There are responsibilities and consequences."

"Yeah. I'm raising one of those consequences right now," Yolanda volunteered, "and it ain't easy."

"Hey, sister, don't look at me. I wasn't the one who got you knocked up." Denzil raised both hands in a gesture of innocence.

"Shut up, Denzil."

"I want to talk about accountability," Brynn said, ignoring the two. "About being mature enough to accept the responsibility for our actions."

"Are you going to lecture us, Teach?"

"No. I'm going to share with you at least fifteen different ways of making love without doing it."

Several of the boys glanced back and forth at each other as if she'd suddenly turned into someone they didn't know.

"I have the feeling I'm not going to like any of those ways," Malcolm muttered.

Pearl stood at her desk and pointed a finger at her chest. "Why is it a guy thinks that because he spends a little money on me, it entitles him to a piece of my soul?"

"Some girls expect it," Malcolm argued just as heatedly. "Half the time the girls are all over me asking for it."

"Yeah," Emilio agreed. "There are plenty of

times I'd prefer not to . . . you know, and if I don't ask, then the girl's feelings are all hurt. It ain't just us men, you know."

"Men?" Yolanda challenged. "I notice you call us girls, but you're men. Why doesn't the *man* who fathered Jason kindly step forward?" With her fists braced against her sides, Yolanda looked around slowly, then released a sigh of disgust. "That's what I thought."

"Enough," Brynn said, putting an end to the argument before it escalated into a shouting match. She could talk until she was ready to faint, and she doubted it would do any good, but she had to try. One thing was clear: her students were as opinionated over the topic as she was herself.

While she had their attention, she spoke from the heart, listing the reasons she felt it was important to wait to experiment with lovemaking until after marriage. The intensity of her feelings must have reached her class because there was a respectful silence when she finished.

"Miss Cassidy," Emilio said when she'd concluded, "I don't mean to be discourteous or anything, but you're living in a dream world if you believe a man's going to wait to make love to his woman."

"Don't be so sure, Emilio. Teenagers across the world are making pledges to keep themselves pure."

"There ain't nothing pure in this neighborhood," someone else told her. "Not even the water."

"But it has to start somewhere," Brynn said, and

walked over to the chipped blackboard. In large bold-faced letters, she wrote I WILL ABSTAIN FROM PREMARITAL SEX. "I say let it start with me." She signed her name below.

Holding up the piece of chalk, she asked, "Anyone else?"

A tense moment passed before Yolanda slid from her seat. With her head held high, the teenager walked up and took the chalk out of Brynn's hand. She wrote her name in huge letters below Brynn's.

Turning around to face the class, she said, "A *boy* will tell you anything you want to hear until you give him what he wants. Then he'll forget he ever knew you. A *man* will make you his wife first."

Pearl Washington walked up and wrote her name down next. She turned around and glared at Denzil. Then, one hand braced against her hip, Pearl returned to her desk. On the walk back to the end of the row, she continued to glare at Denzil.

"I think you just got cut off, man," Malcolm whispered loudly enough for everyone in the class to hear.

"You keep saying how much you love me," Pearl mocked him. "If you love me so much, prove it."

"I ain't adding my name to that list," Denzil shouted angrily.

Pearl blinked several times but said nothing.

"Don't you worry, Pearl, Denzil is nothing but a *boy*," Yolanda said to comfort the other girl.

When she least expected it, Mike rose from his

seat and walked forward. With a bit of flare he added his name to the list, the first boy in class to do so.

"Oh sure, Mike," Malcolm called sarcastically. "You should be so lucky to get laid."

Why the others chose to taunt Mike, Brynn didn't understand. She liked Mike and appreciated the courage it had taken for him to step forward. The desire to defend him was strong, but she realized that would only make matters worse for the youth.

"Mike's more of a man than you are," Pearl insisted. "A hell of a lot more than Denzil will ever be."

Emilio sat on his seat, frowning. After a couple of moments he stood and trekked the short distance to the blackboard.

"Emilio, are you nuts, man?" Modesto asked.

Emilio turned around and faced his friends. "You know what? Miss Cassidy is right. My brother's always talking about what it means to be responsible, and really that's all Miss Cassidy is saying, too. I ain't no priest, but the way I figure it, women will respect me if they know I ain't after nothing."

After Emilio listed his name, three other male students added their promise.

When they'd finished, Brynn took the chalk, stepped to the blackboard, and wrote I WILL PRAC-TICE SAFE SEX. Then she drew a line beneath the words and waited.

"Next we're going to discuss protection," she said.

Later that afternoon, after her class had been dismissed for the day, Brynn felt good about the spontaneous way in which they'd discussed the subject of sex. It might have gone differently had she planned it. Instead the students themselves had contributed their feelings and insights, and because she'd listened to them, they had been willing to hear her out as well.

She studied each name on the two lists and prayed that their talk would make a difference in how they chose to live their lives.

"Miss Cassidy."

Brynn looked up to find Suzie standing in the doorway. "Am I disturbing you?"

"No, of course not." Brynn stood. "How did your session go with Mrs. Christian?"

"All right, I guess. She made an appointment for me at the health clinic."

"That's good, isn't it?"

"My baby's healthy," Suzie said with a shy smile. "I feel him kick and move all the time now." The teenager's gaze moved to the blackboard. "I . . . I heard about what you did. It's all over the school. You talked about birth control and responsible sex because of me, didn't you?"

Brynn couldn't very well deny it. "I didn't break your confidence, Suzie. No one knows what you told me." She felt it was important to assure Suzie of that.

"I knew you wouldn't say anything." Suzie studied the list. "Emilio signed his name." Although it was a statement, the surprise in her voice made it a question.

"Several of the young men in class did."

"Do you think I could add my name?" she asked, diverting her eyes from Brynn's. "Or is it too late?"

"I'd be proud if you did," Brynn told her.

Suzie walked up and added her name to the first list. "I'm going to talk to my mother this afternoon. She'll be angry with me and she'll want me to tell her who the father is, but I won't."

"You can't protect him forever," Brynn said gently.

"I know. Mom will be angry, but not nearly as much as my father."

"Do you want me to come with you?" Brynn asked.

Suzie considered the offer, then shook her head. "No, but thank you for volunteering."

No sooner had Suzie left than Brynn was asked to come down to the office. It was the first time she'd received such a request. She wasn't left to wonder at the reason.

She knew.

If what Suzie said was true, then Mr. Whalen, the principal, had heard what she'd done.

Allen Whalen invited her into his office, and after she'd stepped inside, he closed the door firmly. The sound of it clicking alerted her to the fact that this wasn't going to be a friendly chat.

Brynn respected Allen Whalen. He was a big, no-nonsense man and a fair disciplinarian. He had zero tolerance for drugs and alcohol and didn't shy away from confrontations, often suspending students for fighting or other disruptions. Emilio could testify to that.

"Sit down, Brynn," Allen said, and motioned for her to take a seat on the other side of his desk. More than likely this was the identical chair in which Emilio had sat the first day of the quarter following his fight with Grover.

"First off," Allen said, leaning forward, "I want you to know I've heard good things about you. The kids seem to feel kindly toward you, and that's a plus. I understand you've made a point to visit the families of your students."

"Yes, I—"

"While your efforts are commendable," Allen interrupted, "I don't feel it's a good idea for you to become emotionally involved with your students."

Brynn opened her mouth to explain her purpose, but once again she wasn't allowed to continue.

"You're young, and idealistic. Perhaps a little too young to deal with the reality of our situation here."

"Mr. Whalen, if you'd allow me to explain . . ."

He gestured with his hand, indicating that he wasn't finished. "I had my doubts about this government project. As far as I'm concerned, the less the federal government has to do with the school system, the better. I would never have agreed to this program had I realized . . ." He paused and leaned forward, pressing his elbows against the top of his cluttered desk. "I don't want to get sidetracked here. The reason I asked you to my office has nothing to do with the government or why you're at Manhattan High."

"Yes?" She sat straight, her back as stiff as a steel pipe.

"I received a phone call from two mothers this afternoon," he prefaced, his face growing tight with displeasure. "Don't tell me, Miss Cassidy, that you actually discussed birth control methods with your history class."

Rather than hedge, Brynn answered him in a straightforward manner. "As a matter of fact, I did."

Allen Whalen's eyes drifted closed momentarily. "In your history class, Miss Cassidy?"

"It needed to be said."

"And you felt you were the most qualified to advise a classroom full of young adults? I take it you've attended the course the district requires before teaching sex education?"

"No. The discussion was spontaneous. I certainly didn't plan to spend the afternoon discussing the benefits of condoms."

"In other words, you just decided this needed to be said and you were the one to do it?"

"If you put it like that, then I have no option but to say yes." She had no defense and didn't think it would help her case if she had.

Mr. Whalen mulled over her answers. "In case you weren't aware of it, this community is largely Catholic."

Brynn folded her hands on her lap. "I'm Catholic myself."

"That is no excuse," he said, then stopped abruptly. "You're Catholic?"

"My name is Cassidy and my hair is red." She didn't mean to be sarcastic, but it should have been obvious.

"Then you must be aware of the church's standing on the subject of birth control."

"I am indeed." She didn't blink. Didn't hesitate. Didn't doubt for an instant that he was furious with her.

"I'm afraid, Miss Cassidy, that in light of this admission, I have no choice but to place a letter of reprimand in your file."

Brynn swallowed tightly. "I've always known you to be a fair man. If you feel I deserve to be formally reprimanded for my actions, then I can only assume that you're right."

"You're a history and English teacher. In the future please remember that." He reached for a piece of paper and started writing.

Brynn sat where she was for several awkward moments.

After a while, he glanced up. "You may leave."

When Brynn walked out of the office, she found three secretaries staring at her. Their looks were sympathetic as she whisked past. The whispers started the moment she was around the corner.

* * *

"Hello, Hannah."

Hannah looked up from the novel she was reading. "Carl," she said, unable to hide her surprise and her guilt. No one had told her he planned to stop by that evening. "How are you feeling?" She hadn't spoken to him since his bout with the flu.

Her fiancé claimed the recliner across from her. "Much better, thank you."

Hannah noted that her heart didn't leap with excitement the way it did whenever she saw Joshua. Nor did she experience a twinge of pleasure just because they were together. Carl was Carl. Dedicated, devout, determined. But soon, if everything went as their mothers had planned, he would be more than an unexpected guest. He would be her husband.

"My mother stopped by to talk to your mother," he explained with a wry grin. "They're discussing the details of the wedding."

Hannah's gaze fell back to the pages of the novel. "My mother wants to hire a wedding coordinator," she told him. "I heard her discussing the matter over the phone."

"She must have been talking to my mother, because I heard her say something about it as well."

Hannah smiled and looked away. She noticed with regret that they didn't seem to have a whole lot to say to each other.

"I thought we should set a time to shop for the engagement ring," Carl suggested, almost as if he were grateful for something to discuss.

"That would be nice."

"How about after the first of the year?" he proposed.

"Great." The further into the future, the better.

A disjointed silence followed, as though there were nothing left to say.

"Carl." Her father's face lit up with delight as he walked into the living room. "Ruth didn't mention that you were coming."

Carl stood, and the two men exchanged hearty handshakes. David Morganstern slapped Hannah's fiancé across the back. "By heaven, it's good to see you. You've been making yourself scarce around here these last few days."

"I've been busy."

"Ruth said you'd come down with a twenty-four-hour bug the other night."

"I'm fine now."

Hannah watched as the transformation took place in the man who was to be her husband. It seemed his face brightened as soon as her father walked into the room.

Soon the two entered into a lively debate over some political matter that didn't interest Hannah. While they chatted, Hannah went into the kitchen, brewed tea, and served that along with freshly baked sugar cookies.

Helen Rabinsky and Hannah's mother were engrossed in their own conversation and seemed unaware of her. As she expected, the women were debating the pros and cons of hiring a wedding coordinator.

After a time, Hannah escaped to her bedroom and closed the door. She doubted anyone would miss her.

Sitting on top of her bed, her knees bent, Hannah closed her eyes and remembered her time with Joshua at the skating rink. It wasn't right that she should be thinking of another man. Not with Carl on the other side of the door.

Joshua's business card remained inside her coat pocket, but she didn't need to retrieve it to find the number. In the last two days, she'd stared at that card so often, she'd committed the phone number to memory.

When she feared she might be missed, Hannah returned to the living room. Carl glanced her way and smiled affectionately.

"Carl," she said, "would you like to go for a walk, or something?"

"A walk?" he repeated with a decided lack of enthusiasm. "It's below freezing."

"How about if we went ice skating?" she suggested next.

"Tonight?"

"I don't know what's gotten into that daughter of mine," her father commented, and chuckled. "Two nights ago she walks over to Rockefeller Center and goes ice skating."

"I don't skate," Carl said with a touch of sadness.

"I could teach you," she offered expectantly. "It isn't difficult, and we could have a lot of fun."

Carl looked from Hannah to her father and then back again. "Would you mind if we stayed here?"

"Remember your young man's just getting over the flu, Hannah," her father reminded her gently. "Carl will take you ice skating another time."

She tried to hide her disappointment and must have succeeded. An hour later, Helen Rabinsky announced it was time to leave. Carl stood, and for no reason Hannah could fathom the two of them were left alone. It didn't take her long to realize her family was giving her and Carl a private moment together.

"Thanks for stopping by, Carl," she said.

"It was good to see you again, Hannah." He leaned forward and pressed his mouth to hers. It was a gentle kiss, but passionless. It was unfair to compare the kisses she'd shared with Joshua to the quick exchanges between her and Carl. But Hannah couldn't help it.

Joshua's kisses made her feel as though she'd been hit by a freight train. The emotional impact left her reeling long afterward. She knew that her kisses affected him in the same magical, exciting way. Joshua made her feel like a sensual, alluring woman.

"I'll be calling you soon," Carl promised.

Hannah nodded, afraid to speak for fear of what she'd say. Intuitively she realized she couldn't marry Carl. He didn't love her any more than she loved him. He was as miserable about this arrangement as she was, but they were both caught in the trap. One of them had to break it.

As soon as Hannah and her parents were alone, her mother turned and clapped her hands gleefully. "Helen agrees that we should hire a wedding coordinator. I couldn't be more pleased. She suggested we talk to Wanda Thorndike." She hugged Hannah briefly. "I'll make an appointment with Wanda first thing in the morning."

Hannah wanted to object, to explain that she felt they were rushing matters, but she wasn't given the opportunity.

"I overheard Carl suggest that he and Hannah pick out engagement rings right after the first of the year."

"David," her mother said, sighing, "you can't imagine everything we need to consider for a large wedding."

"We haven't picked a date yet," Hannah reminded her family, dread weighing down her words.

"My dear, you're as naive as Helen and I were about all this. The wedding coordinator will be the one to choose that. She'll know what's available and when. Personally I'd prefer a June wedding. You should be a traditional June bride, but that's barely six months away, and I don't know if we could manage it in that time. One thing I'm going to have to insist we do right away, and that's shop for your dress."

"Mom—"

"Helen was telling me it sometimes takes as long as six months to have a dress made and delivered."

"But—"

"I know, darling, we're throwing a lot at you. Just be patient." Humming happily to herself, Ruth Morganstern returned to the kitchen and the wedding brochures she'd pored over only moments earlier.

Hannah's father chuckled. "I don't know when I've last seen your mother so pleased. This wedding has given her a renewed lease on life."

Hannah couldn't find it in her heart to disappoint them. Not then. Later, she promised herself. She'd sit down with them both and explain that she didn't love Carl.

By noon the following day the deli was filled with the usual lunch crowd. Her father hand sliced pastrami into thick wedges while Hannah and her mother assembled the sandwiches.

Runners delivered orders as fast as they could be packed.

The routine was one in which Hannah had worked most of her life. She never questioned that she would help in the deli; it was assumed.

Around two, the heavy lunch crowd had begun to thin out. Her mother returned to the kitchen to make up a fresh batch of potato salad. Her father was preoccupied with ordering supplies when Hannah looked up to discover Joshua standing on the other side of the counter.

"Joshua," she whispered in a low rush of air.

Just seeing him again had knocked the breath out of her. She couldn't disguise her delight. Her heart went into second gear as she glanced over her shoulder to be sure no one was paying them any mind. "What are you doing here?" she asked in a whisper.

"I came for lunch."

Of course. She reached for a pencil, prepared to take his order.

He read the printed menu that hung on the wall behind her. "I'll have a pastrami on rye and a cup of coffee."

She wrote down his order with trembling hands.

"Are you going to make it for me yourself?"

She nodded, avoiding eye contact. She wouldn't be able to hide how pleased she was to see him again if she looked up.

"You didn't phone," he whispered just loudly enough for her to hear.

"Potato is the soup of the day," she said.

"Hannah, look at me."

"I can't."

"Why can't you?"

She closed her eyes and braced herself. "You shouldn't have come here."

"You don't want my business?"

He was making this difficult.

"You've thought about contacting me, haven't you?"

Again she didn't answer. "Would you care for a bowl of soup with your sandwich?"

He didn't respond for a number of seconds, and then, "The only thing I want is you, Hannah."

"If you'll take a number, I'll have your lunch delivered."

"Will you bring it?" he asked.

Her nod was nearly imperceptible. She saw the tension leave him and couldn't keep from glancing up and offering him a quick smile. It took only a moment or more to finish compiling his sandwich. She carried that and a cup of coffee to his table and was pleased to note he sat as far away from the counter as possible.

"Thank you, Hannah," he said when she placed the plate on the table. "Would you care to join me?"

"I can't." Her hands folded over the back of the chair across from him. She glanced over her shoulder, fearing her father would notice the two of them together.

"Is that your father?" Joshua asked, looking around her.

"Yes. Mom's in the kitchen."

"He doesn't look like the kind of man who would force his daughter into a loveless marriage."

"Joshua, please."

He picked up the sandwich, and once again, Hannah looked back to make sure no one was watching her. "I sometimes walk by the pond in Central Park," she whispered.

Joshua went still. "When?"

"I was thinking of taking a stroll there this afternoon."

"In an hour?"

"Yes."

Joshua's handsome face broke into a wide grin. "I've always favored walking as an excellent form of exercise."

Chapter Eleven

"Are you sure you're up to this?" Trey asked Jenny for the third time since they'd boarded the ferry headed for Ellis Island.

"I wouldn't have suggested sight-seeing if I wasn't feeling better," Jenny insisted. They stood and watched as the New York skyline began to fade into the distance. "I want you to visit Ellis Island," she continued. "It's an emotional experience, at least it was for me the first time I made the trip. I found my great-grandfather's name there."

"Your great-grandfather? How?"

"I looked his name up on the computer. It showed me the year he arrived from Germany and his age at the time. I felt as though I'd stumbled upon an open treasure chest, only this one contained a part of my heritage."

"This was your mother's grandfather?"

Jenny answered him with a quick nod. "Can you imagine packing everything you own in this world in a single suitcase?" she asked, awed by the raw courage and grit her great-grandfather had shown when he was little more than a teenager. "He came to America with nothing but his dreams and the desire for a new life."

"Is that so unusual?" Trey asked.

"Of course it is," she answered, feeling slightly offended that Trey didn't recognize the fortitude and faith her great-grandfather had demonstrated. "He didn't have an easy life here, you know. First off he didn't speak the language, and although he was well educated he was forced into taking a menial job. For years he and my grandmother struggled to make a decent life for themselves and their family. I can't tell you how much I admire them for that."

"What you did, leaving Montana for a chance on Broadway, wasn't all that different."

"Me?" Jenny didn't see the correlation. Of course there was the obvious one, but her great-grandfather had come to America friendless and without the loving support of his family.

"As I recall, when you left Custer you went with a solitary suitcase. You came to the Big Apple without a job, with little money, and with only your dreams to feed you."

"True," she admitted reluctantly, not wanting Trey to continue comparing her with her great-grandfather. Not when she fell so far short.

Trey placed his hand on her shoulder. "It hasn't been easy for you, has it?" he asked gently.

He didn't know the half of it. Jenny turned her face into the wind and let the breeze off the Hudson River buffet against her. The thickness in her throat tightened to painful proportions, and she knew she dared not try to talk. Trey had tried to paint her as some kind of heroine, seeking her way in a new world. In retrospect, Jenny wasn't sure she'd done the right thing to leave Montana. She wasn't sure she was cut out for life in the city. In three years she'd never managed to feel at home in New York.

Jenny didn't see herself as any modern-day champion.

"Jenny?"

Trey's face had knit into a worried frown.

"I'm doing great," she told him quickly, perhaps too quickly, because she felt his close scrutiny. Smiling, just then, would have been impossible.

Trey moved closer to her by the railing. The wind hit against him. His arm came loosely around her shoulder, and, needing him, she pressed her head against his solid strength.

"There's something you should know," she said after dragging a deep breath through her lungs. She closed her eyes, unwilling to continue the pretense any longer. "I'm not what you think."

"Jenny—"

"No, please, let me finish." This was so much more difficult than she'd thought it would be. Trey had come all this way from Montana thinking she was a Broadway star. Either she told him herself or he'd learn it on his own.

A dozen times since his arrival she'd been tempted to blurt out the truth. It had held her prisoner, tortured her, and she couldn't stand the pressure any longer.

"I'm not starring in an Off-Broadway production of *South Pacific*. I'm a waitress, a singing waitress. I lied, and I want you to know how very sorry I am." Her voice pitched and heaved with emotion as she hurried to get all the words out at once for fear she'd break down and weep.

The pressure of his arm around her increased slightly. "I realized that right away."

He knew and hadn't said anything.

"The first place I headed when I arrived in New York was the theater. I wanted to see you perform."

Jenny's throat constricted. "I'm so ashamed to have lied, but I had to tell my family something. It's been so long, and . . . you've got to believe I gave it my best shot, and now, well, now it seems I'm buried neck deep in the lie. Mom and Dad are so proud of me, and they've told everyone, and—"

"Come home, Jenny."

"No." Her response was automatic and sharp.

The brightness in Trey's eyes dimmed, and she turned away, unable to meet his gaze. It sounded as if he were eager to hear she'd failed. Glad of it. Well, she wasn't through yet. She was close, so close she could taste it. If John Peterman didn't want her for this play, then there were other parts, other producers. She wouldn't give up. She refused to turn her back when she was this close. Not even Trey could convince her to do that.

"I may not be the star I led everyone to believe," she told him stiffly, "but I'm an actress, and a damn talented one. I realize I've probably disappointed you, and I'm sorry for that, but I'm not willing to throw in the towel yet."

Trey didn't answer her, and the air between them was strained and tight.

"I shouldn't have asked it of you," he said as the boat neared Ellis Island.

It was as close to an apology as she was likely to get from Trey. She stepped away from him, letting the breeze whip against her face while she mulled over his words.

Trey stepped back, and she noticed the attention he generated with his tall, lean good looks. He was obviously out of place with his scuffed snakeskin boots and weather-beaten Stetson, yet he'd dressed in the height of fashion. Jenny knew more than one male model who would have given anything for that rawboned, natural look.

"Jenny," Trey said, coming to stand next to her, "I don't really think what you did was so terrible. Sure you stretched the truth a bit, but under the circumstances that's understandable."

"But hardly commendable."

Trey didn't agree or disagree. "What you did was burden yourself. It seems to me these New York theater people must have holes in their heads not to realize how talented you are."

This was what Jenny loved about home the most. When it came to talent, the good folks in Custer believed none had more than Jenny Lancaster.

"Those responsible for the theater in New York meet lots of talented men and women with big dreams and a lot of ambition. That was a difficult lesson for me to learn, and I suspect that in some ways I haven't completely accepted it. I'm good, Trey, and I know it, but there are any number of equally talented people just waiting for their big break, the same way as me."

The ferry docked and the passengers disembarked onto the island. Most everyone headed directly for the Ellis Island Immigration Museum.

"There's something I want you to see first," Jenny said, leading Trey toward the flagpole. A brass railinglike border ran the circumference of the island. Embossed in the polished metal were hundreds of names, a small representation of the thousands of immigrants who'd made their way to America between 1892 and 1924. The first time Jenny had visited, she'd walked around the entire island until she'd found what she was looking for.

"My great-grandfather's name is listed here," she told him excitedly. Her fingertips ran over the raised letters. Anton Hellmich. A sense of pride moved her to know that this man's blood ran through her veins. "You can't imagine how excited I was when I discovered this. I called my mother that very night."

She doubted that Trey understood what a rare thing it was for her to phone home. With her finances so tight, Jenny usually wrote letters and made up excuses why it was difficult for her to phone. Talking to her mother, hearing her father's gruff, loving voice, increased her longing for home and her family all the more.

"Anton Hellmich," Trey repeated slowly. He placed his callused hand on top of hers and laced their fingers together. His skin was rough and hard from the long hours he worked his spread. Her skin was silky smooth.

Once again Trey ran the thick pad of his index finger over the raised letters with her. His touch, so warm and caring, so gentle, was like a healing balm to her wounded pride.

Barely realizing what she was doing, Jenny turned so that she faced him. Before another moment passed, before her heart could beat again, Trey's arms were clasped around her as he brought her into his arms.

She watched the transformation come over him, as if he were caught in some winless battle. The muscles in his jaw clenched. Then, moving slowly, as though hypnotized, he lowered his mouth to hers. His lips over hers, moist and warm, were as gentle as lambskin.

Jenny closed her eyes as tightly as she could, seeking to blot out the world and everything around them. Everything but Trey. For the first time since her arrival she didn't want to be subjected to the sights and sounds of the New York waterfront. She didn't want to hear the buzz of aircraft overhead. For this one moment she wanted to be as far away from other people as she could get.

Trey's kiss was everything Jenny had ever dreamed, everything she could have anticipated. She trembled in his arms, needing his strength, his comfort, more than she'd ever needed anything in her life. She clung to him, not wanting him to let her go. Not ever.

Snuggling closer, she stood on the tips of her toes. Her breasts nuzzled his chest, and a new brand of sensations shot through her. Trey recognized the difference, and his tongue went in search of hers as the kiss deepened. By the time they broke apart, Jenny's knees were weak. It didn't seem possible that anything would feel this wonderful.

Jenny had been kissed before, plenty of times. She wasn't a novice to the art, but with Trey all things became new. Everything changed.

When they broke apart, Jenny could feel the heat invade her cheeks. She was actually blushing, which was something that hadn't happened since she was in junior high.

"Trey?" she whispered, pleading with him to explain what was happening to them. She was at a loss to understand, let alone explain.

He answered by kissing her again, this time deeper and with such intensity that her senses spun out of control. When he'd finished, he held her close and whispered, but his words were low and filled with emotion.

"I've waited so long to hold you like this."

"Oh, Trey, I've missed you so much."

His fingers were in her hair, and he angled her head to kiss her again and again. His breathing was harsh with excitement and need.

"Come home, Jenny," he pleaded. "For the love of God, give up on this madness and come back home where you belong."

The pond near Cherry Hill fountain had always been one of Hannah's favorite spots in Central Park. Because she was late, she feared Joshua would have given up waiting for her. Barely taking time to look both ways, she raced across Fifty-ninth Street. Her heart pounded in her throat as she approached the pond. Excitement filled her when she spied Joshua standing along the edge of the water, feeding the goldfish. Hannah half ran to meet him.

"I'm so sorry I'm late," she said breathlessly when she joined him. "It took me much longer to get away than I thought it would."

Joshua glanced at her and enfolded her with a warm smile of welcome. "I was feeding the fish, and didn't notice." He handed her a fistful of stale bread crumbs for her to toss onto the water's still surface. Huge goldfish, some marked with black-and-white blotches, battled for the crumbs, stirring up the water's smooth surface.

"This has always been one of my favorite places," Joshua said.

"Mine too," she admitted. It didn't surprise her that Joshua felt the same way about this place as she did. They appreciated many of the same things.

They stood side by side, content without speaking, satisfied simply to be in each other's company.

"There's something I need to tell you," Hannah said once she'd regained her breath and her equilibrium. Being with Joshua always seemed to pull her off center.

Joshua hesitated, and his eyes sparkled. "Am I going to need to sit down to hear it?"

"No. At least I don't think so." She thought about what she had to say and realized he was the last person she should be telling instead of the first. "I've decided not to marry Carl."

"I know." Joshua tossed the last of the bread crumbs into the pond with a flourish.

Of all the reactions Hannah had expected from Joshua, she'd never anticipated this calm acceptance. She frowned. "What did you say?"

"I said, I knew you weren't going to marry Carl."

"And how could you be so confident of that?" she asked. She hadn't realized it herself until the night before. Once she'd admitted that she couldn't go through with the wedding, she'd felt as though a great weight had been lifted from her heart. It hadn't been an easy decision, and she didn't want him to think she'd made it flippantly.

"I knew you weren't going to be marrying Carl, my sweet, adorable Hannah, for one simple reason. I fully intend for you to marry me."

Hannah blinked back her surprise.

"And yes, if you're wondering, that's a marriage proposal."

"But I'm already engaged to Carl," she argued, saying the first thing that came to mind. He'd shocked her so thoroughly that she wasn't sure how to respond. The second thing that came to mind was that she would have liked nothing better than to be Joshua's wife. She was forced into biting her lips to keep from blurting it out.

He warmed her with another of his bone-melting smiles. "You see, I realized something the very first time we met."

"You did?"

"It's simple, really," he said with the calm reasoning of an attorney. "I realized you and I were meant to be together."

"But what about Carl?" she pleaded. "I was already engaged to him when we met." While that wasn't technically true, for all intents and purposes she might as well have been betrothed to the rabbi's son. In the eyes of both families, all that needed to be decided was if they should or shouldn't hire a wedding coordinator.

"I suppose I sound overly confident of myself," Joshua said, and reached inside his coat pocket for his leather gloves. "I wasn't sure about any of this until recently, though. The night at Rockefeller Center, to be exact. I gave you my business card, remember?"

"I didn't phone you."

"True," he was gracious enough to agree, "and I'll admit I haven't been sleeping well because I fully expected you to contact me long before now." He reached for her hand and raised it to his lips, brushing her knuckles with his mouth. "You and I share something very special, Hannah. I don't know what I would have done had you decided to go ahead with the wedding with Carl."

Hannah dipped her head. "I haven't said anything to him yet." It was far easier to tell Joshua of her decision first. She realized she was behaving like a coward, but she sincerely felt that Carl would experience a deep sense of relief once she asked him to release her from the engagement. She was certain he shared her feelings. They were both eager to please their parents and had allowed themselves unwittingly to be drawn into a self-made trap.

Joshua loved her. The knowledge shook her because she didn't understand how anyone as powerful and intelligent as Joshua could care for someone like her. "I've treated you terribly. I've ignored you, pretended I didn't know you, and shunned you."

"When something is of high value, then it's worth a few inconveniences," Joshua said, and gently bounced his mouth over hers. "In many ways I'm grateful to you."

"Me?"

"I'd almost given up thinking about God until I met you. My life was full and busy, but I felt an aching loneliness. I prayed, but I felt as if my prayers floated away to nothingness. Until the morning of the Thanksgiving Day parade, I was convinced God didn't listen to prayers any longer."

"But He does," Hannah insisted.

"I know. He sent you into my life." Joshua ran his finger down the side of her face. "You'll be talking to Carl soon?"

She nodded. It wasn't a task she relished, but it was one she couldn't delay. To wait for the right moment would only make it more difficult. "I thought I'd discuss it with him first, and then the two of us could explain it to our parents together."

Joshua's gaze narrowed briefly, and she knew he wasn't keen on this part of her plan.

"Carl and I need to present a united front," she explained. "Otherwise I'm afraid they'll manipulate us individually to change our minds."

Joshua considered her words, then asked, "Could they change your mind, Hannah?"

His question fell into a weighted silence. Hannah considered her answer for several thought-provoking moments. "Carl's a good man, and he'll make some woman an excellent husband, but that woman won't be me," she admitted, then added, "Nothing's going to change the way I feel about you, Joshua. Nothing."

"You'll tell him soon, then?"

She nodded. "The sooner the better." She didn't relish this task, but she couldn't put it off, either.

"Do you want me to come with you?" Joshua volunteered.

"No." That would only make matters worse, Hannah realized. Her news would be difficult enough for Carl without adding the complication of her feelings for another man.

Joshua looked at his watch. "I have to get back to the office."

It was easy to forget that Joshua was in important man. If she ever doubted his feelings for her, all she'd need to do was remember the time he took out of his busy schedule to be with her.

"One thing before you go?" she asked, reaching out and gripping hold of his forearm.

"Anything."

She felt foolish asking this of him. "Would you mind very much if we kissed again?"

The warm light that invaded his eyes was all the answer she needed. Joshua wrapped her in his embrace and drugged her with a number of long, slow kisses.

"Is that enough?" he asked.

She couldn't manage anything more than a slight groan.

Joshua closed his eyes and inhaled deeply. "Unfortunately I feel the same way myself. I promise you the day will come when we won't stop with the kissing, Hannah. Frankly the sooner that day arrives, the better."

Joshua left her to return to his office. The warm glow of his kisses carried Hannah all the way to Carl's apartment building. He should be home, seeing that school had been out for several hours. Hannah had been to his place only twice. Carl was an orderly man who kept his quarters meticulously clean. Hannah had never known anyone more gifted in the area of organization than Carl Rabinsky.

Not once on the long walk did Hannah doubt that she was doing the right thing. Only when she arrived at his building did she hesitate. Gathering her courage about her, she squared her shoulders and pressed the doorbell.

Carl's low voice came over the intercom. "Who is it?"

"Hannah," she said, standing on her tiptoes and speaking directly into the intercom to make sure he could hear her.

"Hannah? My goodness, what are you doing here?"

"I came to talk to you. Could I come up?"

"Of course."

A couple of seconds later a buzzer rang and the lock on the front door released, allowing Hannah inside the building. More nervous now than ever, she took the elevator up to Carl's apartment. By the time she arrived outside his door, she was convinced her heart was ready to pound straight through her chest.

"This is a surprise," Carl said, leading her into the living room. The area was nothing like she remembered. Books and papers littered the table. Unopened mail was scattered across the coffee table. This wasn't like Carl. Not once in all the time she'd known him had he displayed any signs of sloppiness.

"Is something wrong?" Hannah asked, watching him.

"I don't think there's any reason to try to hide it any longer," he said, sinking into the chair and covering his face with both hands. "I should have told you sooner."

Hannah didn't know what to think. "Told me what?" she asked gently. She'd never seen Carl like this.

He raised his head slowly, his look tortured. "But then I haven't found the courage to tell anyone."

Hannah waited, knowing Carl would get around to explaining himself eventually. He shifted uncomfortably in his chair and refused to look at her.

"I lost my position with the school," he blurted out, then squeezed his eyes closed. "I couldn't take it any longer, and I got into an argument with Hiram. Since he's the headmaster and I'm nothing more than a teacher, he fired me." Carl raised his head and squared his shoulders. "If you want to call off the wedding, I'll understand. I don't deserve a good woman like you."

Brynn didn't tell anyone about the formal reprimand that Mr. Whalen had placed inside her employment file. There didn't seem to be any need. Everything he'd said was true. She had stepped over the line, but try as she would, Brynn couldn't make herself regret the impromptu discussion with her students. If she'd managed to reach just one member of her class, then it had been worth the trouble.

Her thoughts were heavy as she made her way home that afternoon. Dinner was simmering on top of the stove when her cell phone rang. She reached for it automatically.

"Hello," she said.

"It's Roberto."

Brynn closed her eyes. The sound of his voice, with his soft, lilting accent, was like sinking neck deep into a warm bath in the dead of winter.

"I heard you're teaching sex education now, too." He sounded more amused than angry with her, which was a welcome change.

"I really stuck my foot in it this time," she told him.

"Although he probably wouldn't come out and say as much, I think Emilio was grateful to have someone talk frankly about the subject. Girls can be pushy these days. As pushy as the boys."

"I'm sure that's true." After some of the things she'd seen in the last few weeks, there was little that would shock Brynn anymore.

"Although if you cared to get pushy with me, we might strike some agreement."

Brynn laughed. "Keep dreaming, Roberto."

The mechanic's chuckle slowly faded. "You do that to me," he said, his voice low and serious. "You make me want to dream, but then I wonder . . . Never mind. I didn't call you to talk about dreams."

"Oh?"

"I want to take you to dinner." His voice grew so serious that she wondered if there were some hidden significance behind his request.

"When?" she asked, not that it would have mattered to her. He could have suggested next June and she would have agreed readily.

"Is Friday all right?"

"Yes," she said automatically.

"I'll pick you up at six-thirty." How formal he sounded, as though he were unsure of himself.

"That'll be fine," she assured him. "I'll look forward to it."

"Me, too." The smile was back in his voice, as if to say now that the awkward part was over, he could go back to being himself. "Thank you, Brynn."

"Whatever for?" She was thinking his appreciation had something to do with what Emilio had told her about the class discussion.

"For agreeing to be my date."

Not until Brynn was talking to Father Grady did she realize the significance in Roberto's having asked her to dinner.

She met the parish priest after school, responding to a message he'd sent asking to speak with her. She guessed correctly that Father Grady had heard about her talk with her students.

"Are you going to lecture me about the error of my ways?" she asked him directly. They were walking toward the rectory. Father Grady's hands were folded behind his back, and he avoided meeting her eyes.

"No," he said slowly, "although I fully suspect you know the church's teachings in the area of birth control."

"I know, I just don't happen to agree."

Father Grady released a long, slow breath. "I'm not going to say anything about this again, but I'm disappointed in you, Brynn. I don't know what happened for you to decide it was your duty to discuss this particular subject with your class, but my guess is this entire matter was spontaneous on your part.

"I strongly suspect one of the girls is pregnant. Well, it isn't the first time, nor will it be the last. These things happen."

"Birth control—"

"Promotes promiscuity," the priest argued.

"It would be better if we agreed to disagree," Brynn said evenly. She didn't want to get into a verbal battle with the one person she considered her friend.

They didn't speak for several moments.

"Roberto asked me to dinner Friday night," Brynn said, wanting to break the tension between them.

Father Grady's face broke into a wide smile. "He asked you, did he?"

"Is there something important about this dinner date I don't know about?"

"Not particularly," the priest informed her, "only that it's probably the first time Roberto's dated in the last four or five years."

"You're joking!"

"No. While he was in high school, he held down two part-time jobs in an effort to earn enough money for his mother to travel to the United States. Every penny went toward that goal. There wasn't time for dances or anything else a normal teenager enjoys."

"But he's an excellent dancer." Being in his arms had seemed as right as rain, as the saying went.

"He comes by that talent naturally," Father Grady explained. "But he's never taken the opportunity to indulge in the small pleasures in life. He sacrificed his youth for the sake of his mother."

"I've never met her."

"You won't," Father Grady said sadly. "She died before Roberto had saved enough money."

Brynn felt Roberto's frustration. "I'm so sorry."

"Roberto blamed himself."

"But how could he?" She hated the thought of his taking on blame when he'd already sacrificed so much.

"He seemed to think that he'd failed her."

"Surely he understands that isn't the case."

"Intellectually I believe he does, but not emotionally, although I have hope now that he's taken such a keen interest in you." Father looked well pleased with himself, as though he were the one responsible for bringing her and Roberto together. "You've been good for that young man, but by the same token Roberto has been good for you."

"I like him so much," she whispered. Sometimes it frightened her how deeply she cared for Roberto. He wasn't like any other man she'd dated. He was deep and intense, intelligent and generous.

"I suspected you did."

"Not at first," she countered. "Roberto and I rubbed each other the wrong way in the beginning." Even now they were at different poles on the subject of education. No matter how hard she tried to persuade him, Roberto refused to listen to reason.

Then it dawned on her why Roberto was so opinionated. Father Grady had unraveled the mystery. Roberto had stayed in school and worked, saving his money in order to bring his mother from Mexico. She'd died before he had been able to save enough. If Roberto had been working full-time instead of trying to balance two part-time jobs with his schooling, he might have been able to help his mother. Because he'd stayed in high school the help he had to offer her had come too late.

Chapter Twelve

Emilio followed Roberto around the apartment like a lost puppy, offering him unwanted advice for his dinner date with Brynn.

"First you've got to tell Miss Cassidy how beautiful she looks," Emilio instructed, "then gently take her in your arms and kiss her, but only lightly. Remember that, because it's important. You don't want to start something too soon. Women don't like a guy coming on heavy first thing. They want to be wined and dined first."

"Emilio," Roberto warned under his breath as he tightened the knot in his tie in front of the bedroom mirror, "I can handle this on my own."

"But I know Miss Cassidy better than you do. Don't forget I see her practically every day."

But his brother didn't view her as Roberto did. To Emilio she was his teacher, the first one he'd liked well enough to mention. To Roberto Brynn was a warm, desirable, generous woman. When they kissed the electricity between them was as powerful as Hoover Dam.

In the beginning he'd attempted to ignore the way the air sizzled every time they were together. A touch of antagonism had proved to be his best defense, and it had worked until Father Grady had manipulated them into chaperoning the dance at the church hall. Before he knew what had happened to him, Brynn was in his arms and life hadn't been the same since.

"Where are you taking her to dinner?" Emilio asked, following him across the bedroom.

Roberto splashed on a touch of spice-scented cologne. "I haven't decided yet." Actually he had, but he didn't want his brother dropping by unexpectedly with some phony excuse.

Emilio frowned with disapproval. "That's not going to work, bro, you've got to plan these things well in advance. You should have made reservations for a classy woman like Miss Cassidy."

If the truth be known, Emilio's attitude toward Brynn amused him. The way Emilio talked about her, one would think his brother was half in love with her himself.

"You can't just walk into any restaurant and expect a decent table to be waiting for you."

Roberto reached for his wool jacket. He hoped

Brynn didn't recognize it as the same one from the dance. He owned only one suit, and he wasn't about to go out and purchase another just because of a silly dinner date.

"How do you know all this?" Roberto probed.

"I been around," Emilio answered with a hint of defiance.

That might be true, but Roberto didn't think Emilio had ever taken a girl out on a fancy dinner date.

"You got her flowers, didn't you?"

Roberto hadn't thought of that. "No."

"Oh, man," he said, shaking his head, "you're going to blow this."

"I'll pick some up on the way."

Emilio's face relaxed. "Good idea."

Roberto headed for the door, then stopped for his overcoat and gloves. The leather gloves were new and necessary to hide the car grease he couldn't remove from around his nails.

Once more Emilio followed him. "I know the perfect restaurant," he said excitedly, and snapped his fingers. "It's perfect. Call Mama Celeste's and make a reservation. The food's great and they think you walk on water ever since you repaired their van."

"Good idea." Unfortunately that was exactly where Roberto had already planned to take Brynn. He turned and met his brother, eye to eye. He couldn't remember when Emilio had grown so tall. Nearly ten years separated them, and Roberto had become accustomed to being the older, wiser, bigger brother. He wasn't taller by much, and that surprised him.

"I've already made arrangements to take Brynn to Mama Celeste's," he admitted. "And I don't want you making any excuses to stop by there this evening. Do I make myself clear?"

One corner of Emilio's mouth lifted with a cocky half smile. "What's it worth to you?"

Roberto's eyes narrowed into a dark scowl, and Emilio laughed. "Hey, I was just kidding, bro."

Roberto opened the front door. "Don't wait up for me."

"Are you kidding, man? This is one night I'm going to want to hear about."

Brynn had been less nervous for her first high school prom. She checked her appearance a dozen or more times before the doorbell rang. Her inclination was to rush across the room and throw open the door, but she forced herself to remain calm and collected.

Roberto stood on the other side of the door, so handsome her breath locked in her lungs. It reminded her of the night of the church dance. He'd knocked her senses for a loop then, too.

Looking away, she stepped aside to allow him into her apartment. "Hello, Roberto."

He inclined his head slightly. "You look lovely." Smiling, he stepped into her apartment and tenderly pressed his lips to her cheek.

Surprised and delighted, Brynn raised her hand to her face, her fingers investigating the spot where he'd kissed her.

Next he presented her with a small bouquet of flowers.

"Roberto, how sweet. Thank you." She led the way into the kitchen, where she placed the bouquet of pink carnations and miniature purple irises in a tall crystal vase.

"I didn't think to buy any wine," she said, regretting now that she hadn't thought of that beforehand.

"We'll have wine later," he said.

"I'll only be a minute," she said, and gestured self-consciously toward the bedroom. "I need to get my coat."

The ride to the restaurant, an Italian one from the looks of it, took several minutes. Roberto, the perfect gentleman, helped her out of the car and then escorted her inside.

The moment she walked through the door, Brynn was greeted with the scents of basil and simmering tomato. Garlic permeated the air, and she inhaled deeply, the smell alone enough to make her hungry. No one needed to tell her how good the food would be.

Roberto apparently knew the owners, and standing with his arm tucked around her waist, he introduced her.

"Brynn Cassidy, meet Stefano and Celeste Seti."

She shook hands with the white-haired gentleman

who was smiling broadly. His wife, Mama Celeste herself, planted her hands on her face and mumbled something in Italian to her husband. Brynn couldn't understand a word. Whatever it was appeared to please the grandmotherly woman. With a wide smile she kissed Roberto on both cheeks and promised them, in heavily accented English, the best dinner of their lives.

Soon they were seated at a table. Before Brynn had a chance to smooth the linen napkin on her lap, she was served red wine, thick slices of bread, and a large block of cheese.

The food never seemed to stop coming. Brynn sampled one fabulous dish after another. There must have been three or four different appetizers—shrimp, eggplant, tiny meatballs—before a huge Caesar salad arrived. When Brynn was convinced she couldn't eat another bite, the pasta was brought to their table by Stefano, who insisted she would break Celeste's heart if she didn't take a large portion of the specialty of the house. From the envious looks being sent her way, Brynn had the feeling if she couldn't finish the clam spaghetti, any number of volunteers would gladly step in for her.

"More wine, more wine," Stefano insisted, replenishing their glasses when she'd finished the best pasta she'd ever tasted. Brynn wasn't given a chance to refuse the wine. Stefano filled her glass and carried away their empty plates.

"I've never had such good food in my life," she murmured, and scooted back her chair. She planted her hands on her stomach. "But if I don't stop eating now, I won't be able to walk."

"No dessert?" Roberto teased.

They finished with a cup of dark coffee. Stefano and Celeste visited their table before they left, and this time it was Brynn who was hugged and kissed. Mama's eyes watered, and she dabbed at their corners with the hem of her apron.

Once they were outside, Roberto headed for the car.

"Would you mind very much if we walked awhile?" Brynn asked. Physical movement would help ease the stuffed feeling. Besides, she didn't want the evening to end so soon.

"By all means, let's walk," Roberto agreed. He reached for her hand and set a slow, easy pace. The night was crisp and cold.

"It looks like it might snow."

Roberto glanced skyward. "Wishful thinking on your part," he murmured. "There's barely a cloud in the sky."

He was right. The image of them walking together, hand in hand through lightly falling snow, appealed to her.

Although she'd enjoyed their dinner, her one regret was that with all the food being served, and Stefano checking to be sure everything was to their liking, there hadn't been much of a chance for the two of them to talk.

"Thank you, Roberto, for a wonderful meal."

He released her hand and slipped his arm around her waist. "Thank you for coming with me."

Brynn pressed her head against his shoulder. "What made you decide to ask me out?" She wasn't sure what prompted the question, but she was curious.

"I wanted everything to be right for you."

"Be right?"

He exhaled slowly as though he weren't sure how to explain himself. "You aren't like other women I've known."

Brynn smiled to herself. "Is that a compliment?"

Roberto was taken aback by her question. "I meant it to be. Have I insulted you?"

"No," she assured him.

"You're special, Brynn. Not only to me, but to Emilio and his friends, too. They think a lot of you. I've heard the teens talk about you, and when they do, well, it's with respect. It takes a lot to impress kids these days."

"And how do *you* feel about me?" she asked. It would be far easier for her if Roberto came right out and told her. She'd never been so bold with a man, but this wasn't a normal relationship.

"Me?" He hesitated, taking some time to formulate his thoughts. "You're stubborn and strong-willed."

Brynn wouldn't deny it. "If you think I'm stubborn, you should meet my mother." She bit down on her lip when she realized what she'd said. Reminding him of the mother he'd lost was the last thing she wanted.

"So you inherited the trait." He sounded amused, and Brynn was relieved.

"I care for you, Roberto," she told him softly. "More than I care for anyone other than my family." If he wasn't willing to acknowledge his feelings for her, then she'd be the first one to say it. "Knowing you has blessed my life. When I have a problem, you're the person I want to share it with. When something good happens, you're the one I want to tell. I find myself thinking about you a lot, probably more than I should."

His arm tightened around her middle. "I feel the same way about you. I want very much to kiss you, Brynn," he said with a deep sigh that revealed his longing for her, "but I don't want to do it in public. Not again. I'll wait until we get back to your apartment."

Brynn's heart swelled with emotion as she looked to him. "We could leave now, don't you think?"

Roberto chuckled, and together they raced across the street and back to Mama Celeste's, where Roberto's car was parked.

As they neared Brynn's apartment their amusement ebbed, replaced with a growing anticipation. Brynn's hand shook slightly as she unlocked the front door, knowing that soon she would be in Roberto's arms.

Together they walked into her apartment. Brynn didn't bother to turn on the lights. Once the door was closed, she lifted her arms and reached for Roberto.

With a deep-seated groan, he backed her against the door and kissed her.

The kiss was like fire, a spontaneous combustion of desire and need. Once wasn't near enough to satisfy either of them, and Roberto kissed her again and again. He surprised her with his tongue, and she gasped as he thrust it deep inside her mouth, stroking and teasing her. Gradually her gasp became a whimper that trembled from her lips.

When she was sure they were both about to faint with the intensity of their lovemaking, Roberto pulled away. She noted that his chest was heaving; hers was, too. In the dim light he looked down on her, and she met his look recklessly, unafraid for him to see all the love and longing in her eyes. Her fingers clung to the lapels of his suit as she studied him.

She waited, needing to know he'd experienced the same wonder she had. He closed his eyes momentarily, his breath deep and harsh, as though he needed to separate himself from her, if not physically, then emotionally.

Brynn might have been offended if he hadn't continued to hold her close and with such tender care. She pressed her head to his chest and listened to the strong, fast-paced beat of his heart.

"I don't dare touch you again," he whispered thickly.

"Why not?"

"You make me lose my head."

"That's bad?" she asked.

She felt his smile against her cheek. "Not exactly. It would be very easy to take you into that bedroom and make love to you, but I won't."

"You won't?" She couldn't believe she was asking him this.

"I can't allow that to happen. Once would never be enough with you. I would want you again and again, and that would only lead to—"

A loud knock sounded against the door, startling them both. Roberto's eyes met hers in the faded light. "You're expecting someone?"

She shook her head.

"Who is it?" she asked, struggling to make her voice strong enough to be heard.

Roberto turned on the light switch.

"Emilio," Roberto's brother shouted from the other side.

Roberto stiffened with irritation and opened the front door.

"It's Modesto," Emilio cried as he stumbled into the apartment. His eyes were wide with panic and fear. The teenager slumped onto the sofa and covered his face with both hands. "Modesto's been shot."

Jammed inside Jenny and Michelle's dinky apartment for the potluck Christmas party, everyone seemed to be talking at once. Trey felt as out of place as a bull moose at one of those fancy dog shows, the ones with dolled-up poodles with painted toenails.

Jenny's acting friends were certainly a mixed breed. There were everyday people, the kind he would have been hard-pressed to guess were show people, and then there were the others. The others, he noted, tended to be flamboyant attention seekers.

It made for an interesting evening, he would admit that much. Holding his drink, he found a quiet corner and played the role of casual observer.

A couple of times Jenny drifted his way, but she wasn't able to stay for long. Trey understood. Since she shared hostessing duties with her roommate, she couldn't very well give him all her attention. Though to be honest, that was what Trey would have preferred.

He sipped the wine, a fruity-flavored one he wouldn't normally drink, but all the market had offered. He found himself watching Jenny, mesmerized by her. She was as beautiful as he remembered, more so. Yet he couldn't look at her without his gut twisting up in a knot. This had been his lot when she was growing up. Loving her from afar.

Next to burying his parents, the most difficult thing Trey had ever done was to let Jenny Lancaster leave Custer, Montana, without telling her how much he loved her. He hadn't felt particularly self-sacrificing and noble at the time. He didn't feel that way now. It was just that he had some decisions to make, damned important ones, and they involved Jenny.

He loved her, and although he'd tried to forget her in the last three years, he couldn't. Countless times he'd attempted to convince himself to look for greener pastures.

It hadn't worked.

He'd spent the better part of ten years in love with Jenny, and it didn't appear that time or distance was going to change the way he felt.

She'd been little more than fifteen when he'd first recognized her as a woman. Until then she'd been a pesky kid. Living next door, so to speak, Trey had dealt mostly with Dillon, Jenny's father.

He remembered the day he'd realized she was a woman. He'd driven over to talk to her father about one thing or another and gone into the barn. Jenny had been there, grooming her filly and practicing her lines for a school play, when he'd stumbled upon her by accident. Without missing a beat, she'd continued with a flawless delivery. She'd ended her soliloquy by dramatically throwing herself into his arms, then leaning back and planting the back of her hand against her forehead. Less than a second passed before she'd recovered from her death, leaped upright, and asked him what he'd thought of her performance.

What he'd saw, Trey realized now, was the most beautiful woman he'd ever laid eyes on. Until that moment Trey had thought of Jenny as a kid. But it hadn't been a child he'd held in those few moments.

Trey had scowled and muttered something about

needing to talk to Dillon. Then for the next several years he'd waited impatiently for Jenny to grow up so he could court her. Three long, torturous years. It hadn't been easy watching her date one young buck after another. Nor had he liked her riding over to tell him about her dates and seeking his advice.

Trey suspected Jenny's parents knew how he felt about their daughter. But if they did, neither one said anything to him, and for that he was grateful.

By the time Jenny entered community college, she was dating one particular young man, and it looked for a time as if the two of them might be growing serious. More than once Trey had thought to go to her with his heart on his sleeve and tell her the way he felt.

This happened shortly after his parents had died, one after the other, within a nine-month period, and he was struggling financially. Dealing with his family's estate had drained his ready cash. Unfortunately this was about the same time that beef prices had plummeted. While he was fighting off the banks and barely holding his head above water financially wasn't the time to be asking a woman to be his wife.

By the time he felt he had something to offer Jenny, she'd made the decision to leave Montana for New York.

Trey remembered that Jenny's family had thrown a big going-away party for her. Trey couldn't force himself to attend. He knew if he let her leave, there was a good chance he'd never see her again, at least not the Jenny he knew. New York would change her.

New York would make her into one of those sophisticated women who carried their dogs under their arms while they went clothes shopping.

Letting Jenny leave Montana was a testament of how much he loved her. His love couldn't compete with her dreams. The bright lights of Broadway was her destiny. He was a cattle rancher with damn little to offer someone as talented as Jenny Lancaster.

At the last minute, Trey had stopped by the ranch and managed to wish her his very best. He remembered he'd said something corny about her breaking her leg in New York. Then he'd stood with her family and waved good-bye.

She'd driven off with her friends and taken his heart with her.

Afterward, Trey had gone home and gotten soundly drunk.

The first year after she'd left had been the worst. He'd made a dozen or more excuses to visit the Lancasters and ask about her. He'd been tempted to write her but had promised himself he wouldn't. She was out of his life now and would soon be a big shot on Broadway.

Only it hadn't happened quite like that. By the second Christmas she was away, he'd been semi-successful in pushing the memory of her to the back of his mind. He still asked about her occasionally and was surprised to learn that her name wasn't lighting up any marquees. It was then that he'd begun to hope Jenny would throw in the towel and move home to lick her wounds.

It was the small quiver in her voice when he'd phoned that had first alerted Trey to the fact that something was wrong. He hadn't been able to put his finger on it. After all this time, he didn't expect Jenny to be the same person she'd been when she'd left Custer. He wasn't sure now what he had expected. Instead of sounding happy, she'd seemed sad, and he'd sensed in her a deep pain she couldn't hide.

He'd mulled that over for a number of days, and then it seemed everyone he knew on God's green earth started talking about New York. Before he could question the wisdom of his actions, he'd booked the flight to New York and subsequently learned the truth. He wasn't relieved or glad at her lack of success. His first reaction had been anger that those fancy, worldly men had been blind to her talents.

Trey wanted to take Jenny back to Montana. He wanted to love her, comfort her, and take care of her. More than that, he wanted to wipe away the frustration and disappointment.

He hadn't meant to ask her to come home so abruptly, but the words had refused to remain unsaid. The first time he'd asked, her response had been quick and sharp.

No.

That had been before he'd kissed her. When he'd asked a second time, she hadn't answered.

Someone slipped a tape inside the cassette player, and a fresh batch of Christmas music filled the room. Several started to sing, and soon Trey heard three distinct parts, blending in perfect harmony.

Within a few moments everyone had stopped chatting to sing along. Jenny drifted over to Trey's side. He'd never tire of hearing her sing. This, he decided, was what angels must sound like. Her voice conjured up that image for him.

The old Christmas carols were his personal favorites, and when the first introductory notes of "Silent Night" played, Trey sang along himself. It surprised him how well his deep voice blended with Jenny's.

Pleasure lit up her eyes when she turned to smile at him.

He returned the gesture and draped his arm around her shoulder. A couple of the men in the group glanced his way and frowned. Trey didn't blame them for being jealous. He had battled down the affliction every time Jenny so much as glanced at another man. In the beginning it had damn near eaten him alive, but time and effort had helped him master his feelings.

Soon the music faded, taken over with small talk. The crowd was beginning to get to him, so he decided to step outside for some fresh air. To his surprise, Jenny grabbed her coat and followed him.

"Come with me," she said, and led him to the fire escape. She sat down and patted the space next to her. "I used to sit out here in the hottest nights of summer," she said. Her breath produced clouded puffs in the cold night air. "Out here with the sky bright with stars was as close as I could get to feeling like I was in Montana again," she admitted.

It was hard for Trey to hold his tongue. He'd already asked her twice to come back to Custer with him. He wouldn't do it again.

"I wondered if you ever thought about home," he said.

"Every day."

"Did you think about me, Jenny?" He braced himself, fearing he wouldn't like her answer. He had never said a solitary word about his feelings for her.

When she looked up at him, Trey noticed that her eyes were bright with unshed tears. "I thought about you a lot, Trey. I don't know why, but in the last six months it seemed you were on my mind nearly every day."

"You never wrote me," he reminded her.

Her smile was weak at best. "You didn't write me, either."

That he couldn't argue with.

"Did you . . . did you think about me, Trey?"

"Every damn minute of every damn day you've been away," he admitted huskily. He kissed her then, simply because he needed her so badly. He'd loved her for so long, he didn't know what it was not to love her.

Her ready response left him lightheaded. The kiss went on and on until they were both desperate to breathe.

"Oh, Trey," she whispered, and buried her face against his neck.

It was heaven to hold her and the purest form of torture he had ever experienced. Heaven and hell.

The door abruptly opened behind them, and a couple stumbled out, giggling.

"Sorry!" the male voice charged. "We haven't interrupted anything, have we?"

"Modesto's been shot." Shirley landed on the fire escape with such an urgency that she nearly unseated Mercy.

"My goodness," Mercy said, gasping.

"Did someone call for me?" Goodness asked, joining her two friends.

"Modesto's in the hospital," Shirley blurted out in a dither. "It was a gang shooting . . . someone he didn't even know. We've got to get there."

"What about Brynn?" Mercy asked, following her friend.

"She's already at New York General with Roberto and his brother. Emilio's in a bad way."

"Oh my."

Together the three of them left Jenny and headed across town. They soon descended into the hospital waiting room, where the situation was tense.

Emilio sat in the corner of the room, bent forward, his elbows braced against his knees. Shirley couldn't remember ever seeing the teenager look more stricken. Roberto sat next to his brother, and Brynn couldn't seem to hold still. She paced from one side of the room to the other.

Modesto's mother was weeping softly. His older

sister had her arm around their mother, but she looked as though she were about to break into tears herself.

"They've been waiting two hours," Shirley informed her friends.

"What's taking so long?"

"Modesto's in surgery."

"How did something like this happen?" Mercy asked. In all the time they'd been working together, they'd never been a part of this kind of tragedy.

"I don't know what to do for them." Shirley turned to face her two friends. Always before she'd been the one with the most experience and the one the other two had looked up to for help. She looked desperately to Goodness for help.

"This is just terrible," Mercy murmured, wringing her hands. "Just terrible. Poor Modesto."

"Poor Brynn." Shirley stood near the young teacher and watched her pace. "She's nearly beside herself with worry."

"Stand with her," Goodness urged. "Give her your strength."

"Mine?" Shirley was beside herself. Never had she felt more inadequate. "Gabriel was right. I don't have nearly enough experience to help Brynn the way I should. She needs me and I've failed her."

Brynn collapsed into a chair, and Shirley sat next to her and folded her wing protectively over the young woman.

"Stay with her," Goodness suggested. "I'm going to find out what I can about Modesto's condition."

"I'll go with you," Mercy said, joining Goodness. "Don't you worry about a thing," she said, looking back at Shirley. "I'm sure everything's under control."

The last thing Shirley wanted was to be left alone. She ached the same way Brynn did, worried the same way Brynn did. She shared her charge's feelings of inadequacy. If ever Gabriel was right, it was now.

"Shirley."

Just thinking about him seemed to have conjured up the archangel.

"Gabriel," she said, leaping to attention.

"How are things going?" His presence seemed to fill up the hospital waiting room.

Shirley thought briefly of bluffing her way out of this, then figured Gabriel would be able to see through her in less time than it took for a heart to beat.

"It's about Modesto," she explained, distraught and near tears herself.

"I know all about the boy."

"Can you tell me what's going to happen to him?"

Gabriel inclined his head slightly. "He'll recover in time."

Shirley sighed with heartfelt relief. "Thank God."

"I'll mention it the next time we talk," Gabriel assured her.

Sheepishly Shirley looked to the mighty archangel. "You were right," she admitted sadly.

"That's always nice to know, but exactly what am I right about this time?"

"Me helping Brynn. She's falling in love with Roberto."

"So I understand."

Shirley waited for Gabriel to voice his disapproval, but he didn't.

"Mr. Whalen placed a formal reprimand in her file."

"I heard about that as well."

"Suzie's pregnant."

"Yes."

"Everything's one giant mess, and it's all my fault." She hung her head, not wanting to view the disappointment in Gabriel's eyes.

"Your fault?" Gabriel echoed, then chuckled softly. "You've got it all wrong." Gently he placed his wings around Shirley's burdened shoulders. "I couldn't be more proud had I trained you myself." He paused and sighed deeply. "Come to think of it, I have."

Chapter Thirteen

Hannah returned home from an errand her mother had sent her on, and hurried up the stairs to her family's living quarters. She hadn't taken more than a few steps into their apartment when aunts, uncles, cousins, and her beloved grandmother shouted, "Surprise!"

Hannah blinked back her shock. She stared at the sea of faces and noticed Carl's parents were present as well. Ruth rushed forward and hugged Hannah enthusiastically.

"It's an engagement party," her mother announced when Hannah stared at her, unable to disguise her anxiety.

Hannah looked at Carl, who was thrust into the middle of the room with her. She hadn't seen him since he'd confessed that he'd been fired.

Admitting to his family that he'd lost

his job would have mortified Carl. Hannah might never have learned the truth had she not arrived unexpectedly on his doorstep the afternoon she'd met Joshua.

When she recognized how troubled Carl was over the loss of his job, she knew she couldn't deliver even more depressing news. So she'd been forced to bide her time.

"Apparently this party is in our honor," Carl explained.

Somehow Hannah managed to return a smile, but she didn't know how she would possibly make it through this party.

To be fair, Carl didn't look any more pleased than she did with the unexpectedness of their engagement party. He had told her earlier that since he was no longer employed, they would need to postpone the wedding. The next step was to announce this to their families. Carl had wanted time to tell his parents first, and Hannah had agreed. Now they were being forced to pretend all was well when they were keenly aware that it wasn't.

Once the pressure was off to set a wedding date, Hannah would be free to tell Carl about having met Joshua. He would understand. She was sure of that.

Hannah glanced around the room. It was filled to capacity with family, aunts, uncles, cousins, and longtime friends who'd come to wish her and Carl happiness.

Because it was expected of her, Hannah took Carl around and introduced him to her relatives.

Her grandmother gazed at her fondly from a position of honor, the recliner. Hannah had always felt close to Sylvia Morganstern. Surely she would know something was wrong. Surely her grandmother would recognize that she wasn't in love with Carl. Hannah realized she wouldn't be able to hide her feelings from the one who'd known and loved her all her life.

"Come and say hello to your aunt Edith," Ruth said, placing her arm around Hannah's waist and leading her across the room.

Carl traipsed behind obediently. Hannah didn't know how anyone could look at the two of them and believe they were in love. Nor did she know how she could continue to pretend to be an eager bride when she intended to break their engagement at the earliest possible moment.

Briefly she closed her eyes and hoped Joshua would never learn of this engagement party. Thus far he'd been wonderfully patient with her, but she didn't know how long that would last, especially when he learned she hadn't broken off the engagement with Carl the way she'd promised.

"Hannah, my dear," her grandmother said, and patted the empty seat beside her. "First introduce me to your young man and then sit down. I'm going to be greedy and hog you all to myself for a few moments."

"Carl, this is my grandma Morganstern."

"I'm so pleased to meet you," Carl said formally and with deep respect.

Her grandmother asked him a number of gentle questions, which he answered, although it was clear to Hannah that he was eager to escape. Before he left, he was kind enough to bring Hannah and Sylvia each a cup of punch. Then as quickly as he could, he wandered away.

Her grandmother reached for Hannah's hand and squeezed her slim fingers affectionately. "Now tell me all about you and Carl. How long have you been dating? How'd you meet?"

It demanded all the fortitude Hannah possessed to keep from blurting out the truth. If anyone would understand about her loving Joshua, it would be her grandmother.

"He looks like a good man."

Hannah smiled and agreed. "He'll be a good husband." But not to her. She glanced in Carl's direction and found she could barely look at him and not experience a crushing sense of guilt.

"Hannah?"

Her gaze continued to follow the man she'd promised to marry. It astonished her that she could ever have agreed to be Carl's wife, especially when it was so painfully obvious they were mismatched.

"Carl is a wonderful man. He's loyal and dedicated." Hannah lowered her gaze, hoping her grandmother wouldn't guess the love she nurtured in her heart was for another man.

Everyone seemed to be having a wonderful time. Together Hannah's parents brought one food tray after another out from the kitchen. The buffet-style meal was set on the dining room table. Because her parents were in the food business, this had been a labor of love, and the spread was something to behold.

"I've taken enough of your time," Sylvia insisted, patting Hannah's hand. "It looks like your mother's ready for you and Carl."

It didn't escape Hannah's notice that her grandmother didn't comment on what a nice couple Hannah and Carl made. She was deeply relieved Sylvia hadn't pressed her with more questions. It was difficult enough to deceive her mother and father, but nearly impossible to maintain the pretense in front of her grandmother.

Hannah joined Carl, and it seemed everyone was staring at them, waiting for something to happen.

Carl reached for her hand and whispered, "I spoke to my father."

A sense of relief nearly swallowed her whole, and she turned to face him. "You did?"

Carl's gaze shifted about the room. "He's going to talk to the school board as soon as possible and see what can be done. I'm confident he'll be able to straighten everything out."

"That's wonderful, Carl."

His fingers tightened over hers. "I can't tell you how worried I've been over this."

Hannah had been concerned as well, but not for the reasons Carl assumed.

"Everything's going to work out, Hannah, I promise you that."

"Of course it will." And as soon as Carl's misunderstanding with the headmaster was cleared up, she'd be free to break the engagement.

Hannah's father asked Carl's father, Rabbi Rabinsky, to say a short prayer before they ate. The rabbi stepped forward and placed one hand on his son's shoulder and the other on Hannah's. He closed his eyes, and the room went still.

The prayer was short and potent, asking God to shower His love upon the two of them and to fill their lives with good things.

When he raised his head, there was a murmur of agreement. Her family loved her, Hannah realized, and they wished her and Carl much happiness.

Soon her relatives and other guests were busy filling their plates. Hannah wasn't the least bit hungry, but to not eat might have alerted her mother that something was wrong, so she dished up with the others.

Hannah and Carl were ushered to the seats of honor, and she noticed that he didn't seem to have much of an appetite himself.

The party sat in a large circle, their plates resting on their laps. It was Aunt Edith who asked the question first.

"Well, you two, don't keep me in suspense any longer. When's the wedding date?"

Everyone seemed to wait for Hannah to answer. The room filled with an expectant silence. Hannah looked first to her mother for help and then to Carl. Neither seemed inclined to respond.

"I believe Mother and Helen felt that the wedding coordinator should be the one to decide that," Hannah explained when no one came to her rescue.

"Nonsense," Edith said, dismissing the idea with a wave of her hand. "It's up to the two of you to set the date. Let the wedding coordinator work around the one you've chosen."

"But—" Hannah wasn't allowed to finish.

"I agree," Cousin Hariette intoned. "If you're going to have an outsider make all the arrangements, then it's vital they know from the first who's in charge. A wedding's no small thing, and it's best to get started on the right foot."

"I've wondered about this," Hannah's father murmured, looking to Ruth.

"Springtime," Edith suggested next. "When the flowers are starting to bloom. There's nothing like fresh flowers for a wedding."

"Oh no," Hannah said quickly. "We can't possibly have the wedding so soon . . . there wouldn't be near enough time, would there?" She looked to Carl for support.

"I'm afraid Hannah's right," her mother concurred. "We were thinking June."

"June," Edith repeated. "June would be perfect."

Cousin Hariette brought out a new calendar and flipped through the pages until she located the month.

"I don't think Carl and I are in any rush," Hannah offered, but it seemed no one was listening to her. Both her own mother and Carl's crowded around, peering over Hariette's shoulder, scanning the June page on the pocket calendar.

"The sixteenth sounds perfectly lovely."

"The closer to the middle of the month the better, from what I hear," another aunt offered.

"I don't think we need to choose a date right now, do you?" Hannah tried once more.

Her grandma Morganstern studied her closely, and Hannah realized she'd best not say anything more. Not then, at least.

"What do you think of June sixteenth?" The question was directed to Carl, who had his fork poised in front of his mouth.

"Give the young man a chance to eat," her father said, coming to Carl's rescue.

With his mouth full of food, Carl nodded enthusiastically. Hannah felt he was silently commenting on what her father had said. Unfortunately everyone else in the room seemed to think he was agreeing to the wedding date.

"That settles that," Ruth said cheerfully. "The wedding is set for June sixteenth."

The news of Modesto Diaz's injury spread quickly, and soon a number of Brynn's students had gathered at the hospital. Again and again Emilio was forced to repeat the grisly details of what had happened—first to the police who came to question him, then to the curious and the fearful.

Father Grady arrived, and Brynn was grateful. She felt at a loss as to how to help Modesto's mother and sister deal with the tragedy. After what seemed a lifetime, the surgeon appeared. His look was grave as he announced that the surgery had been a success. Modesto wasn't completely out of danger, and his condition was guarded. But the teen was doing as well as could be expected.

Following a translation of the physician's words, Modesto's mother clenched her hands together, turned her face toward heaven, and wept loudly. His sister cried silently with relief. For the first time since he'd appeared at her apartment door, some color started to return to Emilio's face.

Roberto looked to Brynn and she to him. His relief was evident. Hers, too, she guessed, as she battled down the urge to weep.

While they'd sat through those interminable hours, Roberto had remained beside his brother, offering Emilio his support and love. The younger Alcantara had needed his brother.

Brynn, however, had found sitting impossible, so she'd done what she always did when she was nervous: she'd paced. Back and forth, until she'd feared her path would leave permanent creases in the thin carpet.

Now she felt the need to be close to Roberto. He apparently shared her sudden desire, because he crossed the area. Without a word, he took her into his arms and held her firmly against him. She drank in his strength, absorbed his calm. His hold was tight, almost punishing, as if he planned on never letting her go.

Brynn knew that the two of them had attracted the attention of the others, but she didn't care who saw them together. Gradually Roberto did release her, but not before she felt his muscles tighten. His relief turned to anger as he faced Father Grady.

"It's this neighborhood," Roberto said between clenched teeth. "It could have been Emilio who was shot, or you, or Brynn." His face was tight and fierce. His brother was all the family he had left.

"I know, I know," Father Grady said gently.

Roberto stalked to the far side of the room, his back to Brynn.

She wasn't entirely certain what was happening. Now wasn't the time for explanations, but she knew Father Grady would explain everything to her later.

"I'll take you home now," Roberto announced starkly to Brynn.

She followed him through the crowded hospital corridor outside. The cold night air hit her like an unexpected slap. The wind stung her face and eyes as she hurried to keep pace with Roberto.

For Brynn's sake, Roberto tried to control his anger, but he couldn't think of his younger brother and Modesto facing a nameless gunman on the same streets where children had played only hours earlier. His anger went deep and bordered on rage.

He focused his resentment on the neighborhood and the frustration he felt each time he'd tried to make a better life for himself and Emilio.

It could have been his brother lying in that hospital bed. He could have lost Emilio. The thought terrified him. He'd promised his mother that he would watch after his brother, raise him right. He had failed her in other ways, but not this time. By heaven, not this time.

Roberto glanced over at Brynn, who sat next to him stiffly. She'd never seen this side of him. She didn't know he could be an angry, frustrated brute. This was what happened when those he loved were threatened.

Love.

Just mentally saying the word made him squirm. He was dangerously close to falling for the pretty Irish teacher. He didn't need anyone to tell him what a mistake that would be. It went without saying that a college-educated beauty like Brynn Cassidy had nothing in common with the likes of him. She should be dating a stockbroker or an attorney, not someone who had trouble getting the grease from beneath his fingernails.

He was living in a dream world if he thought anything could develop between them. God had delivered that message loud and clear. Roberto knew what he had to do next.

First off, he had to stop thinking about Brynn as a friend. They'd never been that. As for making her his lover, however much he would like to entertain the notion, she was off-limits. He'd make excuses not to see her again, and soon enough she'd get the message. Their relationship would be over before it ever started. Whatever it might have been was gone now.

Having made that decision, Roberto felt some of the hard ball of anger dissipate. He was in control again. His life was back in order.

One thing he vowed. Somehow, some way, with God's help, he was going to find his way out of this neighborhood.

Brynn's class was quiet and subdued on Monday. Normally her students tested her patience by chattering like monkeys long after the bell rang. Not this day. They filed into the room and sat at their desks and stared at her as though they anticipated some great revelation from her.

"By now most of you have heard about what happened to Modesto," she said.

"It ain't fair, Miss Cassidy," Yolanda said.

"Life isn't fair," Denzil answered.

"Modesto wasn't doing anything."

"He isn't bad, you know."

"Of course he isn't." Brynn felt at a loss as to how to answer their fears, nor did it seem right to dig into her lessons when it was obvious her students needed to talk about what had happened to their friend.

"I went to see him at the hospital," Emilio announced, his voice void of emotion. "They wouldn't let me in."

"Modesto's in intensive care. I know because I called," someone else claimed.

"He's going to live, isn't he?"

Brynn couldn't answer that, so she repeated as best she could what the physician had said. "His chances are very good, but there's always the possibility of complications."

"We weren't doing nothin'," Emilio said to no one in particular. "The police tried to make it sound like we were on the prowl looking for trouble. Man, if I was looking for action, I'd take my posse with me."

There were murmurs of agreement.

Emilio leaned forward and placed his hands over his face. He looked both vulnerable and afraid. Wanting to comfort him, Brynn walked over to his side and placed her hand gently on his shoulder.

He shrugged it off viciously and glared up at her. "Don't touch me," he snapped.

Such behavior wasn't like Emilio. If she considered any one student an ally, it would be Roberto's brother.

She stepped back, but not before Emilio slid out of his seat and stormed out of the room. The glass panel in the door rattled as he slammed it closed.

"Emilio." She started after him. If he was caught in the hall without a pass, he'd be sent to the principal's office. If he mouthed off to Mr. Whalen, he was likely to be suspended a second time, and if that happened, it was doubtful he'd be back.

Brynn stopped at the door. "Suzie," she called, "would you take over for me for a few moments?"

The teenager's eyes widened with apprehension before she nodded.

"Thank you," Brynn whispered, and left the classroom. She was breaking another cardinal rule by doing so. If she was discovered, she would receive another formal reprimand. She weighed the decision carefully before stepping into the hallway. Something was very wrong with Emilio, and she had to find out what.

She found him crouched on the floor next to a dented beige locker at the end of the hall. His head hung between his knees.

"Emilio." She said his name gently.

He didn't look up.

"It wasn't your fault."

"Leave me alone," he said, his voice uncharacteristically hard and cold.

"You can't blame yourself for what happened to Modesto," she offered.

This time he hissed something in Spanish, and for once Brynn was grateful for her limited language skills. One thing was certain: he wasn't inviting her to talk matters out.

"You can't stay here," she said, looking both ways down the hall. "Please, Emilio, come back into the class."

He shook his head.

"If they find you—"

"Yeah, yeah, I know. I'll get suspended. Do you really think I care, Ms. Cassidy? I don't."

"I care."

"Am I supposed to appreciate that?"

"Yes."

He looked away, and it seemed that he was wishing her back into the classroom. "Leave me alone."

"You're hurting, Emilio. I want to help."

He lifted his head and stared at the ceiling. "Modesto's the one who's in pain, not me."

"Do you think Modesto wouldn't be in as much pain if you'd been shot, too?"

"Yes," he shouted, and slammed his fist into the locker directly beside him. The noise exploded in the silent hallway like a cannon shot, echoing off the sides.

For sure they'd be found now. Brynn closed her eyes and inhaled a deep, calming breath. Emilio didn't want her help, didn't need her.

"I'm sorry this happened to you, Emilio," she said softly. "So very sorry." Knowing he wouldn't accept her help, she turned and started back to her classroom.

"I ran."

She paused. So that was what this was all about. Emilio thought himself a coward because he'd deserted his friend and saved his own life.

Brynn turned back and squatted next to him. Her legs ached before she spoke. "I would have run, too. It was probably what saved you from being shot as well."

Emilio said nothing.

"Do you think Modesto wouldn't have tried to escape had you been the one hit first?"

Again Emilio didn't respond.

"You acted instinctively," Brynn tried again. "You had nothing with which to defend yourself. The option had been taken away from you."

A parched cry worked its way through his throat, and he buried his face in his arms with a muffled sob.

Brynn longed to touch him, but she was afraid that her comfort was the last thing he sought. Because her muscles were cramping, she placed her knees on the cold floor.

"There's no shame in what you did," she whispered.

His shoulders shook, and unable to watch him and do nothing, Brynn braced her hand against the curve of his shoulder.

The pain, the doubt, the fears and self-recriminations, broke like a fire hydrant inside him. His shoulders shook violently with uncontrollable sobs. One after another tumbled from his lips until his cries became those of an injured animal.

Kneeling at his side, Brynn gently tucked his head against her breast and held him. Gently she rocked back and forth, fighting emotion while the pain poured from Emilio Alcantara's heart.

"Will you be seeing Trey this afternoon?" Michelle asked Jenny.

"I don't know." They hadn't made plans to get together, and she had to work later in the day. She'd told him her schedule and had expected to hear from him. Thus far she'd been disappointed.

Michelle wandered into their living room, a plastic trash bag in hand. She picked up an empty wine bottle and tossed it inside. "Your friend certainly generated a lot of interest."

Jenny had noticed that much herself.

"I had to tell Julia Leonard to wipe the drool off her chin."

Jenny smiled.

"That guy's a hunk, girl. How come you never mentioned how handsome he is? It's like he walked in directly from the range. Someone asked me if he'd left his horse parked outside." Michelle ditched a paper plate in the trash bag. "There was something else I noticed."

"What's that?" Jenny asked, tossing a beer can into the accumulated garbage.

"He only had eyes for you."

"I've known Trey LaRue nearly all my life," Jenny explained.

Michelle straightened and studied Jenny for a couple of moments. "By the way, what kind of name is Trey, anyway? It sounds like it's French or something."

"His real name's Mark."

"Mark? How'd his family get Trey out of that?"

"His grandfather's name was Mark and his father's name was Mark, and when he was born the story goes that there were so many Marks floating around, they decided to call him Trey."

"Oh, I get it now. Trey for the third Mark," Michelle murmured.

"Right." Jenny returned to picking up the clutter left over from the party.

"Are you going to marry him?" her roommate shocked her by asking next.

"Marry him?"

"Why not?" Michelle asked flippantly. "It's as clear as melted snow the guy's in love with you. When I first met him I thought it was rather sweet of him to travel all this way to see you. It's a definite boost to a woman's ego to have a man from her past idolize her. I could certainly do with a couple of men like Trey myself."

"He's never once mentioned marriage to me, nor will he." Jenny's reply was defensive, and she knew it.

Michelle's eyebrows flirted with her hairline. "You'd be tempted to accept his proposal if he did, wouldn't you?"

"Don't be ridiculous." But she wasn't nearly as confident as she sounded. She didn't know what she'd say if Trey proposed. One thing was certain: she didn't like the turn their conversation had taken. It hadn't bothered her when Michelle mentioned the open curiosity of their friends toward Trey. It hadn't hurt her pride any to have Trey fend off the friendly advances made by the more aggressive of her peers. Frankly, Jenny didn't blame her friends.

Trey had the same overwhelming effect upon her senses.

The few kisses they'd shared before being interrupted had haunted her. She wanted him to kiss and touch her again just so she'd know what they'd shared had been as good as she remembered.

"Can you honestly picture someone like Trey living in New York?" she asked Michelle heatedly. "Within a month he'd go stark, raving mad. Trey's the type of man who needs plenty of wide-open space."

"If he loved you . . ."

"No." Jenny wouldn't consider it. Besides, it was a moot point. The very idea that he'd propose was ludicrous. He was in town only a few days, exactly how many he had yet to tell her. When he left she'd ride out to the airport with him and see him off. But the mere thought of Trey heading back to Montana produced an emptiness she couldn't shake.

"Jenny?" Michelle broke into her musings.

She smiled weakly and resumed her task, but her mind wasn't on it.

"Of course if you married Trey, you wouldn't necessarily need to live in New York. There are—"

"Are you suggesting I return to Montana?" Jenny demanded. "What are you trying to tell me, Michelle? That it's time I admitted the truth, that I'm a no-talent wannabe and that I'll never make it on Broadway or, for that matter, any place else?" She was desperate to breathe by the time she'd finished.

Visibly shocked by Jenny's outburst, Michelle stood frozen and stared at her.

Jenny sagged into the chair. "I didn't mean that."

"I didn't either," Michelle whispered. "I believe in you as strongly as I do in myself."

"I know." They'd been each other's cheering squad for too long for Jenny to doubt her friend now. Over the last three years they'd been through so much together. Jenny knew Michelle wished her nothing but unbridled success. Anything else would have been completely out of character.

The phone rang just then.

The last few days had been a tense time for them both. Michelle was due to hear the results of her second audition with John Peterman. If it were in her power, Jenny would award her friend the role, but it wasn't.

"You want me to get it?" she asked Michelle.

"No, I will," Michelle answered, and walked over to the wall phone. She reached for it and paused, her hand inches from the receiver. "You get it, all right?" she asked, and moved away.

It pealed a third time before Jenny could reach it.

"I should be the one to answer," Michelle said abruptly and ripped the receiver off the hook. "This is Michelle Jordan," she greeted cheerfully, as if she had been sitting idly by the phone without a care in the world. She listened for a moment, then, "Well, hello," she said seductively, eyeing Jenny. "And how are you?"

A second pause while Jenny was left to wonder who was at the other end of the line.

"Of course. . . . No, it's no problem whatsoever." She pressed the mouthpiece against her shoulder. "It's Trey. He wants to talk to you. Do you want me to tell him you're here, or would you rather I made up some excuse and told him you were out for the day?"

Chapter Fourteen

Emilio was absent from school the following afternoon. Brynn's heart sank. She couldn't very well cancel the most important test this term because one student hadn't bothered to show.

Emilio had left school the day before without returning to class, but when Brynn had tried to reach him later, the phone had gone unanswered. With her own commitments, she hadn't been able to seek out Roberto, nor had she been able to talk to him.

Her day felt incomplete without some form of contact with Roberto. Little by little she'd opened her heart to Emilio's older brother. There was such passion in Roberto, such intensity. The other men she'd dated had been neither hot nor cold. Nothing excited them. Not injustice. Not good fortune. Not tickets to a playoff football game. Brynn had been left wondering what would happen if any of them ever won the lottery.

There was no doubt in her mind, however, where Roberto stood on any number of subjects. He rarely hesitated to make his opinions known. Although she often disagreed with him, she appreciated the fact that he was willing to take a stand. He cared deeply for those he loved. That was what had attracted her to him in the beginning.

Every time he kissed her the experience left her shaken. One thing was certain: Roberto Alcantara would never be a lukewarm lover.

"Is everyone ready for their midterms?" she asked the class. Standing in front of the room, she cradled the test papers against her chest.

A low rumble of responses came from her students. As the papers were being handed out, Brynn noted that Emilio wasn't the only student absent that day. Modesto's desk was conspicuously empty. His condition remained listed as serious, but from what she'd heard he would soon be upgraded to satisfactory.

Mike Glasser was gone as well. That disappointed her. She'd tried hard to bring the loner out of his shell, but nothing had worked. His attitude baffled her. When she looked directly at him, she assumed his mind was a thousand miles away, yet when she quizzed him, he knew the answers. The boy was keenly intelligent, but he refused to apply himself.

Brynn walked around the room while her class

took the exam. This was by far the most important test she'd given, and she'd worked long hours composing the essay questions. Her students' responses were the best way she had of gauging how well she'd done her job.

The class discussions were thought-provoking and often heated. Brynn was thrilled that she could make her students care about what had happened in the world sixty years earlier. She felt it was important for them to do more than memorize dates and names.

Her goal was for them to look back at history and learn from the past. She wanted them to gain insight and perspective from a journal written by a teenage Jewish girl, who, despite the years separating their worlds, wasn't unlike them. It excited Brynn when her students recognized that they shared the same dreams, the same aspirations, as Anne Frank.

More important, Brynn wanted her students to reason through this material and willingly share their feelings with her. A number of the test questions had no right or wrong answers. All she wanted was for each of her students to reflect on this time period in American and European history and then express their thoughts.

When Brynn strolled past Suzie's desk. she was surprised to discover that the girl's paper was blank.

Unwilling to break the concentration of any of the others, Brynn resisted the urge to ask Suzie if something was wrong. She noticed that the girl wore a maternity top and wondered if anyone else recognized Suzie was pregnant.

Pen in hand, Suzie briefly acknowledged Brynn, then bent forward and started to write.

As Brynn walked past Emilio's empty desk, she couldn't help wondering what had kept him from class. It wasn't as if he hadn't known about this test or realized its significance. Brynn had been talking about it for several days, reviewing the material so it would be fresh in their minds. Now and again she'd purposely screw up the dates and would take pride when someone, often a student she wouldn't expect to know the difference, would correct her.

After class had been dismissed, Brynn quickly reviewed the test results and was pleased with what she read. Because she was anxious to talk to Emilio, she left school as soon as she could without checking for messages. She rarely received anything more than the dittoed sheets the school printed for all staff members. With the advent of Christmas, and most all the classes winding down, she didn't expect anything of real importance.

Eager to see Roberto, Brynn walked to his garage first. The sky was dark with thick gray clouds the color of tempered steel, and the wind added an extra chill to the late afternoon. Nevertheless, Brynn was happy. She'd had her first real date with Roberto, and even though their evening had ended abruptly, their time together had proved what she'd long suspected. Roberto cared about her the same way she did about him.

Brynn's parents were anxious for her to come home for Christmas, but she'd already decided against making the trip. She hadn't told her mother, and wouldn't, but she preferred to stay right here in New York with Roberto. She'd mentioned him in passing several times, and in the last telephone conversation, she'd confessed she was strongly attracted to him.

The bell chimed over the doorway when she entered his garage. She rubbed her hands together to chase away the chill. No one greeted her.

"Is anyone here?" she called out, thinking it odd that Roberto hadn't locked up the garage.

A minute later Roberto appeared, dressed in greasy overalls. He wiped his hands clean on a rag, his face devoid of emotion. He nodded once and greeted her without revealing any pleasure in seeing her. "Hello, Brynn."

None of the warmth or welcome she'd felt on their dinner date was apparent. Puzzled by his attitude, Brynn felt like walking out the door and coming back to try this all over again.

"Is something wrong?" she asked.

He shook his head. "You tell me."

"Well . . ." Baffled, she wasn't sure what had happened. "Emilio wasn't in class this afternoon."

"Yes, I know."

"There was an important test."

He shrugged as though to say that was of no importance to him.

"Is Emilio ill?"

"No."

"Then where was he?"

"Running errands for me," Roberto informed her briskly.

"You mean to say you knew he was purposely skipping classes and you let him?" Anger swelled inside her, but she did a good job of maintaining her composure.

"Yes. Emilio announced this morning that he didn't feel like going to school, and I told him the choice was his."

This was a discussion they'd had in the past, and they'd always ended up arguing about the importance of education. Nothing she said would change Roberto's opinion, and certainly nothing he said would alter her feelings.

"I want to talk to Emilio," she said, unwilling to be drawn into a verbal battle neither one of them could win.

"He isn't here," Roberto continued stoically.

"When do you expect him back?"

He didn't hesitate. "I don't know."

Brynn could see that discussing Emilio would be a losing proposition. She looked past Roberto, hoping to gain perspective on what was happening between them.

"How was your day?" she asked in an effort to put the conversation back on an even keel.

"Busy." He glanced over his shoulder as though to say there was plenty left for him to do and her silly questions were keeping him from his chores.

Brynn wasn't sure what to do or say. She could play cute word games and dance around the issue, but that would solve nothing. They'd done all that before.

"If you've got something to say to me, Roberto, I'd appreciate it if you came out and said it." She stiffened, knowing instinctively what was on his mind.

A flicker of surprise flashed in and out of his eyes. He hadn't anticipated her being this direct, she guessed. Normally she wasn't. Whenever it was possible she avoided confrontation, but she'd learned that in dealing with Roberto, she was better off taking the offensive.

From the first time since she'd arrived, he hesitated.

"Let me say it for you, then," she offered. "You've come to some monumental decision about us."

"Brynn—"

"Let me finish," she insisted, forcing herself to sound light and airy, as though his attitude didn't affect her one way or the other. "You've decided that it'd probably be best for us not to see each other again. Am I right?"

His jaw had gone white. "Something along those lines, but I don't think now is the time to discuss it."

"It seems to me this is as good a time as any," she responded with a flippant air. "You know what they say about there being no time like the present."

"Perhaps, but—"

"Why, Roberto?" she asked simply. Her chest tightened, and this time she couldn't hide the pain in her voice. "Did I do something unforgivable? Something so terrible that you can't find it in your heart to forgive me?"

"No," he said harshly, and briefly closed his eyes. "For what it's worth . . ." He stopped himself, then started again, his eyes as gentle as she'd ever seen them. He didn't want to hurt her, that much was evident.

"Whatever it is," she whispered forcefully, "we can work it out."

He shook his head. "I never intended to become emotionally involved with you. We're both intelligent enough to realize we're all wrong together." He clenched the muscles along the side of his jaw, and when he spoke his voice was filled with regret. "I blame myself. Matters should never have gone this far."

"What am I supposed to do? Forget I ever met you? When I bump into you on the street, do you want me to turn and walk the other way?"

"No . . ."

"I've never been the type of person who can turn my feelings on and off at will. Tell me what it is you want from me. Just tell me and I promise I'll walk out that door and it'll be as though we'd never met."

For a long time he didn't answer her.

"I'm waiting," she told him. "I'm not a difficult person to talk to, Roberto. At least others don't seem to have a problem. Tell me," she said again, more emphatically this time, "what is it you want."

His hands clenched into fists. "I want you to leave New York," he said, his voice strained. "You don't belong here. You and all this nonsense about teaching these kids to wish for the impossible. Try filling Modesto's head with that garbage now, why don't you? He's fighting for his life. We're light-years away from anything more than survival. You're beating your head against a stone wall, only you haven't learned that yet. Personally I don't want to be the one who's left to pick up the pieces when you do."

His words ripped open her heart, and just then she found it impossible to reply.

"There'll be someone else for you soon enough," he continued.

"Someone else?" She couldn't believe he would suggest she was the type to leap from one relationship to the next in some crazy form of emotional hopscotch.

"Who you date is your own business. All I ask is that you leave me out of it."

It, she reasoned, meant her life. He wanted nothing more to do with her.

Had she possessed a sliver of pride, Brynn would have turned and walked out. Instead she forced herself to stay, even when she knew that it meant more pain.

Her emotions battled with each other. She wanted

to strike back at him, hurt him the same way he'd hurt her. And in the next millisecond she longed to throw herself in his arms and beg him to change his mind.

In the end she did neither. From some reserve of strength she knew nothing about, she scrounged up a genuine, heartfelt smile. "You're right," she told him, "there will be someone else." In time. Then, because she couldn't make herself leave without touching him, Brynn gently placed her hand against his cheek.

A muscle leapt in his face as he steeled himself against her.

"Good-bye, Roberto. God speed."

She dropped her hand and was about to turn away when he reached out and grabbed hold of her shoulder and whirled her around. Crushed against him as she was, Brynn buried her face in his chest and clung. His kiss was hard and urgent, and she knew the moment he released her that he regretted ever having touched her.

"Good-bye, Brynn Cassidy. Have a good life."

She nearly sobbed aloud, but she managed to hold the emotion inside. "You too, Roberto Alcantara."

"How can you stand there and do nothing?" Goodness demanded of Shirley. "Roberto should have his head examined."

"Personally, I agree, but unfortunately he has a free will to decide whatever he wants."

"Free will? I'm telling you right now that's the

crux of the problem with humans. They can do anything they want, and they've let it go to their heads."

"That's the whole tamale in a nutshell," Shirley concurred, then scratched her head, wondering why that sounded wrong.

"I have half a mind to shake up this city."

Shirley wished Mercy were with her. She'd seen Goodness in this mood before, and it was downright frightening. The last time had been in Bremerton, Washington, when Goodness had gotten her hand on an aircraft carrier. The naval command was still trying to figure that one out.

"Goodness, are you thinking what I think you're thinking?"

"Someone needs to shake up this town."

"Personally," Shirley said, trying to be as diplomatic as possible, "I wouldn't advise you to mess with New York."

Goodness appeared unconvinced. "Texas frightens the wings off me, but I can handle New York."

"I still don't think this is a good idea."

"You don't even know what I'm going to do."

Shirley didn't want to know. Oh my, where was Mercy when she really needed her? When Goodness was in this frame of mind, she was more than Shirley could handle alone.

Shirley glanced around her, searching for help.

"Staten Island."

"No," Shirley cried in a panic, leaping in front of her friend, "not the Statue of Liberty!"

Goodness pretended not to notice her, which frightened Shirley all the more. "Let me see," Goodness mumbled, "what could I do to jar a few folks into realizing the error of their ways?"

"Don't you think we should talk this out first?" Shirley asked hopefully. "I mean, just because matters are going poorly with my assignment, there's no reason to take it out on the entire city. There're plenty of good things happening, too."

Goodness hesitated, and hope surged through Shirley that she might be able to reason her friend out of pulling some disastrous stunt.

"I'm sure everything must be going well with Hannah and Joshua." As soon as she spoke, Shirley recognized the error of her ways.

"As a matter of fact, they're not going well at all."

"Oh, I'm sorry to hear that."

"Hannah and Carl have set their wedding date for June sixteenth."

"But I thought . . . didn't you say that Hannah had fallen in love with Joshua Shadduck?"

"She has, and he's head over heels crazy about her."

Shirley assumed this would be good news. "I thought that was what you wanted."

"It is."

Shirley remained puzzled. "The last thing you told me was that Hannah had agreed to break off her engagement with Carl."

"That's what I thought, too," Goodness said with a disgruntled sigh, "only it didn't happen that way.

Instead her family pressured her into setting a wedding date, and before she knew what to do, it was all decided for her. She's scheduled to marry Carl Rabinsky in June."

"Oh, poor, poor Hannah."

"Hannah nothing," Goodness cried. "What about Joshua? He trusted her. She's supposed to be in love with him, remember? The fact is, I don't trust Hannah to do the right thing by Joshua."

"There's plenty of time yet," Shirley said in an effort to placate her friend. "Just because Hannah and Joshua's relationship has gone slightly off course doesn't mean you should do anything so drastic as disrupt the best-known New York landmark."

Goodness didn't agree or disagree with her. "I'm so frustrated with these humans, I could scream."

Shirley was about to suggest just that when to her great relief Mercy arrived, looking serene and happy.

"What's happenin'?" Mercy asked as though she hadn't a care in the world.

While Goodness went into a short explanation about Hannah and Joshua, Shirley studied the other angel. Then it came to her in a flash. Mercy had been up to something herself.

"Mercy, I'm shocked at you," Shirley cried. Oh my, what would Gabriel do if he learned about this?

"What?" Mercy asked, but wasn't able to hide a guilty look.

"Tell me where you've been!" Shirley asked, her eyes narrowing.

"Me?" Mercy had perfected that look of innocence. She might even be able to fool Gabriel.

Although she asked, Shirley knew. "Don't tell me, please don't tell me you've been riding the escalators again?"

Mercy shifted her gaze away. "Just for a little while."

"Mercy." Shirley was outraged. One of them had to show a little responsibility. Why, oh why did it have to be her?

"I can't believe you'd jeopardize our entire mission by doing anything so silly." She closed her eyes and shook her head.

"Actually, I'm in the mood for a little fun myself," Goodness said.

"Goodness, no," Shirley cried.

"You wanna have some fun?" Goodness asked Mercy.

"Oh, I have been, but after what happened this afternoon, I'm game for just about anything."

Shirley opened and closed her mouth. At this point her protests would fall upon deaf ears, and she knew it.

A twinkle sparked from Goodness's eyes as she smiled over at Shirley. "Are you coming along or not?"

"You're headed for trouble."

Goodness laughed. "So what else is new? There's only so much of this being on my best behavior that I can take."

Mercy released an exaggerated sigh. "Boy oh boy, do I identify with that. I can't remember the last time I slid down an escalator railing. By golly, it felt good."

"If you want the truth, I would have thought you'd have discovered the Holland Tunnel before now."

The corners of Mercy's mouth started to quiver.

"What did you do?" Shirley asked suspiciously.

Mercy gave an innocent shrug. "Remember that traffic jam all the newspapers reported not long ago?"

"You caused that?"

Mercy grasped her hands behind her back and shook her head. "Not me. I didn't have a thing to do with it."

Goodness's eyes lit up brighter than a Fourth of July sparkler. "If Mercy can mess around with the Holland Tunnel, then no one's going to mind if Lady Liberty takes a short stroll."

"Goodness, no."

"Oh, come on, Shirley, let your feathers dangle a little. Gabriel isn't going to hear about this."

"I don't think we should risk it," she said cautiously. "Really. Shouldn't we talk this out?"

Goodness shook her head. "Are you in or out, Shirley? It's time to separate the wheat from the chaff."

"Ah . . ."

Goodness and Mercy started to pull away. "I'm

in," Shirley said hastily. "I just hope I don't end up playing a harp for all eternity."

The talk filled the deli all day, until Hannah was sick of hearing about it. Some people, obviously tourists, claimed that the Statue of Liberty had done a 360-degree turn. It was by far the most ridiculous thing Hannah had ever heard.

Someone from the financial district claimed he'd watched the grand lady make the complete rotation. There were said to be news tapes of it as well.

Hannah remained skeptical. Years earlier, some magician claimed to have made the Statue of Liberty disappear. All this talk now didn't impress Hannah. Besides, she had other matters on her mind.

She needed to see Joshua and had been unable to reach him all afternoon. Making phone calls during business hours was difficult for her. Privacy was always at a premium in the kitchen, and she didn't dare risk someone listening in on her conversation.

When she had a free moment, a rare commodity this busy time of the year, she raced upstairs and phoned Joshua's office. Unfortunately he was out, but his secretary promised to give him the message as soon as he returned.

But Joshua couldn't return her call, and they both knew it, so Hannah was left to fret. When she did see him, she wasn't sure she could tell him about what happened.

December was the busiest month for the deli. Her father's meat and cheese trays had a reputation that was citywide. After the normal lunchtime rush, Hannah was left to deal with people who stopped by to order the trays.

She was busy with a customer when she saw Joshua. Although she was desperate to talk to him, this was the worst possible place.

"I think I'll change that from slices of cheddar cheese to Monterey Jack," Mrs. Synder, a longtime customer, was saying.

Hannah bit into her lower lip and watched as Joshua made his way to the counter where her father was making thick pastrami sandwiches.

"Monterey Jack," the woman repeated, louder this time.

"Oh, sorry," Hannah said, and quickly made the notation.

"Do you have Greek olives?"

"Yes. No," she said quickly, correcting herself.

"Do you or don't you?" came the impatient question.

"No, I'm sorry." Hannah forced herself to concentrate on completing the order form.

"How much will that be?"

Grateful that she was close to finishing, Hannah quickly tallied the figures.

"Really? I expected it to be much more than that," Mrs. Synder said, looking pleased.

Hannah immediately refigured the total. She was prime for making a mistake.

"Do you still serve that fantastic cheesecake?" the woman asked.

A male voice answered the question for her. "It's the best in New York."

Joshua.

Hannah's head snapped up. "Thank you," she said, her gaze connecting with his. "My mother makes it herself."

"Throw one in for me, then," Mrs. Synder said, grinning broadly.

"I'll be happy to." Hannah added the cheesecake to the tally. "Everything will be ready for you the afternoon of the twenty-second."

"Thank you for your help."

Hannah's gaze moved past Mrs. Synder to Joshua. His eyes were warm and tender as they met hers.

"Can I help you?" she asked, turning the page on her ordering pad. She could feel the color creep up her neck. Anyone who knew her well would realize that Joshua wasn't just any customer.

"Hello, beautiful."

"Joshua," she mumbled under her breath, "be careful, someone might hear you."

"That doesn't bother me. You are beautiful."

"Thank you. I think you are, too."

He laughed then, but not loudly enough to attract attention. "You phoned me?"

She nodded and chanced a look in her father's direction. She was grateful to see that he was otherwise occupied. Her mother was busy in the kitchen but could appear at any moment.

"You talked to Carl?"

She hesitated, then nodded. "But I wasn't able to break the engagement."

Even from her side of the counter, Hannah could sense Joshua's frustration.

"I couldn't tell him, not then," she hurried to explain. "When I arrived, I learned that he'd been fired from his job. He got in an argument with the headmaster. Carl was depressed and miserable. I couldn't add to his distress."

"What do you plan to do, marry him and make him feel better?"

"Of course not."

"That's what it sounds like, Hannah." His voice was gentle, but she knew he was disappointed.

"I'd never marry Carl. I promise you that. Please, you've got to believe me."

He said nothing, as if placing his faith in her were something he wasn't certain he should do. Hannah fought to keep from blurting how much she loved him.

"Young man, is my daughter helping you?"

It was her father. Hannah tensed, and her eyes pleaded with Joshua's not to reveal their secret. It would only be for a while longer, she promised him silently.

He pulled his gaze away from her. "She's been very helpful," he answered.

"Are you ordering a meat tray?"

"I thought I might give it a try." He reached for a brochure and began to leaf through it. "You're

Mr. Morganstern, aren't you?" he said just when it seemed her father was about to turn away. Hannah didn't understand why Joshua didn't let him leave. Certainly he felt as awkward about all this as she did.

"Yes." Her father's warm smile came through on the lone word.

"Joshua Shadduck," Joshua said, extending his hand across the counter.

Her father hesitated before peeling off the protective plastic glove from his fingers and exchanging handshakes.

"This is my daughter, Hannah."

"Actually, I've met Hannah before," Joshua said, his gaze resting on her.

Hannah tensed, afraid Joshua had completely lost his patience with her and was about to reveal the truth.

"She's delivered lunches to my office a number of times. Hannah's a wonderful young woman."

"Thank you. Naturally her mother and I share your opinion." Her father placed his arm affectionately around her shoulder. "Where's your office?"

Joshua told him.

"So you're an attorney."

Hannah noticed that her father's voice had gone a shade cooler and wondered if Joshua had sensed the difference himself.

"I was recently made a partner in the firm," Joshua explained proudly.

"Congratulations."

"I'm rather pleased myself." Joshua's gaze returned to Hannah.

It must have been the warm way in which he regarded her that prompted her father to continue the conversation. Generally he didn't spend a lot of time chatting with customers.

"We have reason to celebrate as well," he said, gently squeezing Hannah's shoulder. "Our daughter was recently engaged."

Joshua's smile dimmed somewhat. "Then congratulations are in order."

"Thank you," she said without emotion.

"My wife and I feel truly blessed to have our daughter. She's our greatest joy."

"Dad, please, I'm sure Mr. Shadduck doesn't want to hear all this."

"Nonsense. You do my heart proud. The world is a better place because of you."

Hannah was embarrassed, and she was certain Joshua found all this amusing.

"She's a lovely girl," Joshua told her father.

"She'll make a beautiful bride, don't you agree?"

"Oh yes," Joshua was quick to concur.

"I'm sure my wife and I will be sending out wedding invitations to a select few of our most valued customers. Now that the date's been set we can start making up the guest list."

Joshua said nothing, but his eyes narrowed fractionally.

"Daddy, I don't think—"

"The wedding date for your daughter has been set?" Joshua interrupted.

"Yes, we decided that only last night, isn't that right, sweetheart?"

Hannah nodded miserably.

"June sixteenth," her father informed him.

Joshua's gaze didn't leave hers. "Congratulations, Hannah," he said. "I'm sure you and your young man will be very happy." Having said that, he turned and walked out the door.

Chapter Fifteen

Trey didn't dislike New York. If anything, he was pleasantly surprised. He'd
expected it to be the concrete jungle he'd
read about, with treeless, crime-ridden
streets. He was confident there was plenty
of crime, but he hadn't seen any. And even
in the heart of Manhattan he'd noticed an
abundance of trees.

If he had any complaints, it was the
noise. He wondered how a man was supposed to sleep through all that racket. The
traffic outside his hotel never ceased—
horns honking, brakes screeching. And he
was bombarded by an array of sounds he
could never hope to identify; he heard
them all, even twenty stories up in his
hotel room.

The city had its own clamor, nothing
like the sounds in the country: the cry of
a lone wolf, the hoot of an owl as it flew

with the moonlight bouncing off its wing . . . Trey imagined that given the opportunity, he'd become accustomed to city noises. But there was a snow-ball's chance in hell of his ever living in New York City. No, he was a country boy, and like John Denver, he thanked God for that. Too much more of life here and he'd have men with nets chasing him through Central Park.

An early riser by nature, Trey was up and out the door just after dawn, heading for the hole-in-the-wall doughnut shop across the street from the hotel. The hotel served a decent cup of coffee, but there was no way he was going to pay five bucks for a two-bit cup of coffee. The doughnut shop was more to his liking, although he couldn't say that anyone had been all that friendly. He'd been coming in for coffee and a doughnut every morning since he'd arrived, and no one had said much of anything to him.

The same people were there every morning, too. Some businessman who drank his coffee and shared his company with the financial section of the newspaper. A lady who came in wearing tennis shoes and walked out in high heels.

Trey sat at the counter, sipping his coffee and watching the short-order cook, a rotund fellow with a prickly disposition, fry an order of hash browns. A waitress who looked to be in her forties bustled around refilling coffee.

Actually, Trey realized, he wasn't in the mood for

company this morning. He had some heavy-duty thinking to do.

Twice he'd asked Jenny to leave New York and come back to Montana with him. Twice she'd told him no. The time had come for him to play his trump card, give her some incentive to return to Custer.

He planned to ask her to be his wife.

Generally when a man proposed to a woman he was fairly confident of her response. Trey figured his chances with Jenny were less than fifty-fifty. Although he'd worked hard to build up his herd, he didn't have a whole lot in the way of material wealth to offer her. A few hundred head of cattle, a rundown house that badly needed a woman's touch. And a heart so full of love that he nearly burst wide open every time he thought of Jenny and himself raising a family together.

Trey was a realist, and he was well aware that he couldn't compete with the bright lights of Broadway. He didn't have any diamond ring to offer her, either. Not yet.

The fact was, he hadn't thought about asking Jenny to marry him until after they'd kissed that first time. He'd always dreamed it would be like that with them, but the reality had knocked him for a loop. Jenny's kisses gave him hope that she might harbor some tenderness for him.

Never having proposed to a woman before, Trey had no idea how to go about it. Did a modern-day man get down on one knee? Should he remove his hat and place it over his heart? None of those things sounded right to him. But since he was asking Jenny the most important question of his life, he didn't figure he should do it without showing some semblance of respect.

On impulse, Trey slipped off the stool and looked around the doughnut shop. As usual, the place held the same five or six people who frequented it every morning.

"Can I have your attention, please," he said in a loud voice.

The businessman lowered the newspaper. The cook turned around, the spatula raised in one hand.

"My name's Trey LaRue," he said. "I've been having coffee here every morning since I arrived in this city, and it seems time I introduced myself. I take it you folks all know each other."

The five other customers stared back blankly.

"You don't know each other?"

"No." It was the woman with one high heel and one tennis shoe.

"Well then, don't you think it's time you introduced yourselves to one another? I'm Trey, and I'm visiting from Montana."

"Hello, Trey," the waitress responded. "I'm Trixie."

"I'm Bob, and I'm in advertising."

"I'm Mary Lou, and I'm an assistant editor at a publishing house." She waved one shoe in greeting.

The others went around the compact space and

introduced themselves and told what they did for a living. Trey acknowledged each one with a brisk nod.

"What brings you to New York?" The question came from the cook, whose name was Steve.

"I came to ask a special woman to be my wife."

"Has she agreed?" This came from his editor friend.

"Not yet." He splayed his fingers through his hair, feeling less confident about his decision. "The fact is, I haven't asked her yet. I'm not exactly sure how to go about it."

"Just come right out and ask her," Bob advised.

"But wine and dine her," was Trixie's advice.

"Yeah," Bob teased, "get her good and soused first."

Mary Lou shook her head slowly. "Don't you listen to any of that. You tell that young woman what's in your heart. That's all you need to do, and if she feels as strongly about you as you do about her, nothing else will be necessary."

"I shouldn't take her to a fancy dinner, then?" Trey asked. His newfound friends confused him more than they helped.

"Dinner and champagne won't hurt," Trixie assured him, "but Mary Lou's right. Just tell this special lady what's in your heart and go from there."

That sounded like a lot less trouble than getting down on one knee, Trey decided.

"You might try singing to her."

Everyone turned to stare at Steve, Trey included.

As far as Trey was concerned, there were certain things a man didn't do, and break into song was one of them. One of Jenny's male friends might consider that, but not him.

"Women like romance, and there ain't nothing more romantic than to sing. You don't even have to have that great a voice," Steve added, a cigarette hanging from the side of his mouth.

"I won't be doing any singing," Trey said emphatically.

"You love her, don't you?" Steve smashed the cigarette into an ashtray.

"Yeah."

"Then romance her."

"He's right about that," the assistant editor acknowledged. "There isn't a woman alive who doesn't want to be courted by the man she loves."

Singing was out of the question, but there were other ways to prove he was as tenderhearted as the men she'd dated in the big city. "What about flowers and chocolates?"

Only the day before, Trey had walked into one of those fancy sweet shops by accident. He'd been blown away at the prices. Why, a man could feed a horse for a month on what they wanted for a box of chocolates! French ones.

Mary Lou shook her head. "Be more imaginative than that."

"Jenny loves those fat pretzel vendors sell on the street corners here," he said, thinking out loud.

"You can't woo a woman with pretzels," the guy

in advertising insisted. He folded the newspaper and tucked it under his arm. "I've got to get to the office. You'll let us know what happens, won't you?"

"Sure thing," Trey promised. He checked his watch. It was early yet. Jenny would still be sleeping, but he'd told her he'd be by to pick her up this morning. She wanted to take him up to the top of the Empire State Building.

Trey left some change on the counter. "I appreciate the advice," he told his newfound friends.

"Good luck," Trixie said with a smile.

"If he's getting married, he'll need it," the short-order cook teased, then laughed when Trixie swatted him across the backside with a dishrag.

An hour later Trey stood outside Jenny's apartment complex. He paced the sidewalk in front of her building, rehearsing in his mind what he wanted to say. It took another ten minutes before he'd gathered up enough gumption to go inside.

He'd no sooner knocked than the door flew open and there was Jenny, standing on the other side. When she saw him, her face lit up with a smile as bright as a July sun. As long as he lived, he'd never grow weary of seeing Jenny smile.

"Mornin'," he greeted her, touching the edge of his hat in a genteel salute.

"Oh, Trey, you'll never guess what."

Before he could prepare himself, she leapt into his arms. Whatever it was that brought Jenny this close must be good, he thought.

"Irene phoned this morning!"

"Irene's your agent, right?"

"Right." Then, not giving him an opportunity to ask anything more, she blurted out, "John Peterman phoned and asked if she had an audio of me."

Trey didn't know who this John Peterman was, but he was fairly certain he wasn't going to like the other man.

As soon as she could, Hannah left the deli to find Joshua. If she explained how she'd been pressured into setting a wedding date, surely he'd understand. Surely he'd be sympathetic and willing to listen to reason.

The angry, pained look in his eyes haunted her, especially knowing that she was responsible for putting it there. Joshua didn't deserve to be treated as if she were ashamed of loving him. Yet she could find no fair way out of this dilemma.

Her first stop was at Joshua's office. When he wasn't there, she didn't know what to do. Depressed and miserable, she started walking, barely aware of her destination. She was unconscious of the street sounds, the people who moved crisply past her; all she could think to do was walk.

She appreciated Joshua's feelings. If the situation were reversed, she'd feel the same way. Joshua was an honorable man, and it went against his grain to be involved with a woman engaged to another man. Nor was he comfortable meeting her without her parents' knowledge.

Hannah didn't like that aspect of their relationship, either, but for now it couldn't be helped. She didn't want to break the engagement with Carl until this matter with the school had been cleared up.

Suddenly aware of her surroundings, Hannah realized she was close to her grandmother's apartment.

Sylvia's tired eyes brightened when she opened the door. "Hannah, my dear, this is a pleasant surprise!"

Hannah kissed her grandmother's cheek.

"I just brewed myself a pot of tea. Join me, please."

"I'd love some tea." Hannah followed her grandmother into the kitchen, then carried the tray with two dainty china cups into the living room.

Hannah loved this room, with its personal touches. An end table with a small clock that had been in the family for close to a hundred years. Antique photographs. Hand-crocheted doilies. An array of family photos lining the fireplace mantel.

Hannah's favorite picture was one of her grandfather taken when he was a young man recently emigrated to America. Another favorite was of her father as a youngster, less than ten years of age.

"Sit," Sylvia instructed after settling herself in the oak rocker she loved. She took a sip of tea, then held the delicate china cup with both hands. "Actually, I wondered when you'd come. I've been waiting, you know."

"Waiting for me?" Hannah turned from the familiar photographs and met her grandmother's keen eyes.

"I know you far too well not to recognize when something is bothering you."

Hannah lowered her gaze. She didn't bother to deny that she was troubled. Nor was she surprised that her grandmother had guessed. She suspected Sylvia had known her true feelings from the moment she'd introduced Carl.

"You look tired, Hannah."

She was unbelievably so. But the bone weariness that drained her energy had little to do with the long hours she worked at the deli or the number of customers she served. It was a fatigue of the heart, of pretending to love Carl, of giving the impression that she was happy.

"You don't need to tell me anything you don't feel comfortable sharing." Her grandmother's tone was loving and tender. "Just sit with me a spell and soak in the silence. I don't know how a person can sort everything out unless they can hear themselves think."

Sylvia swayed gently in the oak rocker and sipped her tea. A soft creaking noise eked up from the hardwood floor beneath the braided rug.

"It's about Carl and me," Hannah said after a long while. She stood and walked over to the fireplace, where a gentle flame flickered over the logs. After running her hand against the top of the mantel, she turned and faced her grandmother.

"I guessed all this involved Carl."

Hannah smiled to herself, appreciating Sylvia's insight. She sat on the braided rug next to her grandmother. Sylvia's hand stroked the top of Hannah's head.

"I've been praying for you for a good many years, Hannah. Long before you were born, I asked God if He would see fit to give my son a child, and He gave us you."

It was a story Hannah had heard often. Her childless parents had longed desperately for a baby. The doctors had told them it would take a miracle.

Like Hannah in the story of Samuel, a familiar one in the Bible, her mother and family had prayed diligently for a child. Samuel's mother, like her own, had wept and pleaded with God in the temple with such anguish that Eli, the priest, had assumed she was drunk. When she spoke of her longing for a son, Eli had assured her that God had heard her prayer and that in a year's time she would have a son.

After nearly twenty years of marriage, Ruth had conceived, and the Morganstern family had rejoiced. When David learned his wife was pregnant, he'd been the one to decide on his daughter's name. Hannah had been named after Elkanah's wife, whose faith had been richly rewarded.

All her life Hannah had been loved and cherished. That was what made disappointing her family so difficult.

"Through the years, I have continued to pray for you," Sylvia went on. "As you entered your teen years, I added your husband to my list."

"My husband?"

"The man you would marry. It seemed to me that

God in his almighty wisdom would choose an extraordinary man for you. A man of character, a man of wisdom and discernment. A man who would love you with all his heart."

Her grandmother's gentle words caused Hannah's throat to thicken with tears. "I don't love Carl," she whispered brokenly.

Sylvia's hand didn't pause as she continued to stroke Hannah's crown. "I realized that almost immediately. You've met someone else, haven't you?"

"Yes, and Grandma, he's a good man, just the way you say. I can't tell you how fortunate I feel to even know him. I love him so much that it frightens me. . . . I'm so afraid I'm going to lose him."

"He loves you?"

Hannah nodded. The knowledge should have filled her with an incredible sense of wonder that a man as wonderful as Joshua would care for her.

"Then why would you lose him?" her grandmother questioned.

"Because of Carl."

It was as if Sylvia had forgotten Hannah were engaged to the other man. "Ah yes, Carl."

"Carl's a good man," Hannah whispered. She didn't want to hurt him, either.

"Carl's a fine young man, but he's not the one for you."

"Joshua is." There was no doubt in Hannah's mind about that.

"Joshua," Sylvia repeated slowly, as if testing the name on her tongue. She shook her head once and said decisively, "If you love him the way you claim, then you have nothing to fear."

"But everyone expects me to marry Carl. You saw what happened, how we were pressured into setting a date for the wedding."

Her grandmother said nothing, which increased Hannah's guilt.

"I wanted to break the engagement," Hannah said all at once, running the words together. She didn't think it was fair to tell her grandmother that Carl had recently lost his job; the fewer who knew, the better. The best way to handle it was to be diplomatic, she decided.

"This is a bad time for Carl," she offered. "He's under a lot of pressure right now. I wanted to tell him about meeting Joshua. I've tried—honest, I have—but something always happens. For a long time I figured that it was too late for Joshua and me. I even tried not to see him again."

"That wouldn't have worked."

Hannah glanced up at her grandmother, wondering at the strength and conviction in the older woman's words.

"You and Joshua were meant to be together," Sylvia elaborated.

Hannah rested her head against her grandmother's knee. "Joshua came into the deli this afternoon."

"David knows him?"

"He's a frequent customer."

"Then he knows good food when he tastes it."

Hannah smiled.

"Tell me what happened," Sylvia encouraged.

"Joshua wanted to talk to me, but it was impossible there. I'm sure he was about to suggest that we meet elsewhere—we've done it before—but he didn't get the chance.

"Somehow Joshua and Dad got involved in a conversation, and then Dad told him that Carl and I had set the wedding date. He actually invited Joshua to the wedding."

Her grandmother sighed heavily. "I don't imagine Joshua was pleased."

"He looked so hurt." That was the only way she could think to describe the anguish she'd witnessed in Joshua's eyes. "He congratulated me, and before I had a chance to explain, he left the deli. I got away as soon as I could and hurried to his office, but he wasn't there and his secretary couldn't tell me when he'd be back. I've got to talk to him." She squeezed her eyes shut, berating herself silently.

"What would you have said if he had been at his office?" her grandmother questioned.

"I longed to explain how Carl and I had been coerced into picking a date for the wedding."

"Do you think that was what he wanted to hear?"

"No," Hannah murmured miserably. "He wants to hear that I've told Carl about us. He needs to know that I've broken off the engagement, and that my family's been told that I won't be marrying Carl."

"My guess is that he'd be willing to speak to your parents with you."

Hannah dreaded telling her parents most. She'd

never considered having Joshua stand with her and immediately knew that he would want to be there. He'd never ask her to confront her family alone.

With an energy that had escaped her earlier, she leapt to her feet. "I've got to talk to him."

"Joshua?" her grandmother asked.

"No, Carl. I can't worry about his feelings any longer. He doesn't need me to hold his hand."

"Good girl." Her grandmother's face beamed with pride.

"Joshua is the man I love, he deserves my loyalty. As soon as I've talked to Carl, I'll speak to Joshua."

Sylvia looked well pleased. "That, my dear, sounds like a plan."

The anger inside Roberto simmered just below the exploding point. His patience was gone, his temper unreasonable, his mood black. He'd probably offended every customer he'd dealt with in the last couple of days. Matters would improve drastically, he realized, if he could stop thinking about Brynn. But that seemed impossible.

He wished to hell she'd leave. Pack her bags, hand in her resignation, and go back where she belonged. Because she sure as hell didn't fit in this neighborhood. A delicate, beautiful rosebud among thistles.

The only way to convince her he wanted nothing more to do with her was to shove her out of his life. His chest ached with a crippling tightness for all that he'd lost. He hadn't meant to do it then and there, but she'd forced his actions, coming to him the way she had.

Modesto's injuries had convinced him of the terrible risk Brynn was taking working in this neighborhood. She was an easy target. Too easy. She refused to listen to reason and defied him at every turn. Fine. She could do as she damn well pleased, but he would have no part of it. Or her.

If she wanted to sacrifice herself over a bunch of screwy, idealistic goals, so be it. But he wasn't standing by idly to watch her fall on her face. Nor would he be there to pick up the pieces.

For her own good, she had to leave this neighborhood, and she wouldn't as long as he encouraged her to remain. That was exactly what their relationship was doing.

It was over, and nothing would change his mind. Not this time. Not with Modesto in the hospital, a bullet hole in his chest, and his brother screaming with nightmares.

Roberto heard a movement behind him and glanced over his shoulder to find Emilio standing just inside the garage.

"You gonna bite my head off?" Emilio asked.

"That depends on what you want."

"Nothing."

"Then what are you doing here?" Roberto threw a wrench toward the work bench. It landed with a discordant clanking sound. He never abused his tools, but then there was a first time for everything.

A first time to fall in love. A first time to turn his back and run from what he wanted most.

"I'm bored," Emilio confessed. "I thought it'd be fun to stay home."

"Then go back to school," Roberto said without emotion. He hadn't changed his mind about education, but he was willing to agree that Brynn might have a point. For a long time he'd thought Emilio would work with him at the garage. He could teach his brother, and the two of them could be partners. But Emilio didn't have the knack for working on cars. He liked people, liked being around them.

"I don't want to go to school," his brother confessed, walking all the way into the garage. He planted the tips of his fingers in his jeans pockets. This was the stance he chose when he had something to hide. His brother tended to be transparent about such things, and frankly, Roberto was grateful.

Unwilling to reveal he knew something was amiss, Roberto continued to work on the car, removing the carburetor from an engine. "I thought you liked your classes."

Emilio shrugged. "The best are the ones Miss Cassidy teaches. She makes learning fun, but she isn't an easy teacher. Sometimes after school me and the others talk about her."

Roberto stiffened, then asked nonchalantly, "What do you have to say?" Emilio and the other boys in the class weren't blind. Brynn was as beautiful as she was naive.

"She talks about things that make a person think, about war and prejudice, and stuff like that. Just about every day she gives us a writing assignment and then has us read what we wrote and talk about it."

"Like what?"

Emilio's eyes brightened as he spoke. "We're reading this book about Anne Frank. She was this Jewish girl, who—"

"I know who Anne Frank is."

"You do?" This appeared to impress Emilio. "Well, Miss Cassidy asked us to pretend we were the ones in hiding. To share this compact space with another family, to live in constant fear of discovery."

"And?"

"And we did, and then she had some of us read what we'd written, and I was surprised, you know, by how she tied it in to what's going on in our world today. Social issues and that sort of thing. The guys and me sometimes talk about the same things we did in class. I don't do that with any of my other subjects."

"She's a good teacher, then."

"The best I've ever had."

That did and didn't surprise Roberto. He knew Brynn was popular with the kids, but that didn't say much about her ability to teach a class.

"Then go back," Roberto said as though it should be an easy decision. He never did understand Emilio's sudden desire to quit. The teenager certainly wasn't any help here at the garage, mooning around, looking miserable. Everything he'd asked Emilio to do thus far, with the exception of errands, he'd had to do over.

"I can't."

His brother's low, trembling voice caused Roberto to look up. "Why can't you?"

Emilio shrugged.

"If you like school, then go."

"I'm not going back," Emilio insisted with a ring of rebellion.

Roberto frowned and gave Emilio his full attention. Something was very wrong. "First you said you can't go back, and now you're telling me you won't? Which is it?"

Emilio looked decidedly uncomfortable. "Both."

Leaning against the work bench, Roberto crossed his arms. "You'd better explain that."

Emilio took a short stroll around the garage. "I can't go back because . . ." He hesitated.

"Because why?" Roberto pressed.

Emilio whirled around, his eyes flashing with open defiance. "Because I'm embarrassed, that's why."

"Embarrassed about what?" He hadn't a clue what his brother could possibly have done that would cause this reaction.

"I made a fool of myself in front of Miss Cassidy." He admitted this between clenched teeth, as if to say that was all he was willing to admit.

Roberto snickered and shook his head. Emilio wasn't the only one to play the fool when it came to dealing with the beautiful redhead. All at once it dawned on him that Emilio might have fallen in love with her, too.

His brother seemed to read Roberto's thoughts. "It's not what you think," he snapped. "She's your woman, not mine."

Roberto returned to the carburetor rather than look his brother in the eye. "She's not mine, either," he said forcefully, "and that's the way I want it. The less you say about it the better. Understand?"

Emilio didn't say anything, but Roberto felt his brother's scrutiny. He regretted having said this much, but Emilio would have figured it out sooner or later.

"Now get your butt over to school."

Emilio didn't budge. "Why is it so hellfire important for me to get an education? I thought you said it was a waste of time. What changed your mind?"

The last thing Roberto wanted was to be dragged into an argument over the pros and cons of education. "You changed my mind. I gained nothing in high school, least of all a decent education. But it's different for you. Now don't make me embarrass you further by dragging you back."

Emilio hesitated, as though he didn't know what to do. "You'd do it, too."

Roberto grinned. "Don't doubt it. Now get your sorry ass over there."

"I'm going to tell Miss Cassidy you forced me to come."

"Fine, tell her." He'd rather Emilio didn't mention

his name, but he wouldn't give his brother something to hold over him, either. Swallowing his pride was a small gift he could give the two people he loved most in this world. His brother would have his education, and Brynn would have the pleasure of knowing that he'd changed his mind about school.

The decision made, Emilio disappeared.

Roberto heard the door slam and paused long enough to look out the window to see Emilio racing down the street, kicking up his heels in his eagerness to get back to school.

It didn't seem an hour had passed before Emilio was back. He looked more like his usual self than he had over the last couple of days, loitering around the shop, disgruntled and miserable.

"I thought you went back to school," Roberto said with a scowl.

"I did go back. School's over."

Roberto glanced at the clock above the door. Emilio was right.

"A couple of the guys are waiting for me. We're going to visit Modesto. He can have company now, and we thought we'd see if we could find any good-looking nurses."

"Then what are you doing here?"

"I got a message for you from Miss Cassidy."

Roberto steeled himself. He didn't want to play any games, notes back and forth, that sort of thing. It was over, and the sooner she accepted it, the better.

"I don't want it," he said forcefully.

"It?"

"The note or whatever it is she gave you."

"She didn't give me anything. She just wanted me to tell you something."

"Fine," he said stiffly, "tell me."

"She said thank you."

"For what?"

Emilio's look told him the answer to that should have been obvious. "For me coming back to school. I told her you were the one who insisted I did, and she got all teary eyed and asked me to tell you she appreciated that."

The pain in Roberto's chest tightened. "You've told me, now get out of here. I've got work to do."

Chapter Sixteen

Jenny didn't know what to think about Trey. He hadn't been himself for nearly two days. She'd spent as much time with him as her schedule would allow, but that was only an hour or two each day. Perhaps he was disappointed in her.

She'd taken him to all the tourist spots. Only recently they'd been up to the top of the Empire State Building and to the United Nations building.

By nature Trey was a man of few words, but he'd been less communicative than usual the last couple of days. That worried her.

"Are there any other sights you want to see?" Jenny asked as they strolled lazily through Central Park, feeding the birds.

"I can't say that there are," Trey said,

tossing birdseed to a flock of people-friendly pigeons. Others flew over instantly from a variety of directions, looking for a handout. Their wings made a ruffling sound that carried with the wind.

Jenny tossed a fistful of seeds and laughed at the way the silver birds battled over the goodies.

"I was thinking maybe we could go to dinner this evening," Trey said unexpectedly.

"Dinner," Jenny repeated. She'd promised Michelle they would have their own small Christmas that evening, since her friend would soon be heading home for the holidays. Jenny's schedule at the restaurant had changed a number of times with other girls needing time away. She'd worked all the extra hours she could. The only night she'd been free in nearly two weeks had been the evening of the Christmas potluck. Surely Michelle would understand.

"I'll need to check with Michelle first." She didn't tell Trey the reason, because another, more intrusive thought immediately came to mind.

Trey was going back to Montana.

Dinner would be his way of telling her good-bye. An empty feeling, one that chilled her heart, came so swiftly it felt as if someone had slapped her viciously across the back.

"When's your flight?" she asked point-blank.

Trey didn't answer her right away, and she thought he might not have heard her. "Two days' time."

So she was right.

"I can't stay any longer, Jenny. I'd like to, but

I've got a herd of cattle to worry about, and I can't leave Pete alone much longer."

"I understand." If anyone could appreciate his need to return, it was she. After all, she was a rancher's daughter. That Trey had stayed in New York this long was something of a surprise. Just when she was growing accustomed to having him with her. Just when her heart felt whole again. He was going to leave her. "Maybe you'll be able to visit again soon," she said, fighting to disguise the ache in her heart. Next time. The only way she could deal with his leaving was to look into the future and the promise of his return.

The birdseed gone, Jenny experienced the need to sit down. She walked over and sank onto a park bench.

Trey joined her. "When will you be able to talk to Michelle?"

For a moment Jenny didn't know what he was talking about. "Soon," she said, and then remembered Trey had asked her to dinner. A fond farewell dinner. A "gee, but it's been swell" good-bye dinner.

Her stomach clenched, then tied itself into a knot that tightened with each breath. As the ache intensified, Jenny realized how much she wanted Trey to stay. How much she needed him in her life.

Sitting on the edge of the park bench, her hands buried deep in her coat pockets, Jenny tried to compose herself, fearing she'd embarrass them both by breaking into tears.

"Jenny—"

"Michelle's at the apartment now. We can go ask her," she suggested cheerfully. That she could fool Trey into thinking nothing was amiss was a testament to how truly talented an actress she was.

"Michelle's there now?"

Jenny checked her watch. "If not, she will be any minute. Why don't we go back to the apartment? It's about lunchtime anyway. I can fix you a sandwich. I make an excellent peanut butter and jelly."

He didn't answer her right away. "If that's what you want."

"Sure," she said, rushing to her feet as though tickled pink to return to her small, cramped apartment and slap together two pieces of bread.

It didn't escape Jenny's notice that Trey didn't speak a single word on the way home. Perhaps it was the subway, which she knew confused him; it had her in the beginning, too, but now she was a pro when it came to finding her way around the city. Of course she didn't take it at night, and never when she was alone.

She unlocked the apartment door and stepped inside.

"It doesn't look like Michelle's back," Trey murmured.

"She'll be here any time," Jenny said confidently. Now that she was home, in familiar surroundings, she didn't know how much longer she'd be able to keep up the pretense. The tightening, empty feeling in the pit of her stomach had spread to her heart and her throat. Tears threatened to spill down her cheeks.

"Make yourself comfortable and I'll get you a sandwich," she said, eager for an excuse to leave him. She needed this time to compose herself, to figure out how she was going to see him off and do it with a smile. No one was that good an actress.

"I'm not hungry."

"You will be soon enough," she said, hoping she sounded enthusiastic. "If you don't want it, I'll eat it later." She walked into the kitchen and braced her hands against the kitchen sink and closed her eyes. Inhaling deep breaths didn't seem to help.

Trey was going back to Montana, where he belonged—where she belonged, too. Only she was too proud to admit it, too stubborn to throw in the towel. For three years she'd given all that she had, looking for a chance to prove herself. All that effort, all her talent, had gotten her was a job as a singing waitress in a two-star restaurant.

Leaning forward, she propped her elbows on the kitchen counter and pushed the hair away from her forehead. She tried taking in short breaths, followed by deep ones. Nothing seemed to help.

Damn it all, she was going to cry. Trey would see, and then he'd want to know what was wrong. She didn't know what she would tell him.

If Michelle came home, perhaps her friend could distract him until Jenny had collected herself.

She felt the first tears slip from the corners of her

eyes. She'd held them back for so long that it was as if a dam had burst inside her. The tears marked more than Trey's return home. They represented the frustration, the disappointment, of three hard years of her life. Three long, fruitless years.

"Jenny, is something wrong?" Trey stood directly behind her. She could feel the warmth of his body so close to her own.

"I'm fine," she answered in a strained voice. She straightened, wiped the telltale moisture from her face, and reached toward the bread box.

"You don't sound fine. Turn around." His hand fell gently on her shoulder.

She might have been able to pull it off if he hadn't been so tender with her. The moment he touched her, she knew she was lost. The sob was a painful tightening in her chest that worked its way up to her throat.

She turned in his arms and let his torso muffle her cry. Her shoulders shook as he wrapped her in his embrace.

"Jenny, my heaven, what is it?"

She didn't answer him; she couldn't.

His hand stroked her hair, and Jenny was confident he had no idea what to do with her. She feared her tears embarrassed him as much as they did her.

"Oh my," she said, breaking away from him. She smeared the traces of tears away from her cheeks and from some hidden reserve of strength offered him an apologetic smile. "I wonder what that was all about."

Trey didn't respond. Instead he tucked his finger beneath her chin and lowered his mouth to hers. They'd kissed before, and the hot sensation between them had shocked Jenny. He kissed her again and again, each kiss gaining in intensity and momentum until she was struggling for control.

"Jenny, sweet Jenny," he whispered, his voice husky and low. "I don't think you know what kissing you does to me."

"I do know, because you do the same thing to me." She ran her tongue along the underside of his jaw and felt his body tense against hers. She'd never experienced such a powerful sense of control over a man.

He cupped her face between his hands for another deep, breath-stealing kiss.

"Tell me why you were crying," he whispered.

Jenny closed her eyes. Her hands bit into the material of his shirt, her hold so tight that her fingers lost feeling. "I . . . I'm going to miss you, Trey."

He stiffened, and she wondered if she'd said something wrong. "You don't need to worry," she hurried to assure him. "I'm a big girl, really."

He led her into the living room and sat her down in the chair, then he started moving around as though he needed to sit himself but couldn't find an available seat.

"Trey?"

He held out his hand. "I've got something to ask you. I was going to wait until tonight at dinner, but now seems as good a time as any."

"Ask me what?"

He looked decidedly uncomfortable. "I'm not sure how to do this. I've never done it before, and hell"—he paused and dragged a deep breath through his lungs—"I damn well never plan to do it again."

"You've never done what?"

"Propose," he snapped, then seemed to realize what he'd said. He ceased his roaming and stood directly in front of her. "I love you, Jenny Lancaster. I've loved you from the time you were fifteen years old. . . ."

"Fifteen? But you never let on . . . you never told me."

He frowned. "If I'd said anything, your father would have had me arrested, as well he should have. I never wanted you to leave Montana, but you deserved your chance. You've had it, and now it's time to come home. With me, with the promise you'll be my wife." His eyes grew dark and serious as he got down on one knee in front of her. "Come home with me, Jenny. Marry me, and mother my children. I don't have a lot to offer you, except a heart that will always be yours."

Jenny was too stunned to respond. She pressed her hand over her mouth and battled down a fresh batch of emotion.

The front door opened and Trey stood up abruptly and, irritated, glanced over his shoulder.

"Hello, everyone," Michelle greeted as she whirled into the room like a prairie dust storm. She hesitated and looked from Trey and Jenny. "I'm not disrupting anything, am I?"

"Yes," Trey answered before Jenny could.

"Oh, sorry. Do you want me to discreetly disappear for a few moments?"

"That would be much appreciated." Again it was Trey who responded.

Michelle had just started to tiptoe from the room when the telephone rang. "I'll get it," she said, and then tossed Trey an apologetic look. "I've been waiting for a call all week."

Trey rubbed his hand along the back of his neck and gave her an impatient nod.

Michelle answered on the second ring, and her gaze swiveled automatically toward Jenny. She placed her hand over the mouthpiece. "It's for you."

"Me?" Jenny asked.

"It's Irene."

Jenny leapt off the sofa and hurried to the phone. "Irene," she said eagerly, unable to hide her delight. When her agent phoned it was generally with good news.

"Jenny." Irene sounded excited. "I just got off the phone with John Peterman. He wants you for the second lead in his new musical. This is it, kiddo. All your hard work has finally paid off. We couldn't ask for better money or better terms. You're on your way now."

Dumbstruck, Jenny listened while Irene relayed the details of her contract. When her agent had finished, Jenny replaced the receiver and turned to Michelle, who stood beside her expectantly.

"I got the second lead," she whispered, her voice revealing the extent of her shock. "John Peterman wants me."

Michelle let out a wild scream and hugged her enthusiastically. Then the two of them did a dance about the room, laughing, crying, their joy spilling over like champagne poured too fast from the bottle.

A good five minutes passed before Jenny remembered Trey, and then she couldn't find him.

"Where'd he go?" Jenny asked her roommate.

Michelle gave her a blank look. "I don't know. He must have left."

The minute Brynn walked into the school she knew something was very wrong. One of the secretaries sat at her desk, weeping silently. A handful of teachers stood in the corner of the office, talking in whispers. The tension in the room was thick enough to slice and butter.

Not knowing what was wrong, Brynn walked over to her cubicle and cleared out the space. As she suspected, there were a number of printed sheets detailing information about the winter break. The teachers' Christmas party was scheduled for that evening. Since her surname began with a C, she was responsible for supplying a main dish. Another paper detailed the period schedule for the last day.

Brynn slipped the papers into her bag. A white envelope fluttered from her space and landed on the floor. It was addressed to her personally, and she wondered who had put it there. On closer inspection, she realized the handwriting was familiar. It took a moment to recognize it was from Mike Glasser.

"Did you hear?" Doug Keast asked as he reached for his own papers.

"Hear about what?" Brynn had never been particularly fond of Doug. Not since the day he'd been so eager to have Emilio hauled off to the office. She had no problem with the school's policy regarding fighting, but she questioned the other teacher's attitude. It seemed Doug had welcomed the opportunity to see Emilio expelled.

"Mike Glasser."

"What about him?" she asked.

"He blew his brains out." Doug pointed his finger to his temple and pulled an imaginary trigger. "His mother found him late yesterday afternoon." Doug hesitated. "Say, isn't he one of the kids in your program?"

Mike, dead? A suicide? It was as if Doug had pulled the floor out from under her. The information came at her like a fist in the dark.

Brynn gasped and slumped against the wall. It demanded every ounce of strength she possessed to remain upright. Involuntarily she started to hyperventilate, and she reached out and grabbed hold of the back of a chair.

"Brynn?" Doug's arm came around her. "Here, sit down. Do you need something?"

"Water. Could you please get me a glass of water?" A shocking, total numbness shrouded her.

"Of course. Listen, I'm sorry." Doug steered her to a table and sat her down. "I guess I shouldn't have told you like that." His voice was full of apology.

Brynn was too numb to respond.

Dead. Mike, the young man she'd tried so hard to reach, was dead. There would be no more tomorrows. No dreams for Mike. No future.

The letter. Mike had written her a letter. A suicide note. No. No, please, please no. Had he written it to her as a desperate cry for help? Dear God, please no. She hadn't collected her messages in two days.

Her hands shook so badly that Brynn was barely able to retrieve the long white envelope from inside her bag. She ripped it open and pulled out a single sheet.

Miss Cassidy,

By the time you read this, I'll be dead. I'm not going to go into the reasons why I'm doing this because that wouldn't solve anything. For me death is the only solution. This is what I want. Life is simply too painful.

I imagine you're wondering why I'm writing you. There's someone I care about, and she's going to take this hard. I don't know anyone who can help Suzie through this, except maybe you.

Suzie's the best thing that ever happened to me, and I love her. She tried to help me, but she couldn't. No one could.

My dad killed himself when I was a kid. I used to get upset about it, but now I understand why he did it. Dying is easier than living.

Unable to continue because her eyes had blurred with tears, Brynn paused long enough to search for a tissue, then returned to Mike's letter.

You don't owe me any favors, but I know you like Suzie.

Talk to her for me, would you? Tell her I'm sorry. Tell her . . . Shit, you'll know what to say. It isn't her fault. It's no one's fault. Not Suzie's. Not yours. Not mine. It's better this way for everyone.

I know I don't have any right to lay this on you, but there's no one else I trust. If you would, I'd appreciate it if you said something to my mother, too. You're good with words and you'll know what to tell her.

Since this is the last thing I'll ever write, there's something I'd like to know. I wish I could have traded places with Anne Frank. She wanted to live, when all I could think about was dying. You're a good teacher, Miss Cassidy. You made me care.

Mike

Doug Keast returned with a paper cup filled with water. Brynn thanked him with a brisk nod as she folded the letter and placed it back inside the envelope.

"Are you sure you're all right?" he asked.

Brynn nodded. She wanted nothing more to do with Doug Keast and was grateful when the first bell rang.

"Brynn," her fellow teacher pressed, "do you want me to call someone? You don't look so good."

"I'll be fine." But she wouldn't be. It would be a long while before she would feel right again. Brynn couldn't keep from thinking that she should have known something was wrong. She should have been able to reach Mike. Should have realized the depth of his despair.

And Suzie. Poor Suzie. Brynn was certain the teenager had never told Mike she was pregnant. Suzie had loved him and tried to protect him. Mike had loved her enough to ask Brynn to help her through her grief. Brynn didn't know what she could possibly say that would comfort Suzie and Mike's mother.

By some miracle, she made it through the morning, teaching by rote. Not everyone had heard about Mike's death, but then only a handful of her morning students knew him.

At lunchtime, still numb, still in shock, Brynn returned to the office to ask about Suzie Chang. As she suspected, Suzie was absent. She wrote down Suzie's home address, tucked it inside her pocket, and returned to her classroom.

Her heart ached. Her body ached, and she wondered if she would emotionally survive this day. The burden of explaining and comforting seemed beyond her.

When it was time for her afternoon class, Brynn sat at her desk. One by one, her students paraded single file past her. Mike's desk in the center of the room sat empty. Brynn found she couldn't look at it without experiencing a tremendous sense of loss.

Everyone appeared to be watching her, waiting for her to say something. Brynn walked to the front of the room. The silence was deafening.

"By now I'm sure you've all heard about Mike," she said, and was shocked at how thin her voice had become. She struggled with her composure. "Talking about it might do us all some good. Perhaps you can help me understand why Mike would take his own life?"

"It's stupid," Pearl Washington said.

"But Mike wasn't stupid," Brynn insisted. "When I could get him to express his feelings, I found his essays to be full of insight." She realized as she spoke how dark his writing was, how bleakly he saw the world. Then and now. Guilt swamped her senses. She should have seen it coming, should have realized how much pain he was in.

"He should have told someone," Emilio suggested.

"Who?" Brynn asked. "Told them what?"

"We weren't exactly his friends," Yolanda reminded everyone sadly.

"He didn't want no friends," Denzil insisted.

"Okay, so he wasn't Mr. Personality, but he wasn't so bad, you know."

"Are you sorry he's dead?" Brynn asked.

A chorus of regrets chimed back, and Brynn knew that the class was suffering just as she was. Mike had asked her to talk to Suzie, to help Suzie. What he hadn't realized was that they were all going to need help dealing with his death.

"He never let on, you know?" someone complained.

"I don't think he knew how to share his pain," Brynn suggested.

Yolanda started to cry. "It makes me mad."

"What does?" Brynn questioned, struggling not to weep herself.

"That he didn't give any of us a chance to tell him good-bye. When Modesto was shot it was bad, but this is worse because I feel like there was something I should have done, something I should have said. Maybe if I'd been friendlier, it would have helped."

"I don't think any of us had a clue how much emotional pain Mike was in," Brynn told them solemnly. "Death was obviously something Mike had been entertaining for a long time. It was wrong, and now each one of us is left with recriminations."

Brynn paused at the sharp pain in her chest. "I can't blame Mike, but I wish I'd known how much he was hurting. I might have been able to help him. Like Yolanda said, we never got a chance to say good-bye."

"I want to get in his face and make him listen to

reason," one of the girls shouted. "He's hurt so many people."

"He was in pain himself."

"I wish I could talk to him."

"You can," Brynn whispered.

"But how?" Denzil asked. "It isn't like we can write him a letter."

"Why can't we?" Brynn asked, remembering how much writing had helped her deal with the death of her beloved grandmother five years earlier. "It's true Mike won't be reading it, but writing Mike might help each of us deal with the shock of what he did."

"Miss Cassidy's right."

Binders opened and spiral notebooks appeared as her students automatically reached for a fresh piece of paper. They did this without Brynn so much as asking.

The remainder of the time was spent writing Mike. Brynn wrote her own letter and found herself struggling to hold in the emotion as she placed feelings of doubt on the page. When she glanced up, she found several of her students were weeping.

Afterward, those who were willing read their letters aloud.

Emilio volunteered first. Looking shaken but determined, he faced the class. "Mike, don't do it, man. Don't do it." Then he slid back onto his seat.

Pearl stood beside her desk. "Why do I hurt so bad? I barely knew you, and yet I feel some responsibility for your death. You sat three desks away from me. Three desks and you couldn't reach that far? Three desks and I couldn't see your pain? I'm sorry, Mike. Forgive me."

Yolanda, tears streaming down her face, volunteered next. "Thank you, Mike, for what you taught me. I wasn't your friend, but I wish I had been. I never took the time to talk to you. But you touched my life. Never again will I sit in a classroom and not look around me. I wish I'd known how much pain you were in. I'd like to think you would have told me had I asked. Only I never asked. Next time will be different. Next time I'm going to look."

When the bell rang her class filed out of the room with little of the enthusiasm they generally showed at the end of a day.

"Will you find out about Mike's funeral?" Emilio asked.

The other kids stopped and waited for Brynn to respond.

"We want to know," Yolanda said.

"I think it would help if we went."

There was a chorus of agreement.

"You were the only friends Mike had," Brynn said.

"It's too bad we didn't do a better job of it," Yolanda said just loudly enough for Brynn to hear.

Brynn left the school as soon as she could. She had Suzie's address with her and walked over to the teenager's apartment. The girl's mother greeted her at the door and was painfully polite as she ushered Brynn into the living room.

"Is Suzie home?" Brynn asked.

"No. She with Mike's mother."

Brynn studied the delicate Chinese woman who struggled with English. "My daughter has torn heart."

Brynn placed her hand over her own heart. It did indeed feel as if it had been torn. "Please tell Suzie that I'm looking for her."

"Yes. Thank you very much to coming." Her English was heavily accented and barely understandable.

Before she left, Brynn placed her hand on the other woman's shoulder. "Suzie is a wonderful girl. I feel honored to have been the teacher of such a fine student."

The delicate woman's eyes avoided Brynn's, but she thought she might have detected a smile.

When Brynn arrived at Mike's, his mother was at the funeral home, making the arrangements for her son's burial. Brynn left feeling as if she'd failed everyone. Mike. Suzie. His mother. Her students. Herself.

Her apartment was cold and bleak. She walked inside and stood in the dark, feeling as though she carried the burden of the world on her shoulders. With a heavy heart, she turned on the light switch and walked over to her desk.

It might have helped her had she been able to cry, but there were no tears left inside her. With a steady, sure hand, she wrote out her letter of resignation to give to Mr. Whalen in the morning. When school resumed after the first of the year, she wouldn't be there.

Roberto was right, and had been from the first, she realized. She didn't belong here. She'd failed Mike, but most of all she'd failed herself.

"She isn't actually going to quit, is she?" Mercy asked.

Shirley stood with her hand planted protectively over Brynn's shoulder. Mercy knew that her friend had been with her charge from the moment Brynn had learned about Mike's suicide.

"What happened with Mike wasn't her fault." Mercy wished there was something she could do. Poor Shirley was at a loss as to know how to help.

"I know."

Brynn leaned forward and pressed her forehead against her folded arms.

"Isn't there something we can do for you?" Mercy asked.

Shirley shook her head.

It was then that Mercy realized her friend was weeping. "Oh, Shirley."

"I'm sorry," the other angel said softly. "It's just that I can't bear to see Brynn feeling this defeated."

"What's going to happen?"

Shirley rubbed her hand under her nose. "I don't know. Gabriel's the one who can tell us that. But . . ."

"Yes?" Mercy prodded.

"I think it might be best if Brynn returned to Rhode Island."

Mercy was shocked. "But why?"

"She cares too much. If she'd had a more experienced angel assigned to help her . . ."

"You can't blame yourself," Mercy cried, outraged at the suggestion.

"She needs Roberto," Shirley added.

"Then let's get him," Mercy suggested. There were ways of dealing with stubborn men, and she wasn't opposed to using them. If Roberto Alcantara thought that he could trample over this sweet young woman's heart, well, there was a thing or two Mercy could teach that man. She'd take a great deal of pleasure in doing it, too.

"No," Shirley said with surprising strength. "Leave Roberto out of this."

"But—"

"He has what he wants."

"You're sure of that?" the strong male voice spoke from behind them.

"Gabriel." Mercy was quick to jump to attention.

"How's Jenny?" the archangel asked her.

Mercy brightened. "Great. At least she was the last time I checked. She was chosen for a major role in a new musical. It's the chance of a lifetime. She couldn't be more thrilled."

"What makes you think that?"

Mercy hesitated. This sounded like one of those trick questions. "I . . . I . . ."

"What happened to Trey? The last I heard he'd disappeared, and Jenny was looking for him. He'd checked out of the hotel by the time she arrived."

"Trey, well, that is a bit unfortunate." Mercy did feel bad about the young man who'd set his heart on loving Jenny all these years. "I'm afraid he's gone."

"Gone?" Gabriel frowned, and when he did, he was something fierce to behold.

Mercy edged closer to her friend. "Yes, he left New York. He had a little trouble changing his airplane ticket, but managed to catch an earlier flight."

Brynn's doorbell chimed, and she straightened and wiped the tears from her face.

"Who's coming?" Shirley directed the question to Gabriel.

"Suzie Chang," he answered. "Apparently there is a letter Brynn needs to share with the girl."

Chapter Seventeen

Talking to Carl proved to be so much more difficult than Hannah had thought it would be. She'd waited all day for him, practiced in her mind how to break the news as gently as possible.

She'd left her grandmother's filled with conviction. In the time since, her clear purpose had become clouded with the time-honored traditions of duty and honor.

"I know you're wondering why I asked to see you," Hannah said as she brought Carl a cup of tea and set it on the table in the family kitchen. She was nervous, and the hot liquid sloshed over the edges of the cup.

Hannah didn't worry that her parents would interrupt them. Her family seemed to think it was important that Hannah and Carl have time together alone, and for once Hannah was grateful.

"I've been wanting to talk to you, too," Carl said, smiling broadly. He looked happy, more so than she could remember in a long while. She suspected the situation with the school had been cleared up, and she was pleased for his sake.

"My father had a go-round with the school head-master himself," Carl said, gloating a little.

So she was right.

"I have my job back, Hannah, and if anyone's position is in jeopardy, it's Hiram Steinfield's."

"I couldn't be more pleased," she said, but before she could relay her own, less welcome news, Carl continued.

"As you might guess, my mind is greatly relieved."

"Of course, and now . . ."

"We can seriously start planning for our wedding," he finished for her.

"As a matter of fact, that was what I wanted to talk to you about. . . ."

"Now I agree June is an excellent time of year, but personally I'd prefer May." Once again Carl wouldn't allow her to continue.

"Carl, would you please listen to me?"

"In a minute. There are a number of reasons I prefer May."

"Carl!"

"My mother's birthday is in May, and then there's Mother's Day. I've always found it convenient to cluster certain dates together whenever possible. It helps to keep track, and if we're going to need to buy . . ." He stopped abruptly when Hannah stood up.

She walked over to the stove. Now she understood what it was about Carl that had always disturbed her. He refused to listen.

"Hannah?" he asked gently. "You're upset, aren't you?"

"Yes," she said between gritted teeth, unwilling to hide it.

"Your heart's set on June, isn't it?"

"No," she said forcefully, and whirled around. "I'm not going to marry you." There, she'd said it, but in far less diplomatic terms than she'd wanted.

A stunned, disbelieving silence followed. At last she'd found a way to capture his attention.

"You're honestly breaking our engagement?"

He seemed to need confirmation. "Yes," she said firmly.

He scratched the side of his head. "Don't you think that's a bit drastic, considering that I'm willing to give up the May date? I'd like to think I'm a reasonable man. If you don't want the wedding in May, why don't you just say so?"

"I don't want the wedding in May or June or any other month of the year." She folded her arms and released a deep sigh of frustration. "This is the crux of the problem between us. You don't hear me. I'm trying to tell you something important, and either you don't care or you've already got your mind made up."

He stiffened. "I don't see it that way."

Hannah had never intended for them to discuss their basic personality differences. "I want to break the engagement, Carl. I deeply regret hurting you, but I'm fairly certain you aren't in love with me."

"Don't be ridiculous," he snapped. "Of course I love you. I think you're wonderful. You'll make me a good wife, you're supportive and—"

"You're doing it again," she cried, clenching her fists at her sides. Hannah so seldom raised her voice that it shocked even her.

Carl looked genuinely baffled. "I don't understand. Hannah, listen, tell me whatever it is that you find offensive. I can change."

"It doesn't matter."

"But of course it matters. I realize that marriage is an important step and you're bound to have second thoughts, every woman does. Now it's true," he said, and raised his right hand with a dismissive gesture, "that I've been wrapped up in my own problems of late. I haven't paid you nearly enough attention, have I? Naturally you're feeling short-changed in the romance department, and frankly I don't blame you."

"Carl," she whispered, "you don't love me."

"Nonsense. I asked you to marry me, didn't I?"

"Okay," she whispered, her patience wearing paper thin. "Let's try this from a different angle. I can't marry you, Carl, because *I* don't love *you.*"

He laughed. The man had the nerve to actually laugh aloud.

Dumbfounded, all Hannah could do was stare at him.

"Of course you love me," he countered, sounding relieved. He placed his hand on his chest as if to restrain the bubbling amusement welling up inside him. "Hannah, these doubts of yours are only natural. I had them, too."

"And now you don't?"

"Occasionally," he was willing to admit. "But I've worked through those feelings, and given time, you will, too."

Hannah had hoped that she could talk to Carl without telling him about Joshua. It was one thing to break the engagement and something else entirely to mention she'd fallen in love with another man. She'd hoped to spare Carl that.

"The problem as I see it," Carl said, talking to her as he would one of his students, "is that people are rarely willing to see through their difficulties. Our society is caught up in fast-food restaurants, 'pay later' mentality, and instant gratification. My dear Hannah, what you're feeling isn't so difficult to understand. But we've made a commitment to each other, and we can't treat it lightly."

"Carl, I'm terminating our engagement." She couldn't say it any plainer than that.

"It's times such as these that we need to hold on to each other instead of letting go of the most important relationship of our lives."

Hannah's heart was pounding so hard and fast, it

felt as though her ribs were about to break. "I've met someone else," she said forcefully.

Her words stopped Carl cold. His eyes narrowed. "Who?"

"You don't know him."

"Don't be so sure. Tell me his name."

"What does it matter what his name is?" she demanded. "I love him and he loves me."

Looking completely taken aback, Carl pulled out a kitchen chair and slumped onto it.

"To be honest, Carl, I didn't think you'd care."

"Not care?" he cried as though her comment had outraged him. "Of course I care. Some man, some stranger, has stolen my bride, and you seem to think that it really shouldn't matter."

Hannah knew it was his ego speaking and was sorrier than she could say. "If you're looking to blame anyone, blame me," she told him gently. "I never intended to tell you about him, but then I couldn't make you listen, and—"

His head jerked up. "You weren't going to tell me?"

"All I wanted to do was break the engagement, but you refused to believe me . . . you weren't hearing me."

"Don't be ridiculous. I heard every word you said."

Hannah wasn't going to get into an argument with him, but this was too much. "You keep discounting me, offering excuses and reasons for my wanting to call off the engagement. You've given me no option but to tell you about Joshua."

"Joshua . . ." He repeated the name as if he were reading it off a post office poster.

"I'm genuinely sorry."

"You're serious? This isn't some stupid joke?"

"I can't marry you, Carl, nor can I go on pretending I love you."

The silence that followed fell like a butcher's cleaver into the middle of the room.

Carl reached for his jacket, swinging it over his shoulders like a shawl in his rush to get away from her. "Do your parents know?"

Hannah hesitated. "They will soon enough."

He walked toward the stairway, his steps abrupt and urgent. "If this other man is who you love, then all I can say is you're welcome to him. Just don't come crying to me when you've regained your senses."

"Joshua isn't going to break my heart," she assured him softly. "I realize this is painful, Carl, but I'd like it if we could be friends."

"Friends?" he echoed as though it were a ridiculous suggestion. "You've got to be kidding. Frankly, Hannah, I doubt that I'll ever want to see you again." Having said that, he stormed out of the apartment, slamming the door behind him. The pictures on the walls shook with the force of his exit.

"Hannah?" A moment later her father called from the bottom of the stairs.

"Yes," she said, hoping she sounded calm and assured.

"Is everything all right between you and Carl?"

She didn't hesitate, and the relief in her voice was evident. "Don't worry, Dad, everything's the way it should be."

There came a time in every man's life when he had to admit he'd made a mistake, learn from it, and move forward. Joshua had reached that point the afternoon he'd heard Hannah's father invite him to his daughter's wedding to another man.

Even now he couldn't find it in his heart to be angry with Hannah. Her inability to break her engagement highlighted what had attracted her to him. She was loyal to a fault, caring, and tender-hearted. Family took priority.

A part of him would always love her, he realized. Knowing her for this short period had blessed his life, but now it was time to own up to a few home truths.

First off, his love was hurting her. Because of the tenderness he held for Hannah, he couldn't continue to make her miserable. The truth was, he'd found her too late.

His decision made, Joshua had hoped to experience some sort of emotional release, but he didn't. If anything, he felt considerably worse. He'd stewed and fretted, doubted and reasoned, until he was blue with the effort. Nothing would ever change. Hannah loved him, but it went against the very grain of her being to defy and disappoint her family.

The snowstorm that had been predicted for that afternoon had already darkened the sky. Another night of sitting home alone, thinking about Hannah, would solve nothing.

Unfortunately all his favorite escapes had been ruined. He couldn't walk past Rockefeller Center now and not remember the time he and Hannah had skated together. Nor could he forget how good she'd felt in his arms.

This was the real problem: he couldn't forget.

The time had come to seek greener pastures, and he had just the woman in mind. He reached for the phone and dialed Carol's number.

"Hannah," her mother called to her from the hallway. "Your father and I need to talk to you."

Hannah opened her bedroom door, her coat draped over her arm.

Ruth's eyes widened with distress. "You're not going out, are you?"

"Yes."

Ruth hesitated and looked to her husband.

"Did you need me to get you something?" Hannah asked, then added, "I don't know when I'll be home."

"No. . . . I just received a call from Carl's mother. Is it true, honey, have you broken the engagement with Carl?"

Hannah should have realized something like this would happen. Carl had gone directly to his family and listed her sins. Hannah regretted that she hadn't prepared her parents for the news, but she'd been hoping to confront them with Joshua at her side.

"I don't love Carl," she told her mother gently. "I'm sorry, Mom, I know how much you and Dad like him, but I don't feel the same way."

"There's someone else?" her mother questioned, her voice revealing the depth of her disbelief. "Helen seems to think you've been seeing another man on the sly, without any of us knowing. I assured her that couldn't possibly be true."

David Morganstern stood behind his wife, his hand on Ruth's shoulder. His eyes, dark and inquisitive, rested on his daughter.

"His name's Joshua Shadduck," she admitted. "He's an attorney."

Her mother gasped softly and covered her mouth with her hand. Hannah wasn't sure if this was because she'd admitted to dating someone while engaged to Carl or because Joshua was an attorney.

Her father frowned. "Didn't I recently meet this young man?"

Ashamed that she'd deceived them both, Hannah lowered her gaze. "Yes. He was in the deli."

"How could you have fallen in love with him?" her mother asked, her voice raised with disbelief. "How could you hurt Carl like this? He's such a good man. We couldn't ask for a better husband for you."

"Joshua will make me a good husband, too."

"I forbid you from seeing this Joshua again," her father said sternly.

"Daddy, I've never defied you. I've always done what you've asked, but I love Joshua with all my heart. I need to see him. I need to be with him."

Her parents stared back at her, too shocked to respond right away.

"How did you meet him?" The question came from her mother a moment later.

"We met at the Thanksgiving Day parade. Then, before I had a chance to analyze how I felt about him, Carl asked me to marry him. I didn't want to agree, but at the time it seemed like the best thing to do. You and Dad were so pleased, and you both like Carl."

"He's been like a son to me," her father admitted sadly.

"I'm sorry, Dad," Hannah whispered. "I didn't mean to disappoint you." Before either one could say anything more, she rushed out of the apartment.

"Hannah, please, don't go," her mother shouted from the top of the stairway, but Hannah pretended not to hear. Never in all her life had she ignored her mother and father.

Hannah caught a taxi outside the deli and read the driver the Riverside Drive address Joshua had written down on the back of his business card.

"It looks like it might snow," she said, glancing toward the darkening sky. The sooner she reached Joshua, the better. She needed him now as never before. When she told him what had happened, he'd come with her and together they'd talk to her family and make everything right.

The driver mumbled something in return that she didn't understand.

Several minutes later the cabdriver pulled over to the curb and flipped off the meter. Hannah gazed out the car window at the high-rise apartment building and experienced a sense of relief. The man she loved, the man she'd defied her family to marry, lived in this building.

"Lady, are you going to stare out the window all day?"

"No, sorry." She returned her attention to her purse and pulled out her wallet. From the corner of her eye, she caught sight of a familiar figure. Looking up, she saw Joshua coming out of the building. She raised her hand and was about to call him when, suddenly, she stopped. The happy shout died in her throat.

Joshua wasn't alone.

Standing beside him was the most beautiful, elegant-looking woman Hannah had ever seen. Joshua slipped his arm around the other woman's waist, bent down, and kissed her gently on the lips.

Her heart pounding like a locomotive chugging uphill, Hannah hurled herself back against the seat, not wanting him to see her.

"Lady, are you going to pay me or not?" the cabbie asked a second time with far less patience.

"Yes, yes, of course." Hannah leaned forward just far enough to peek at Joshua. It was apparent the two were long-term acquaintances. The woman with him gazed up adoringly, as though this were the happiest day of her life.

"Please," Hannah whispered. "Take me home."

"You got the money or don't you?" the taxi driver asked.

She handed him a twenty-dollar bill for security. "Now take me back," she pleaded. She'd go home because she had nowhere else to go. With her tail between her legs, her heart heavy with pain, she'd return to her family, who would love and support her despite the fact that she'd deeply embarrassed and disappointed them.

"All right, if you want to go back, then fine, I'll take you." The driver hesitated, and Hannah met his gaze in the rearview mirror. "Is everything all right?" he asked gently.

"No," Hannah whispered.

She was too late. Joshua had found someone else.

Mike Glasser was buried two days later. Father Grady was scheduled to say the funeral mass and had spent considerable time counseling Mike's mother, Louise.

Brynn was one of the first to arrive at the church. She slipped into the pew and knelt down on the padded kneeler. Since hearing the news, she hadn't cried. It might have helped if she'd been able to release her grief, but she held on to it with both hands, clenching it to her breast, fearing what would happen if she ever let go.

Mike's death was a constant, painful reminder of how badly she'd failed him and her other students. How badly she'd failed herself.

Emilio walked into church and sat in the pew directly across from her. Yolanda and Pearl arrived together and sat in front of Brynn.

The huge church was nearly half full with a number of other students and faculty members from Manhattan High. Mike's suicide had had a powerful impact on those who'd known him.

Organ music, deep and somber, filled the church. Mike's mother and a handful of other relatives arrived. Together they walked down the center aisle. Louise Glasser's shoulders were bent under the weight of her grief. She appeared to be leaning heavily on the girl walking beside her. The two clung to each other. It didn't take Brynn long to realize the one with Mike's mother was Suzie Chang. They needed each other.

Brynn had met with them both, separately. They'd come together as strangers with a common bond. Both had loved Mike. Both deeply grieved his death.

Organ music surged through the church as a man's voice, hauntingly melodic, rang loud and clear from the choir loft. The voice, a baritone, reached out and consoled with music those who'd gathered to mourn Mike's death. Brynn recognized the singer's voice immediately.

Roberto.

Even from this distance his voice filled her with a bitter sadness. It settled in the pit of her stomach, and a chill came over her as she closed her eyes and soaked in the comfort of the song. She pretended it was Roberto's arms around her.

Since her last meeting with Roberto, Brynn had tried to push all thoughts of him from her mind. By the sheer force of her determination, she'd partially succeeded. Despite her efforts to purge him from her thoughts, she couldn't keep from feeling that something important, something vital, was missing.

Once, a year or so before, Brynn had lost her purse. A knot had formed in her stomach that refused to go away until she was able to replace everything that had been lost. A similar sensation had been with her since her last meeting with Roberto. She was lost, and the way she felt just then, nothing would ever be right again. She supposed her thinking was melodramatic. In time she'd be able to put these weeks in New York behind her.

As Roberto had encouraged her from the beginning, she would return to where she belonged. But she wouldn't go back to Rhode Island the same as when she'd left. No, when she headed home, she'd be bringing a lot of emotional baggage with her.

Father Grady said the mass. A wake was scheduled in the parish hall immediately following the service. Brynn knew she was expected to show. It was as good a time as any to tell her students that she wouldn't be back in class following winter vacation. Already they'd been assigned another teacher, one with more experience than she.

Most of Brynn's apartment was packed. Depending on road conditions, she should be ready to leave in another day, two at the most.

When the service was over, Mike's family filed out first, then each row followed in turn.

Brynn stayed behind. She wanted a few moments alone before she headed over to the parish hall. With her head bowed, she tried to pray. Lately it had been a losing battle. Every concern she gave to God had claw marks all over it.

Not only had her abilities as a teacher been questioned, but her faith, once so stable and sure, had been badly shaken. She recognized that in time it would right itself again, but just then even that looked doubtful.

Footsteps sounded on the tile floor behind her. Brynn kept her head lowered, resenting the intrusion. She needed this time alone. She wasn't ready to join the others.

To her surprise it was Roberto who slipped into the pew and sat next to her. He didn't say anything, simply sat at her side, his head bowed in prayer.

After a while he touched her forearm. "The others are waiting."

"I know," she whispered back. "Tell them I'll be there in a few minutes."

He didn't leave.

"I'm fine, Roberto. I appreciate your concern, but there's nothing to worry about." She hoped her weak smile would convince him she was telling the truth.

He didn't budge. "I know you too well to believe that."

She stiffened. His words set fire under her. "You don't know me at all, you never did."

Seeing that he wasn't going to leave her, she stood abruptly and made her way out of the pew and down the side aisle. Her crisp steps echoed in the empty church.

She must have risen too quickly, because she hadn't gone more than a few feet when her head started to swim and the room began to spin. Reaching out to the end of the wooden row, she caught herself in time to keep from collapsing.

Roberto was at her side in an instant. He murmured something impatient in Spanish and led her to the back of the church.

"Stay here," he insisted, and disappeared. No more than a minute passed before he returned with a glass of water.

"There's nothing wrong with me," she insisted. She didn't want him to touch her. Didn't want him close to her. He was the one who wanted her out of his life. She'd go. Kicking and screaming, she'd abided by his wishes. However difficult, however painful. He had no reason to complain.

"When was the last time you had anything to eat?"

Brynn couldn't remember, but she wasn't about to let Roberto know that. "I'm fine," she insisted stiffly. "I'd appreciate it if you'd kindly leave me alone."

"Brynn, please listen."

"If I understood you correctly, you don't want anything more to do with me. All I ask is that you respect my wishes, as I have yours."

He hesitated, and Brynn felt a small sense of satisfaction, knowing her words had hit their mark.

"Allow me to escort you to the wake. Please." She knew that the "please" had cost him a great deal.

"Why?" She didn't understand the necessity of this.

"It's a little thing, isn't it?"

It would be petty to refuse him, so she agreed. His arm came around her shoulder. She meant to shake it off, but the moment he brought her close to his side, the tears that had refused to come broke free in a surging dam of grief.

Brynn sank into the pew at the back of the vestibule and wept as though her very soul had been ripped from her body.

"It's all right," Roberto whispered, cradling her in his arms, pressing her head to his chest.

She didn't mean to cling to him, but her pride be damned, she needed him as she'd never needed anyone.

He spoke again in Spanish, his voice low and soothing. Tucking her head against his shoulder, he rocked back and forth gently.

"You were right," she admitted when the shoulder-shaking sobs had abated. "You tried to tell me, but I wouldn't listen. Now Mike's dead and—"

"You can't blame yourself."

On a conscious level Brynn agreed with him, but deep inside she felt she carried a portion of the blame. Mike had trusted her enough to write her. She was the one person in all the world to whom he felt comfortable enough communicating his last wishes. Yet she'd been oblivious of his pain, deaf to his needs. The boy had been desperate, and she had been blind.

In retrospect Brynn realized that Mike had been trying to tell her in subtle ways of the hopelessness he experienced. His essays had been full of it. The dark side. Despondent words from a despondent youth.

Abruptly, Brynn pulled away from Roberto. In addition to his comfort, his embrace was a painful reminder that he wanted nothing more to do with her. If this was a contest, she was declaring him the winner.

"I won't be coming back," she announced firmly, surprised at the strength of her voice. "I've already given Mr. Whalen my letter of resignation. In January the kids will have a new teacher."

"Do Emilio and the others know?" Roberto asked.

"Not yet."

"When do you plan to tell them?"

"Now."

Something flashed in his eyes. "It's for the best."

She noticed that Roberto didn't try to talk her out of leaving. She realized that was what she wanted, what she longed with all her being for him to do.

She stood. "I'll do it now," she said, and boldly walked out the door.

"What are we going to tell Gabriel?" Shirley demanded of her two friends. The three had gathered in the choir loft following Mike's funeral, at a loss as to how to report their progress to the archangel.

"This is the first time we've failed. He'll understand," Mercy offered.

"He might accept one failure, but all three of us?"

"What happened this year?" Goodness threw her arms into the air, thoroughly disgusted by this unexpected turn of events.

Shirley cast them a disgruntled look. "It might have helped matters if you two hadn't been playing on escalators and writing on billboards in Times Square."

"Blaming each other isn't going to help."

"But it's nearly Christmas Eve," Mercy protested. "I can't possibly see us turning everything around at this late point."

"Maybe there's a chance if we work together."

Shirley shook her head slowly. "It seems to me working together is what got us into this mess."

"All right, let's each report what's happening with our charges," Goodness suggested, and gestured for Shirley to go first.

"Well, as you can see," Shirley said, pointing to

Brynn, who sat in the corner of the parish hall, "Brynn has said good-bye to her class. She's miserable, and blames herself for Mike's death."

"What's going to happen to her?"

"I haven't a clue," Shirley said, and sounded thoroughly miserable. "Gabriel was right, this assignment was too much for me. I'll leave him to pick up the pieces. It's going to take an archangel to bring about some good from this tragedy."

"Roberto loves her," Goodness said, studying Emilio's brother.

"Yes, I know," Shirley said sadly. "Letting her leave is a sign of how much he cares for her."

"There's nothing more you can do?" Mercy asked. "Perhaps what Brynn needs is a little talking to from the three of us."

"I'm afraid that would send her packing faster than anything."

"Okay, okay," Goodness said, looking to Mercy. "What's happening with Jenny?"

"I thought she'd be overjoyed to get this chance to star on Broadway. It's been her dream."

"And she isn't happy?"

Mercy shrugged, apparently unable to come up with an explanation of her charge's behavior. "She's moped around the apartment for two days now. I'm afraid she wants Trey with her *and* a chance to star on Broadway, but she can't have both."

"Oh boy," Shirley muttered. "And what is Gabriel going to say about that?"

"I don't know, but I have the distinct notion he's

going to think I was responsible for getting the play's director to notice her. I wasn't, truly I wasn't."

"I believe you," Shirley murmured, but her opinion wasn't the one that mattered, and all three knew it.

"That leaves me to tell you about Hannah," Goodness said, and her disappointment was keen. "She broke off the engagement with Carl."

"Good." Both Shirley and Mercy brightened.

"But it was too late." Goodness told them that Joshua was dating Carol seriously now.

"Joshua found someone else?" Shirley asked. "I don't believe it."

Mercy crossed her arms and pursed her lips. "Men can be so fickle."

"In my opinion he still loves Hannah."

"But he doesn't know that Hannah broke her engagement with Carl, does he?"

"It might have made a difference," Shirley insisted.

"It's too late," Goodness informed them sadly. "Hannah saw him with the other woman."

"We can fix that," Mercy said confidently. "This sort of thing is right up our alley."

"It won't work. Not this time."

"Why not?" Shirley insisted.

"Because Joshua has decided to cut his losses and look elsewhere for a wife."

"And Hannah?"

"Hannah will live with her parents the rest of her life and never marry."

"Just a minute," Mercy said, and rolled up her

sleeves. "We can fix that, and while we're at it, there are ways to deal with men as stubborn as Roberto."

"What about you and Jenny?" Goodness asked.

Some of Mercy's brightness dimmed. "I don't know what we can do about Jenny and Trey."

Shirley rubbed her chin. "I have an idea. All isn't lost yet."

Chapter Eighteen

From inside his office Joshua heard the raised voices of the receptionist and an angry man. He stepped into the hallway and heard David Morganstern, Hannah's father, demanding to see him.

"It's all right, Julie," Joshua said, coming forward, "I'll see Mr. Morganstern."

David shot the receptionist a look of triumph and straightened the cuffs of his coat sleeves. "I told you Mr. Shadduck would see me."

"He doesn't have an appointment," Julie told Joshua, "and he refused to make one."

"It's all right, Julie."

Joshua escorted David into his office. The older man paused in the doorway and looked around. He didn't seem overly impressed. "Mighty fancy digs you have here."

"Thank you." Giving the impression

of nonchalance, Joshua sat down at his desk and invited Hannah's father to make himself comfortable. "What can I do for you, Mr. Morganstern?"

David sat on the cushion as if he expected it to jump up and bite him at any moment. "I've come to ask you a few questions, young man. I recently learned, through no fault of my daughter's, that you've been sneaking around with Hannah. I want you to know I don't like it one bit."

Joshua folded his hands on top of the desk and waited.

"I wanted to meet the man face to face who played havoc with my daughter's life." It was clear David's feelings ran strong and fervent. The older gentleman bolted out of the chair and stood directly in front of Joshua's desk.

Joshua wondered exactly how much David knew about the two of them and feared saying more than he should.

"Your silence tells me everything I need to know," David said, spitting out the words, revealing his distaste. "I find you to be the most despicable kind of man."

Joshua didn't blame Morganstern. His behavior had been less than honorable. He'd never been comfortable meeting Hannah on the sly, kissing her, urging her to continue their relationship while she was engaged to another man. He wasn't comfortable now, offering excuses.

"How is she?" Joshua couldn't keep himself from asking.

"How do you think?" David demanded.

"You have my apology," Joshua said, hoping the other man understood the full extent of his regret.

"What about Carl? Are you willing to apologize to him, too? What about Hannah? My daughter gave you her heart, and it meant nothing to the mighty, powerful attorney. You people seem to think you have the right to disrupt lives. It's time someone made you accountable for your actions."

"You want me to apologize to Carl?" Joshua asked, willing to do whatever he could to appease Hannah's family and make matters easier for her. Personally he thought the less Carl knew about him, the better.

David considered his offer, then shrugged. "No. Carl and our family aren't exactly on speaking terms."

Joshua leaned forward slightly, wondering if he'd heard him correctly. "Why aren't you?"

David sat back down and eyed Joshua suspiciously. "You mean to say you honestly don't know?"

"I wouldn't ask if I did."

"Hannah loves you."

The confirmation of her feelings should have brought him joy; instead he was filled with a deep, painful sense of loss. "I love her, too."

"Not in my book," David fumed. "You leave her to face Carl alone, and when she breaks the engagement, you dump her."

It was Joshua's turn to bolt upright. "Hannah broke off the engagement?"

David frowned and nodded. "You mean to say you didn't know?"

Joshua came out from behind his desk. "No."

"She defied both her mother and me when we insisted she not see you again. Then less than a half hour after she leaves, she returns, tells us how sorry she is for having upset us, and goes to her bedroom. She hasn't been herself since. She won't talk about you or Carl, but it's plain as the nose on my face that she's miserable."

"She never told me. I knew how difficult all this was for her. She didn't want to hurt anyone, least of all her family and especially not Carl. Every time she promised to break the engagement something more would happen to prevent it. I felt the only thing I could do was step aside."

It was clear David wasn't interested in hearing explanations. "Do you or don't you love my daughter?"

"I love her," Joshua said with conviction.

"Then what are your intentions?"

He didn't hesitate. "I want to marry her."

David glanced around the office once more, this time with a less critical eye. "Talk to Hannah first, and then you and I might strike some kind of agreement. We could do with a lawyer in the family." He started toward the door, then stopped abruptly and turned around. "Are you coming or not, young man?"

Joshua laughed and reached for his coat. "Coming."

David nodded once, profoundly. "Good, that's exactly what I wanted to hear."

Hannah was working the counter when Joshua walked inside the deli, her father at his side.

"Hannah," David shouted, "you've got company. Take him upstairs and serve him a piece of your mother's cheesecake."

Hannah ignored her father and directed her question to Joshua. "What are you doing here?"

"I came to talk to you. I suggest we go upstairs as your father advised." They'd already attracted more than enough attention.

"Go," Ruth Morganstern insisted to Hannah. "This way, young man," she said, and directed Joshua around the counter, pointing the way to their private quarters.

Joshua followed Hannah up the stairs. She paused halfway up and turned to face him. From her position on the stairway they were at eye level. It required more discipline than he'd needed in quite some time not to kiss her right then and there.

"What did my father say to you?" she demanded. Her eyes were full of fire. "I don't need your pity, Joshua Shadduck."

"My pity?" This came at him out of the blue. "If anyone is asking questions, it should be me. The last thing I heard was your father inviting me to your wedding to another man."

Hannah's shoulders went stiff. "The last time I saw you, you were kissing another woman."

He frowned. "Who?"

"How should I know?" she flared.

The door at the bottom of the stairs opened. "Upstairs, Hannah. The entire deli is listening in on your conversation."

If ever Hannah needed an incentive, this appeared to be it. She raced up the remainder of the stairs.

Joshua was left with no choice but to follow her, which he did gladly. He found her standing in front of a window looking out, her back to him, her arms folded around her middle.

"Her name's Carol," he said gently, wanting to clear the air as soon as he could so they could move on to the more important matters. "I've known her for a number of years."

"You should marry her," she suggested, turning to face him.

"I can't. She's a wonderful woman, but she isn't you. You're the one who owns my heart. You have from nearly the first moment we met. I had to let you go, Hannah, surely you understand that. My love was hurting you. The family pressures on you to marry Carl were overwhelming. Stepping aside was the only decent thing to do."

"It didn't take you long to recover, did it?"

She was jealous of Carol, and Joshua thrilled at the realization. "I see it's done a bit of good for you to know how I've felt these last few weeks. It wasn't easy on me when you were spending time with Carl. It was probably the most difficult thing I've ever done."

"I always loved you, and you knew it. You never had a single reason to be jealous."

Joshua longed to hold and kiss her too much to argue the point. "Are you going to marry me or not, Hannah Morganstern?"

Her eyes searched his as if she questioned the sincerity of his proposal.

"I love you," he added tenderly, and held open his arms to her.

It didn't take her long to find her way into his embrace. When she slipped her arms around his middle, Joshua sighed with a sense of peace, of homecoming. He'd been waiting all his life for this woman, and now that she was his, he didn't intend to lose her.

Tunneling his fingers through her hair, Joshua positioned his mouth to kiss her.

"I've been so unhappy," she admitted on the tail end of a soft moan.

"Me, too." He kissed her again.

"But you weren't lonely," she accused. "I was miserable and lonely."

"I love you, Hannah," he said, laying his heart at her feet. "You're going to marry me, aren't you?"

"Oh yes."

"Good." He held her against him protectively. "It's the oddest thing," he mumbled, nuzzling his face close to hers.

"What is?" she said, thrilling him with small kisses along the underside of his jaw.

"Your father claims I gave him my business card. I never did. I haven't a clue where he got it."

"Me either," Hannah said. "Does it matter?"

Joshua chuckled. "Not in the least."

The last thing Brynn anticipated when she was ready to leave New York was car problems. Ever since Roberto had worked on her carburetor, her Escort had been running like a dream. Now, however, the engine wouldn't so much as crank.

The first thing she did was contact her family and tell them. Her parents were concerned about her, and they weren't happy to have her traveling home alone, but she couldn't very well desert her vehicle.

Sitting inside her apartment, she thumbed through the telephone directory, looking for a garage listing, knowing full well her chances of finding someone willing to work on her car on Christmas Eve were damn near impossible.

Her doorbell chimed, and disheartened, Brynn slipped off the stool. When she checked her peephole the first person she saw was Emilio, but there were a number of others she recognized with him.

After flipping open the latch, she found herself facing a throng of her students and their parents.

"What's going on here?" she asked. There must have been close to fifty people jam-packed into her hallway.

"We don't want you to leave, Miss Cassidy,"

Emilio said, serving as spokesperson for the group. "After Mike's funeral a number of us went and talked to Mr. Whalen. We asked that the school refuse to accept your letter of resignation."

"I don't know how much we were able to influence him," Yolanda said, laughing nervously. "I think our parents had a far greater impact."

Suzie Chang's delicate mother pressed forward and in halting English said, "You say it honor to have Suzie in class. We say it greater honor to have you for teacher."

A cry of agreement followed the Chinese woman's words.

"We love you, Miss Cassidy."

Brynn couldn't speak for the lump in her throat. Never in all her dreams had she expected anything like this.

"Mr. Whalen says you can have your job back, if you want it," Denzil's mother told her. "For the first time in his life, my son's doing well in school. He's talking about something other than video games."

"What do you say, Miss Cassidy?"

Frankly, Brynn was left speechless.

"Say something," Emilio urged.

"I don't know . . . I just don't know."

"Give the girl some room to breathe." Parents and teens parted so Father Grady could make his way to the front.

"Father Grady!"

"You didn't know I was here? My dear, I was the one who drove the bus."

"You brought the church bus?" Brynn placed both hands over her mouth to keep from laughing out loud.

"Roberto's driving it around the block, looking for a place to park now."

"Roberto." Brynn whispered his name.

"I'm telling you right now, Teach," Emilio advised from the corner of his mouth, "you have to be patient with my brother, but once he learns something, you'll never have to teach him again."

She caught sight of Roberto just then, hurrying down the corridor, breathing hard. He slowed his pace when he saw her.

"Will you stay, Miss Cassidy?"

Brynn reached out and touched Yolanda's face. Then, because it seemed to be so important to everyone else, she nodded.

A loud cheer went up, and Brynn's next-door neighbor opened the door and stuck out her head. "Ralph, I told you there was a party going on in the hallway. Come and look."

"Hello, Mrs. Camden," Brynn called, and waved.

"Is everyone invited?" her neighbor asked.

"Of course," Father Grady answered. "Come with us. We got what we came for." One by one they filed down the hallway. Lorraine Camden and her husband joined the line, chattering as they went.

"Where are we going?" Brynn heard the older woman ask.

"To the bus," someone answered.

"Ralph, they have a bus."

"Yes, Lorraine, I heard."

Soon only Brynn and Roberto were left. She led him inside her apartment and closed the door. With her back pressed against it, she studied him.

Finally, when she couldn't stand not to know any longer, she asked, "You want me to stay, too?"

He avoided eye contact. "It's a dangerous neighborhood."

"You didn't answer my question."

"Yes!" he shouted as if it made him mad to have to say it. "I want you to stay."

"Why?" She wasn't going to make it easy for him.

"Because you're a damn good teacher and there isn't a student in your class who didn't protest when they learned you were leaving."

She took two steps away from the door. "I'm not talking about my students. I'm asking why you don't want me to leave."

"Me?" He swallowed uncomfortably, then pointed to the door. "Father Grady might have a problem driving the bus. It would be better if we continued this conversation some other time."

She laughed softly. "Not on your life, buster."

To her amazement, Roberto broke out laughing. "Buster. That's exactly why I love you so damn much, Brynn Cassidy. The worst you can think to call me is Buster." He whispered something in Spanish.

"If you love me, then why were you so eager to be rid of me?"

He channeled his fingers through his hair and

sighed audibly. "Because I love you. This neighborhood has a way of dragging people down. Eventually it would happen to you, and I couldn't bear to sit by and watch that."

"As long as you're with me that's not going to happen. We can help one another."

He buried both hands deep in his pockets. "I'd like to be self-sacrificing and send you back to that fancy girls' school, but I can't. The problem is I need you as much as Emilio and his friends."

"That's a start," she said, smiling through her tears. She held her arms out to him.

Roberto reached for her and kissed her gently.

"I need you, too, Roberto . . . so much," she whispered, kissing him freely and fully.

Roberto groaned and forced her lips to part beneath his. His tongue probed hers in a silken dance, then plunged forward, unleashing a fiery passion.

At last, groaning, he broke away. "Come with me."

"Where?"

"Onto the bus. Father Grady can't drive worth beans."

"Where are we headed?"

"Church," he told her. "Do you mind?"

She laughed. "No, I don't mind. It seems like the perfect place for us to be on Christmas Eve."

The weather was perfect for such a night. Trey glanced at the clear, bright sky as he made his way from the house to the barn. When he'd finished feeding the horses and settling them down for the evening, he planned on stopping off at the Lancasters' for some of Dillon's wassail. It had become tradition that he join Jenny's family for the Christmas Eve celebration.

He'd eat dinner with them, and then they'd attend church services together. The last couple of years the family had invited him to stay for the gift opening, but Trey had refused.

He'd often spent time with the Lancasters on the off chance they could tell him something about Jenny. This year he knew everything there was to know. He'd come for dinner and attend the evening church service, and then, as always, he'd head home. Alone.

Jenny hadn't contacted him since he'd left New York, not that he'd expected she would.

Pausing in the hallway, Trey picked up the box of fancy chocolates he'd bought for Jenny's mother. He figured every woman deserved a box of expensive French candies one time in her life. Besides, he owed Paula.

The Lancaster house was bright with outside lights. Trey never could pull into their yard and not think of Jenny. The tightness around his heart felt almost physical as he climbed down from his truck and headed inside.

His timing was perfect. Charlie, Jenny's brother, and his fiancée, Mary Lou, were carrying serving dishes to the dining room table.

"Hello, Trey. Welcome." Paula kissed him on the

cheek. Trey tucked the chocolates under the tree and shook Dillon's hand.

"Think it'll snow?" Dillon asked. It was the same question his friend proposed every Christmas Eve.

"Not this year," Trey told him, knowing it would disappoint Dillon.

The smells coming from the kitchen were tantalizing enough to convince a confirmed bachelor to find a wife.

Dillon offered him a glass of hot wassail, but Trey declined. He didn't figure there was enough time to finish it before dinner was served.

"Mom, are these the linen napkins you were looking for earlier?" a soft voice asked from the vicinity of the hallway.

It was a good thing Trey hadn't been holding a drink. Sure as hell, he would have dropped it. The voice he heard belonged to Jenny. She paused momentarily when she walked into the room. "Hello, Trey. Merry Christmas."

Trey felt as if someone had knocked him behind the knees with a baseball bat. He stared at Dillon. "What's Jenny doing home?"

Dillon looked well pleased. "You'll have to ask her that yourself."

Trey intended on doing exactly that. He followed her into the kitchen and stood behind her while she dished up a mound of steaming mashed potatoes.

"When did you arrive?" he asked.

"This morning." She answered him as though

there were a hundred other more important items occupying her mind at that moment. "I do need to talk to you, however. I didn't take kindly to your leaving New York without saying good-bye."

"Trey, would you mind putting the relish plate on the table?" Paula asked.

"In a minute." He wasn't budging until he had the answer he wanted.

"The potatoes are ready," Jenny announced, and handed the bowl to her brother, who promptly delivered them to the table.

"What about the play?" Trey insisted.

"What about it?"

"I thought you said the rehearsals started before Christmas."

"They did." Jenny dipped her finger inside the gravy boat and licked it clean. "Mom, this is your best ever."

"Thank you, darling."

Charlie returned, and Trey handed Jenny's brother the relish dish. He followed Jenny to the other side of the kitchen. "Shouldn't you be there?" he asked.

"Where?"

He figured she was being deliberately obtuse, and it irritated him no end. "Practicing," he said louder than he intended.

"Not really," she mumbled, then said to her mother, "As far as I can see, everything's on the table."

"Great. Call your father and we'll sit down."

"Dinner," Jenny called, and the family started to gather around the dining room table.

"Jenny." Trey's hand on her arm stopped her. Silently he pleaded with her to tell him what was going on. "Why aren't you in New York?"

"You honestly don't know?"

Baffled, he shook his head.

"I'm marrying you, Trey. We've got the next fifty years to discuss all this, but right now dinner is getting cold." She left him standing in the middle of her mother's kitchen with his mouth sagging open so far, it damn near bounced against the floor.

By the time he'd recovered enough to walk into the dining room, everyone was seated and waiting for him.

"Trey, would you care to say grace?"

Everyone looked to him, but for the life of him Trey couldn't take his eyes off Jenny long enough to do as her mother requested.

"It seems Trey's otherwise occupied," Dillon said, chuckling. "I'll be happy to say the blessing."

The Lancaster family bowed their heads while Dillon offered up a short prayer of thanksgiving. When he'd finished, he looked to Trey. "Sit down, Trey. Your place is directly across from Jenny. Once you're seated, would you kindly pass the mashed potatoes?"

Trey was certain he gave them all a good laugh. The first thing he did was pour gravy over the sweet potatoes. He couldn't help it. Nothing could make him stop staring at Jenny. He doubted he ate two bites of the entire dinner.

Twice she looked up and smiled, and it was damn near all he could do not to reach for her right there.

"I'd appreciate a few minutes alone with Jenny after dinner," he said, looking to her parents.

"You don't need our permission," Dillon responded. "Jenny makes her own decisions."

An eternity passed before the meal was over. Jenny tormented him during dessert by licking the whipped cream off the back of her fork—her eyes locked on him the entire time.

When she announced she was too full to take another bite, Trey nearly picked her up out of the chair in his eagerness to get her alone.

"How about a stroll to the barn," she suggested.

"Fine." He didn't care if she suggested New Zealand; he wasn't waiting another minute for her to explain her earlier statement.

The night was clear and crisp. Trey led her by the hand into the barn. "All right," he demanded without turning on any of the lights. "Did you mean what you said earlier?"

"I said a number of things. Which one do you mean?"

"Jenny, for the love of heaven." He jerked her into his arms, and it wasn't until she slammed against his chest that he realized how willingly she'd come.

"You big oaf," she said, solidly planting her lips over his before he had a chance to kiss her. Wanting her as badly as he did, for as long as he had, Trey nearly crumpled to the floor under the weight of his joy. The kiss was slow and deep and moist.

"Oaf?" he repeated, holding her head so he could kiss her again and again. Fifty years wouldn't be nearly enough to satisfy him.

"You didn't stick around long enough for me to answer. If you're going to propose to a woman, the least you can do is wait for the response."

He kissed her just long enough to cut off her tirade. "Answer me now."

She threw back her head and laughed. "First I think I'll make you suffer."

She hadn't a clue to how much he'd already been suffering. His breath came fast and heavy as she brought his mouth down to hers once more.

"Jenny, I love you."

"Yes, I know. We're going to be very happy, Trey. First we're going to get married, then we're going to start our family. I want a house full of children. I've been so hungry for family."

His throat went thick. "That sounds perfectly fine with me." He kissed her a dozen times, and even the gentleness between them, the love and tenderness, were far from being sated. "What about New York?" He had to know.

"Michelle got the part."

"But I heard . . . Irene asked to talk to you."

"It's true they offered it to me first, but when I declined, the role went to Michelle."

"But this was your big dream."

"I loved New York, but I love you more. Montana is where I belong, right here with you. I knew it a long time ago, but was too stubborn to admit it. I'm home now."

The back porch light went on, and Dillon appeared on the top step, although there wasn't any chance he could see them. "Hey, you two, it's about time for church. Are you ready or not?"

Trey's hand squeezed Jenny's. "We'll be inside in a minute."

"Is there going to be a wedding?"

"Yes, sir," Trey shouted back. "Soon, too, the sooner the better."

Dillon laughed. "Welcome to the family."

Trey kissed Jenny one last time, and with their arms wrapped around each other, they headed for the house.

They hadn't gone more than a few steps when thick, flat flakes of snow drifted down from the sky.

"I thought you said it wasn't going to snow," Dillon challenged, waiting for them on the back porch.

Trey looked up to the bright, clear sky. "I don't know where it's coming from," he mumbled, puzzled.

"Maybe someone up there is telling us how

pleased they are to hear we're going to be married," Jenny suggested.

Trey kept his eyes trained on the cloudless sky. "Maybe you're right."

"It seems to me we've met in a similar spot before," Gabriel said to Shirley, Goodness, and Mercy as they sat in the choir loft of St. Philip's. The congregation crowded into the church for the Christmas Eve ceremonies. Candles brightened the interior, and pure red poinsettias decorated the altar.

"Hello again," Shirley said, leaning over the loft to get a better view of Brynn and Roberto. The two sat together, holding hands and singing. They appeared to have eyes only for each other.

"Brynn's decided to stay," Shirley told Gabriel, although it was unnecessary. The archangel was well aware of Brynn's future plans.

"You outdid yourself, Shirley. You all did. I'm proud of you."

All three prayer ambassadors blushed with pleasure. "Thank you," Shirley said.

"There is that one small matter involving Brynn's car, however."

Shirley glanced guiltily toward her two friends, whose attention seemed to be conveniently occupied elsewhere. "I had to do something, and fast," she rushed to explain. "She was about to leave, and the church bus was due any time."

"Don't worry about it," Gabriel said benevolently.

"Tampering with a car engine is small potatoes compared to horsing around with the Statue of Liberty."

That captured Goodness's and Mercy's attention.

"What does the future hold for Brynn?" Shirley asked in a diversionary tactic.

"Ah yes, Brynn."

"Will she marry Roberto?" Shirley asked.

"Yes, next year at this time, to be exact. Eventually Roberto will find a way out of this neighborhood, too. His shop will inspire other Hispanics to start their own businesses."

"What about Emilio, Suzie, and the baby?"

"Emilio will go on to college and become a teacher himself. The day will come when he'll be at Manhattan High once more, but not as a student."

"Emilio?" Shirley didn't bother to disguise her amazement.

"He's an intelligent young man."

"What about Suzie and Modesto?"

"Suzie will have a baby girl in the spring. She'll decide to raise the child herself, and with the help of Mike's mother and her own family she'll be able to attend college. Suzie is going to major in medicine and do great work in the study of depression and its treatment."

"And Modesto?"

Gabriel frowned and shook his head sadly. "Not long after he recovers from the gunshot he'll become heavily involved in drugs and waste his life."

"Oh, dear."

"What about Trey and Jenny?" Mercy asked.

"Ah yes, Jenny." Gabriel turned his attention to Mercy. "Isn't it amazing that snow would fall from a cloudless sky?" He watched his favorite prayer ambassadors squirm and had a difficult time not chuckling.

"They'll marry on Valentine's Day," he informed her.

Mercy clapped her hands together. "That's perfect."

"In the next six years they'll add two girls and two boys to their family. The girls will be as talented as their mother, and the three will form a singing group and frequently perform at church functions. The boys won't be able to carry a tune to save their lives."

"That's sweet. Will Jenny have any regrets about giving up her chance to perform on Broadway?"

"Not a one," Gabriel assured Mercy.

"Hannah and Joshua?"

"Ah yes . . ." Gabriel scratched the side of his face. "They'll marry this June, and Hannah's mother will fight with the wedding coordinator from the first moment they meet. The wedding will be one of the most talked-about affairs in New York. It'll be lovely." Gabriel smiled to himself. "Ten years from now, when their son and daughter are still young, Joshua will run for state senator and win. Joshua realizes that Hannah is not only his wife and partner for life, she's his greatest political asset as well.

"Are you ready?" Gabriel asked, gesturing sky-ward.

The three nodded. In the distance the archangel could hear music from the harps of heaven. It was a night wrapped in glory and time for them to head home.

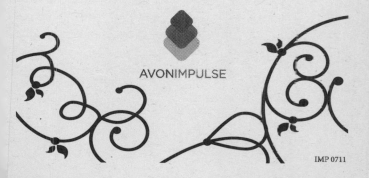